HOT SEAT

HOT SEAT

Simon Wood

CRÈME de la CRIME

This first world edition published 2012
in Great Britain and the USA by
Crème de la Crime, an imprint of
SEVERN HOUSE PUBLISHERS LTD of
9–15 High Street, Sutton, Surrey, England, SM1 1DF.

British Library Cataloguing in Publication Data

Wood, Simon, 1968-
  Hot seat.
  1. Automobile racing–Fiction. 2. Suspense fiction.
  I. Title
  813.6-dc23

ISBN-13: 978-1-78029-023-2 (cased)

All Severn House titles are printed on acid-free paper.

Severn House Publishers support The Forest Stewardship Council [FSC],
the leading international forest certification organisation. All our titles that
are printed on Greenpeace-approved FSC-certified paper carry the FSC logo.

Typeset by Palimpsest Book Production Ltd.,
Falkirk, Stirlingshire, Scotland.
Printed and bound in Great Britain by
MPG Books Ltd., Bodmin, Cornwall.

ACKNOWLEDGEMENTS

My thanks go to Mike Whelan, Edward Stores, Jenni Oglesby, Jack McGowan, Ryan Green, Jim McLeod, Robert O'Neal, Roy Carroll and Carrie Gordon Watson who answered my 'casting call' and donated their names to this book. Enjoy your roles, people.

AUTHOR'S NOTE

The European Saloon Car Championship is a fictional racing series, although it does share its roots in a number of championships past and present.

'If everything seems under control, you're just not going fast enough.'

Mario Andretti

First Lap

I was backstage listening to my new boss, Richard 'Rags' Ragsdale, and new teammate, Kurt Haulk, being interviewed. Public speaking wasn't my forte, but in a couple of minutes, I'd be joining them.

'Ragged Racing has been the "It" team for several seasons,' George Easter said. He'd been the voice of motorsport since before I was born. 'Do you expect that to continue?'

'All indicators say yes,' Rags said. 'The cars are performing well and I have great confidence in my drivers.'

Rags wasn't wrong. Haulk was fast becoming a saloon-car legend. He was two-time Dutch Touring Car Champion, British Saloon Car Champion, and the current European Saloon Car Champion.

I'd graduated from Formula Ford to the European Saloon Car Championship. The ESCC pitted the likes of the Honda Accord, Audi A4, BMW 3-Series and Ford Mondeo against each other. With the engines limited to two litres and power to 300bhp, it kept the racing tight.

Claudia Bernard appeared next to me. Her grin helped alleviate my nerves. She was the media liaison for the ESCC. She was French and typically so, with a self-assuredness that only the French seemed to possess. She was pale, thin and wore her hair in an asymmetric pageboy cut that would have failed on ninety-nine per cent of women.

She leaned in close and whispered in my ear. 'When you 'ear your name called, you go on.'

Claudia's English was impeccable, but she suffered from that French trait of not saying her h's. I found it comforting that she wasn't entirely perfect.

'Don't be nervous. You'll do great. I 'ave faith in you.'

'That makes one of us.'

Her grin shone in the backstage gloom.

Today was my great unveiling at the *Pit Lane* magazine Racecar Show and Exhibition. Held every year at Earls Court, the show drew everyone who had anything to do with motorsport, from the fans all the way to the auto giants. Exhibits surrounded the centre stage where interviews played out across the exhibition hall and, in two minutes, I'd be on stage addressing these people.

George Easter's voice filtered backstage. 'Speaking of driving talent, I'm very excited to bring a fantastic up-and-coming driver and the new addition to Ragged Racing to the stage.'

Claudia beamed. I wanted to throw up. I hadn't adapted to the publicity side of my sport yet.

'Please welcome *Pit Lane* magazine's Young Driver of the Year and the son of the late, great Rob Westlake, Aidy Westlake.'

Ah, there it was, that familiar qualifier attached to my name – the son of the late, great Rob Westlake. My dad had climbed the ranks to Formula One, but had died in a car crash with my mum before he ever took part in a grand prix. Since then, my dad had taken on a mystical quality in the racing community. His name came up every time I met someone for the first time. It didn't rankle me. I loved and admired my father, but it would be nice to be introduced as just me for once.

Claudia held back the blackout curtain and I walked on to the stage. Bright lights hit me in the face and the silhouettes of over a hundred people looked back at me. My inability to see the faces of the audience helped keep my nerves at bay.

All three men stood up as I walked by the Honda Accord I'd be racing next month. I shook their hands and sat down in the remaining chair.

'Congratulations on becoming *Pit Lane* magazine's Young Driver of the Year,' Easter said.

I'd won the drive courtesy of a driver shootout. *Pit Lane* had invited six young drivers who'd impressed them last season to take part in a two-day audition. My against-the-odds third place finish in the Formula Ford Festival and World Cup last October had won me the gold ticket invitation. The driver with the best across-the-board scores received a one-year contract with Ragged Racing, ten grand from *Pit Lane* and a one-year lease on a Honda Accord courtesy of Honda.

'You knocked off some pretty impressive talent to win the drive.'

I had. I'd beaten the cream of Britain's young talent.

'What does it feel like knowing you'll be driving for the top team in the ESCC?' Easter asked.

'A dream come true. It's going to be great driving for the defending champions.'

Ragged Racing had risen to prominence in the last five years and blown away the competition to take the ESCC drivers' and manufacturers' title three years in a row. Last season, they'd dethroned Townsend Motorsport as the official factory-backed team for Honda.

'Rags, what made you decide on Aidy?' Easter asked.

'It wasn't my sole decision. I took input from Kurt as well as my engineers.'

'And the stopwatch?' Easter said and got a laugh.

'Yes, we're all slaves to lap times. But we know that a good driver is more than just being quick. Aidy not only put up some fast times, he worked well with the pit crew. I tested the contenders' mechanical prowess. The team manufactured a mechanical or electrical fault for each driver so we could see what they brought back to the crew. Aidy nailed the fault. That's the kind of driver I need during the heat of the race. That incisive feedback could be the difference between a result and a DNF.'

'It looks as if your grandfather taught you well, Aidy,' Easter said.

My grandfather, Steve, had worked the Formula One pit for Lotus during the sixties and seventies and now ran a classic-sports-car restoration business when he wasn't helping me. He was well known for his uncanny ability to read a car. 'He's a good teacher,' I said.

'What I liked was his adaptability,' Haulk said. 'Aidy was coming off his first full season in Formula Ford and we put him in a saloon car. He responded well to the instruction I gave him.'

'So, Kurt, is he the complete package – brains and skill?'

'I hope not, or my title is in trouble.'

I struggled with this lovefest and blushed. OK, I knew there was a certain amount of grandstanding going on to make the team look good for the public, but wow, Kurt Haulk was complimenting the shit out of me.

'But seriously.' Haulk stretched out an arm and patted me on the back. 'I think Aidy has a lot of potential. This year will be a massive learning curve for him, but I won't be surprised to see him at the front of the pack.'

'I bloody hope so,' Rags said. 'I can't afford for him not to do well.'

Rags wasn't wrong. The budget for my car alone was a quarter

of a million. For the first time in my short racing career, there
was expectation and all the pressure that came with it. Rags was
taking a big chance with me, just out of my rookie year. I
was replacing saloon- and sports-car legend, Tim Reid, who was
out of contract and moving on. Over the last twenty-five years,
he'd won the 24-hours of Le Mans, the World Touring Car
championship, and just about everything else you could win in
saloon and sports cars. I hoped I was up for the task.

'With all this praise flying around, what have you got to say
for yourself, Aidy?'

'It's all deserved.'

Now, I got a laugh out of the crowd.

'I love a confident man,' Rags said.

'But are you overconfident?' Easter added.

'I don't think so. I'm very excited by the opportunity and the
faith in me shown by Rags and the team. I'm going to do my
best to win.'

'After me, you can be first,' Haulk said.

'Not if I can help it,' I fired back with a smile.

A collective 'Oh' rose from the crowd.

'It looks as if you're going to have your hands full with these
guys.'

'I like to think they're going to have their hands full with me,'
Rags said.

The interview was going really well and actual enjoyment seeped
into me. I looked over to the side of the stage where Steve and my
best friend, Dylan, stood. Dylan flashed me a thumbs-up and Steve
beamed at me. They couldn't be more proud.

'What would your dad say if he were here today?' Easter
asked me.

'He'd want to know why the bloody hell I was driving tin tops
and not sticking to single seaters.'

Dad was a purist. His interest began and ended with formula
cars. Me, I was more like my racing hero, Jim Clark. He was a
double Formula One champion, but he'd driven everything –
sports cars, saloon cars, Nascar, and even rally cars. While my
dream was to reach Formula One, I'd drive anything.

Easter hit me with a couple more questions and eventually
wrapped up the interview. The crowd applauded and Easter went
down the line shaking everyone's hand. When he reached me,

he said, 'I'm looking forward to keeping up with your progress. If you can emulate your old man, you'll go far.'

'Let's hope so.'

Rags dropped an arm over my shoulder. 'Nicely done.'

We all filed off the stage. Claudia was there to welcome us.

'You did very well, gentlemen. Performances like that make my job very easy.'

As I went to pass, Claudia hooked an arm in mine and guided me away from the others. 'Aidy, can I 'ave a second? Your story and the Westlake name 'ave a lot of media potential. I want you to be the face of the championship this year. You represent the next generation in this sport.' She grinned at me. 'Expect to be at my beck and call.'

I didn't know if I should read something into that last remark. I can read a track I've never seen before, but I'm clueless when it comes to women. She pulled out her mobile, punched a number into it and disappeared before I could find out.

Steve and Dylan walked up to me.

Dylan grabbed me in a bear hug and since he's a foot taller and four stone heavier than me, he lifted me off the ground. 'I knew this would happen. I'm so pleased for you, mate.'

'Put him down,' Steve said.

Dylan released me and I straightened my clothes.

'I think Madame Touchy-Feely likes you,' Dylan said.

'She's not married, so that would make her Mademoiselle Touchy-Feely.'

'Pardon my French.'

'Ignore him,' Steve said. 'You did well up there.'

'You didn't make a tit of yourself,' Dylan said.

'Classy. Thanks.'

'Just trying to keep you grounded before you forget who your real friends are.'

'You got time to wander through the exhibition?' Steve asked.

'No. I'm booked solid with one publicity thing or another. I'll be back at the ESCC stand later this afternoon. I can talk then.'

I saw the disappointment on Steve and Dylan's faces. This was a bittersweet moment. Up until now, they'd been there for every part of my racing career, from karts to Formula Ford last season. It had seemed as if we'd always be a team, but after one season, I was leaving them behind. Growing up. Moving on.

As much as the upcoming season was going to be a full and fun one, I could see it being a lonely one.

'Go do your thing and we'll see you at home,' Steve said.

I left the guys and headed for the exit. Next up for me was a private luncheon with Honda at an Italian restaurant a few streets from the exhibition hall. As I reached the main concourse, I was walking towards Brian DeYoung and Chloe Mercer who were coming the other way. They were the Brad and Angelina of motorsport. Brian was tipped to have a ride with Lotus F1 next season and Chloe was the top female driver in European motorsport. She'd been the only female driver in the *Pit Lane* driver shootout last November.

I put out my hand and said, 'Hey, Chloe.'

They ignored me and kept walking.

'Ouch,' someone said from behind me.

I turned. My predecessor, Tim Reid, was standing there. I hadn't seen him since the shootout either. Like Haulk, he'd put me through my paces during the competition.

'That was awkward,' Reid said. 'I guess not everyone is excited about your success.'

I glanced over at Brian and Chloe, who were striding away through the crowd. 'It sure looks that way.'

'She really thought she had the shootout in the bag,' Reid said. 'But not everyone is like her. I'm so pleased for you.'

'Thanks. How are you set this season?'

'I've got some very interesting offers on the table.'

'That's great.'

'Enough of that,' Rags said, appearing behind me with Haulk in tow. 'You're back on the clock, my boy.'

The rest of the day descended into a blur of meetings, interviews and greeting the public at the ESCC exhibit. The day's highlight was the head of marketing for Honda presenting me with my privately leased Accord. It would have been even sweeter if I got to keep the car and not hand it back Cinderella-style in twelve months. Up until now, I'd been underwriting most of my racing costs, which meant sacrificing luxuries like home ownership, holidays and a personal vehicle. If I needed a car, I either borrowed Steve's much-cherished Capri RS2600 or his Transit van. Tonight, I'd be driving home instead of taking the train back to Windsor.

The day ended with a team dinner that stretched into the night. Rags told us to enjoy it because after tonight it was work, work, work. By the time he settled the bill, it was after ten p.m. Everyone headed back to their hotels and I walked back to Earls Court to collect my new car. I could have stayed at a hotel, but with Windsor so close, I preferred to spend the night in my own bed. The European season was going to keep me away from home a lot over the next six months.

I walked past my car and stopped in front of the massive Ragged Racing transporter. It was big enough to hold two cars. A larger-than-life representation of the Honda Accord covered each side of the trailer in full racing colours. Painted on the rear door were two names – Kurt Haulk's and mine. I choked up at the sight of my own name. The drive was real. Not a fairytale. I didn't give a shit what Chloe Mercer thought. I deserved this.

The big question was where it would all lead. A good showing could result in a renewed contract or a contract with a different team. If I wanted to realize my dream of following my father into grand prix racing then I couldn't afford to dawdle too long in tin tops. I'd be turning twenty-two in April and I was already behind in the age stakes with my peers. Chloe had two seasons on me and was a year younger than me. If I worked this opportunity to my advantage, I could use it to land a Formula Renault or Formula Three drive next season. It was all pie in the sky stuff, but it looked pretty delicious from where I was standing.

I reached up and touched my name on the transporter. I closed my eyes and said, 'Please be a good year.'

The sound of choking snapped me from my moment. A rush of embarrassment washed over me at my display and I jerked my hand away.

A scrape of heels drew my gaze downward to an outstretched leg sticking out from under the rear of the transporter. It kicked at the ground but the person it belonged to never got to their feet. The sound of the choking intensified.

'Hey, are you OK?'

A gurgling that turned my stomach came as a reply.

I ran to the rear of the transporter. A man lay on his back, clutching his throat. Street lights caught the steady stream of blood leaking from his fingers.

'Jesus Christ,' I murmured.

I dropped to my knees at the guy's side. I did my best to ignore the stark contrast between the cold asphalt and the man's warm blood seeping through my chinos.

'It's going to be OK,' I said, believing my words until I saw the source of the man's bleeding. Someone had cut his throat. A combination of blood and air bubbled up from the ugly and efficient wound.

I didn't know what to do. Apply pressure? Not apply pressure? I tried to pull his hands away, but he fought me.

'Let me help.' I pulled a handkerchief from my pocket and pressed it against the gash. I felt his blood and breath through the cotton.

He fixed me with a stare that turned my heart to stone in my chest. The fear in his eyes terrified me. He was on the edge of death and he was willing me to save him.

He tried to speak, but only a distorted gurgle made it out.

'Don't speak. Save your strength.'

Pointless words for a pointless situation.

'Help!' I yelled. 'I need help here. Please help.'

The sound of a single pair of feet striking the asphalt like a thunderclap split the night-time silence. The dying man swung an arm in the direction of the receding footfalls and pointed. I whipped my head around and saw no one.

'Help!' I yelled again, so loud my single plea burned my throat. Where the fuck was security?

I removed a hand, reached inside my pocket and pulled my mobile out. My bloody fingers slipped on the buttons, but I pressed nine-nine-nine.

By the time someone answered the phone and asked me the nature of my emergency, security guards were swarming towards us and the man was dead.

Lap Two

'Jason Gates. The name means nothing to you?' Detective Inspector Joan Huston said. She was slim, about my height and wore her hair in a style a good ten years out of date. She looked more like someone's mum than a cop, but she was much tougher than that. It was there in her eyes. 'He's a mechanic for Townsend Motorsport. Sure you don't know him?'

'I've never met him before.'

'I find that hard to believe.' She glanced over at Detective Sergeant Robert O'Neal sitting in the corner. He was a typical-looking cop, tall and broad-shouldered, and he hadn't said a word since introducing himself.

I was in a police station interview room not far from Earls Court. I didn't know which one. I'd been in a daze since finding Jason Gates. I'd never seen someone die before, not like that, not up close. Last October, I'd seen Alex Fanning's fatal crash at the Stowe Park circuit, but that had been a death at arm's length, insulating me from its horrors. Jason had been different. I'd been there for pretty much every step of his brutal death. I'd felt his blood spill between my fingers and heard his last breath leave his body. I'd been so ill-equipped to handle the situation that I'd kept pressure on the wound long after he was dead. Paramedics had to peel me off him when they arrived. I'd washed the blood off my hands when I reached the station, but I still felt it buried deep under my nails.

My clothes were a mess. A scenes of crime officer at the station had given me a pair of trousers to replace my blood-soaked chinos, as they were evidence, but I still wore my Ragged Racing polo shirt with Jason's blood speckling the front.

Huston said something, but I didn't catch it.

'Sorry. What?'

'I was just saying that Jason's throat was cut with a cutthroat razor or a knife with a finely honed edge. Did you see anything like that?'

I shook my head.

'For the tape, Mr Westlake.'

'No, I didn't.'

'OK. Maybe you can answer me this instead. What were you doing there? The exhibition had closed for the night, but for some reason you were hanging around.'

This was a new tack for Huston. Until now, her questioning had been preoccupied with what I'd seen and done after discovering Jason. She hadn't been warm and friendly, but this latest question came with a hard, accusing edge that got my attention.

'You wouldn't understand,' I said.

'Try me. You'd be surprised by my powers of understanding. This job makes you very open-minded.'

I noticed she didn't sit, despite the free chair. This forced me to look up at her at all times. I guessed there was some psychology to that.

'Today was a big day for me. This is my first time with a major team and the unveiling was a special moment.'

Huston cocked her head to one side. 'Correct me if I'm wrong, but wouldn't that have happened inside the exhibition hall when the public was there?'

'It did.'

'So that still doesn't explain why you were in the Earls Court car park after hours.'

'I wanted to see my name on the side of the transporter.'

'You wanted to see your name,' Huston said, her sarcasm beginning to show.

I knew I was struggling to get my point across. 'Seeing my name made it real.'

'And inside the exhibition wasn't real enough?'

'I told you that you wouldn't understand.'

'Try harder.'

I sighed. The demand drained me of every drop of energy. 'I wanted a private moment away from the crowds, the team and sponsors. So when I came back to collect my car, I stopped to look at my name painted on the side of the transporter.'

'A chance to gloat about how good you are?'

Huston was being purposely combative, but she wasn't far off the mark. I was being prideful of my luck and success. It was petty of me, but it felt good to do it. 'You usually have to have someone around to gloat.'

Huston flashed a nasty grin that robbed her of her maternal looks. I'd said something wrong, but I didn't know what.

'The car you came by to collect – that's the one Honda gave you?'

'Yes.'

Huston leaned against the wall and made a big production of processing what I'd told her. 'I suppose the thing I don't like is that you chose to have your private moment at the same time someone cut Jason Gates' throat.'

'That's just coincidence. Someone was going to find the poor sod at some point. If it wasn't me, it would have been a security guard on his rounds, the clean-up crew emptying the bins or someone parking their car. I was just the unlucky twat who found him first.'

A knock at the door broke the moment.

'Interview suspended, twelve sixteen a.m.,' Huston said and hit stop on the recorder.

She opened the door. A uniformed officer stood in the doorway holding a T-shirt.

'I got Mr Westlake a shirt. Sorry, it's a little on the large side.'

'That's OK,' I said and stood.

The officer held out the shirt, but before I could cross the cramped interview room, Huston snatched it and lobbed it at me. Reflexively, I caught it left-handed.

Huston and O'Neal exchanged yet another look. I must have been emerging from my state of shock because I caught the significance of the moment.

'I'm going to need your shirt,' the officer at the door said.

I peeled off my polo shirt and dropped it into an evidence bag the officer held out. He sealed it without touching the shirt and left.

I noticed Huston checking out my body as I pulled on the clean shirt. I knew she wasn't ogling. She was looking for cuts or bruises picked up from a fight.

'Did I pass or fail the test?' I asked.

'I don't know what you mean,' Huston said.

God, she was a terrible actor. She pressed 'record' and announced that the interview was resuming.

'What test, Mr Westlake?'

'You wanted to see if I was left- or right-handed. I'm guessing you know which hand was used to cut Jason's throat.'

'That's privileged information,' she said.

'Do you think I'm involved in this?'

'You tell us,' Huston said.

'Let's stop playing games. If you think I did it, then say it, charge me and stop wasting my time.'

'Mr Westlake, I suggest you remember where you are.'

'And I suggest you remember that I'm a witness. If I'd cut Jason Gates' throat, why would I call nine-nine-nine, yell for help and try to save his life?'

'That's a good question and I think I know the answer. You and Jason Gates got into a fight for some reason. Maybe he

found you in the middle of your private moment and embar-
rassed you—'

'And I cut his throat?' I finished for her. 'That's a weak reason
for killing someone.'

Huston shrugged. 'Maybe you found him trying to make off
with that shiny new car you'd been given. Oh, that's a motive I
like because I understand you. Your big day. Your moment in the
spotlight. You're the next Nigel Mansell, Jenson Button and Lewis
Hamilton rolled into one. You're a cocky little sod because of it.
You're on top of the world. And guess what, some poxy grease
monkey tries to half-inch your motor the day it's given to you.
Now, who wouldn't forgive you for launching into one?'

You, I thought. 'Detective Huston—'

'Detective Inspector Huston,' she corrected.

I knew that misquoting her rank would needle her and it gave
me a little pleasure.

'Detective Inspector Huston, ignoring what I did with the
weapon and a thousand other holes in that stupid scenario, I think
that statement says more about you than me.'

Huston burned me with a glare.

'I came here as a witness, but if I'm a suspect, then charge
me. Right now. If not, I'm going home.'

I knew she couldn't charge me. She was trying it on. She
didn't know all the facts, so she was chancing her luck. Part of
that process was giving me a hard time. I understood it, but I
didn't like it.

Huston walked over, leaned down, fixed me with an ugly stare
and said into the tape recorder, 'Interview suspended at twelve
twenty-seven a.m.'

Lap Three

O'Neal lived up to his mute status during the drive back
to Earls Court. I wondered if his silence was a tactic
designed to force me into opening up. If it was, it failed.
I didn't feel any compunction to talk.

He handed me back my mobile. Jason's blood had been cleaned

off. It had been covered in the stuff when Huston had claimed it as evidence. She'd no doubt checked my call log to see if I'd had any contact with him.

We arrived at Earls Court to an active crime scene with investigators combing every inch of space around the transporter for evidence. The cordon included my new car. I heard O'Neal speak for the first time when he cleared the way for me to collect it. A crime-scene technician gave O'Neal the all clear and he drove it off the hallowed land of the crime scene.

'Aidy. Aidy!' It was Rags jogging around the cordoned area. It didn't surprise me to see him here. He ducked under the cordon tape, shook my hand and squeezed my shoulder with his free hand. 'They told me what happened. How you doing, son?'

'OK.'

'Did you see the killer?'

'No. Heard him. I think.'

'Christ, you were lucky.'

'What do you mean?'

'A minute either way and you could have walked in on this prick. If you had, I'd be identifying your body right now.'

That thought hadn't occurred to me and my naivety left me cold.

'I need to get out of here,' I said.

'Yeah. Of course.'

'I'll see you in the morning.'

'No, you're done. Stay home. As soon as I get the all clear from this lot –' he jerked a thumb at the police at work – 'I'm pulling the team from the show. I don't want a circus forming over this, especially around you. OK?'

It was probably the best thing to do.

'You stay out of the limelight. Anyone comes sniffing around for a comment, refer them to me. Got it?'

'Got it.'

'Good, now get off home. Put this behind you and take it easy. I want your head in the right place for testing on Monday.'

Rags managed to pack concern for me and the needs of the team into a single statement. It just went to prove that life did go on, kindness and callousness coexisting in perfect harmony.

O'Neal held my car door open for me as I slipped behind the wheel. He'd been watching my exchange with Rags with his customary silence. 'We just want to find the killer, Mr Westlake. No offence intended.'

I said nothing, closed the door and drove away.

I threaded my way through the London streets. At one a.m. on a school night, the traffic was light and I drove on autopilot. I opened my mind to white noise and random thoughts. I hoped the monotony of shifting gears and dancing between the clutch, brake and accelerator would put me in a Zen-like mood of vacant thought, but images of hot blood on cold tarmac and Jason Gates' burning gaze filled the void. There was no forgetting. It was too raw. Too fresh.

I picked up the M4 motorway and pushed the Accord up to seventy.

O'Neal wanted to let me know that he and Huston were just doing their jobs. I wondered how seriously they viewed me as a suspect. Cops being cops, they weren't going to tell me. I'd know in the next couple of days. If Huston came with handcuffs in hand, then I'd know how she viewed me. I didn't bother contemplating that one any further.

I replayed Jason's final moments again in my head. I couldn't believe that I'd been so caught up in myself that I'd missed a man bleeding to death just a few short feet from me. That single thought stalled my mind's replay. How long had I been standing there revelling in my success? Two minutes? Five? If I'd gotten to him the second I returned to the transporter, could I have saved him? Would those extra couple of minutes have made a difference? No, I didn't think so. Jason was dead the moment the killer sliced his throat open.

It wasn't worth contemplating what I couldn't change, but maybe I could still help. What had I seen? What had I heard? Any detail could be vital. I replayed my steps from the moment I'd entered the Earls Court car park, but came up with nothing. No one had passed me. I hadn't heard an argument. I didn't remember anything out of place. One thought did hit me hard. The killer would have been close when I discovered Jason. He had to be. At best, Jason had minutes to live after his throat had been slit. So how close was the killer? His footfalls had been loud as he escaped. Had he watched me trying to save Jason? My skin prickled at the thought.

I didn't remember hearing a car engine start after the footsteps. That meant the killer was on foot or parked a long way out of earshot. So did he live local or use public transport as a means of escape? If he'd jumped on the tube, security cameras would have picked him up. Huston might find that information useful.

Before I knew it, the Slough and Windsor junction came up and I followed the slip road down to the roundabout and took the Windsor Relief Road. Almost home. I lived with Steve off Maidenhead Road across from the horse track. Since I'm only five foot four, Steve always said I could have been a jockey if I hadn't wanted to go into motorsport. Despite having grown up across from the racecourse, I never had any desire to ride. Racecars were in the family blood, not horses.

A BMW 5-Series flew by me. A few years earlier, I would have chased after the car. As soon as I got my licence at seventeen, I trawled the streets looking for a street race. Oddly, ever since I'd gotten into motorsport, I'd lost the desire for it. No street race could ever emulate the raw adrenaline rush of a motor race.

I followed the BMW off the Windsor Relief Road. By the time I turned on to Maidenhead Road, my speedy friend was long gone.

Just as I drew level with the entrance to Windsor Racecourse, a bang rocked my car. The steering wheel turned to lead in my hands and pulled to the left. It was a blowout. I knew it without even having to get out. I let the car go where it wanted to go and pulled over. I climbed out and prodded the flat tyre with my foot. I'd had the car less than twenty-four hours and I'd already picked up a flat. It was the icing on a very shitty day.

Something stuck from the tyre and I jerked it free. It was an eight-inch length of laminate flooring with nails hammered into it. Obviously, someone thought it was funny to shred people's tyres.

'Wankers,' I murmured.

I looked back down the road. Three more nail strips sat in a row in the roadway. I gathered them up. No one else deserved my luck tonight.

Headlights from the opposite direction lit me up. The BMW that had passed me a few minutes earlier stopped next to me. The driver, a middle-aged guy in a suit, leaned out of his window.

'You all right?'

'Puncture.' I held up the nail strips. 'Somebody left these out.'

'Some people are real shitheads. I'll give you a hand changing the wheel.'

'Nah, it's OK. I live a couple of streets away. I'll change it in the morning.'

'Don't be daft. You drive anywhere and you'll shred the tyre and ruin the rim. It's not worth it. We can have the spare on in ten minutes.'

He was right, so I nodded.

The BMW driver pulled over while I tossed the nail strips in the boot and dragged out the spare tyre.

My good Samaritan jogged across the empty street. 'What's your name, mate?'

'Aidy Westlake.'

'I'm Dominic Crichlow.'

He put out his hand. I went to shake it, but as I extended my hand, Crichlow ignored it and pressed something against my stomach. I heard a click-click sound before electricity coursed through me. Every muscle in my body clenched. My jaw slammed shut, my hands balled into fists, my back arched and my neck snapped back. I tried to pull away, but I remained frozen until I finally gave out and collapsed to the tarmac.

Feeling leaked back into me. I tried moving, but my body still vibrated to the stun gun's tune.

Crichlow rolled me on to my back and taped my hands together in front of me. He produced a hood from his suit jacket pocket and pulled it over my head.

'Stop! You don't have to do this. You want the car? Take it.'

'Sorry about this, Aidy, but it has to be done.'

He wrapped his arms around my neck, cutting my breath off. I kicked out, but the strength hadn't returned to my legs. The sound of my blood pumping roared inside my head. I fought for breath, but the air in my lungs turned sour and burned. My grip on consciousness melted, then I saw blackness darker than the inside of the hood.

Lap Four

A bump in the road woke me as my head bounced off the carpeted floorboard. The hood was still on and my wrists were still duct taped. The world was moving underneath me. I was in the BMW's boot.

My body ached and I still felt on the verge of throwing up, but the stun gun's jolt had helped me wise up. It was a shame I hadn't seen through Crichlow's little stunt. It was obvious that he'd set the nail strips for me to drive over since his car hadn't been affected and he had no reason to come back my way. Not that it mattered anymore. He'd gotten what he wanted – me. Now, what did he have planned for me?

I listened. The engine revved at a constant speed. I felt no rapid acceleration or deceleration. We were on either the motorway or a dual carriageway travelling fast away from my home and safety.

It was hot under the hood. The thing was sodden from my breathing. He'd taped my hands in front of me, so it wasn't hard to tug the hood off. It was a relief to breathe unhindered and the rolling nausea and pounding headache eased. I didn't know if breathing through the hood or Crichlow's Vulcan death grip had caused the symptoms, but I felt a hell of a lot better with the hood off. I let out an involuntary groan of relief.

'You alive in there?' Crichlow said. 'Almost there.'

What the hell was going on? How had the best day of my life descended into this mess? I didn't bother him with my questions. I knew they wouldn't be answered.

The BMW slowed. It turned right and we left the road for uneven ground judging by the choppy ride. Dirt and gravel peppered the underside of the vehicle.

The 5-Series rolled to a halt. My heart quickened when the engine stopped. This was it, whatever it was.

'Aidy, do you have the hood on?' Crichlow asked. 'It's important that you don't know where you are.'

Unless we were somewhere near famous landmarks, I wouldn't know where I'd been taken, but I didn't bother arguing the point and pulled the hood back on. 'It's on.'

Crichlow popped the boot and pulled me from the car. His hands fell on my shoulders. 'I'm going to guide you. Just walk and I'll steer you.'

The whine of a door sliding back told me I was somewhere industrial. I went forward and my footfalls rang out on a concrete floor. It took a couple of seconds before the echo of my footfalls came back to me. This building was big.

The door drew back behind me and Crichlow tugged the hood off. We were alone in a disused factory.

Crichlow removed a flick knife. I stiffened at the sight of
the four-inch blade. He flashed a hint of a smile at my fear before
cutting the tape around my wrists. I peeled it off.

A bank of fluorescent tubes lit up a portion of the factory.
Disabled and derelict machinery stood silently in the shadows
and debris covered the floor. A tubular steel chair with a cracked
wooden back sat under the lights.

A stocky man, around fifty, with blond hair emerged from the
shadows. Just like Crichlow, he was dressed in a suit. 'Come
have a seat, Aidy.'

Crichlow gave me a gentle shove and escorted me to the chair.
I sat and it creaked under my weight.

'Do you know who I am?'

I shook my head.

'I'm Andrew Gates, Jason's brother.'

Oh, shit. An unstable family member. Just what I needed.

'From your expression, I see that my name means something
to you.'

I shook my head. 'Until now, I didn't know Jason Gates had
a brother. In fact, until a few hours ago I didn't even know
Jason.'

'OK, a quick history lesson,' Andrew Gates said. 'I'm a very
wealthy man. I earned it the nasty way – from loan sharking –
which didn't exactly endear me to my family. No one wants a
monster for a son. My baby brother was different. He loved me,
regardless of who I was and what I did. I changed my way of
life for him. For the last ten years, I've been a reputable property
developer. Until tonight.' He palmed away a tear. 'What I once
was, I am again. Stand up.'

I put my hands out. 'Look, I didn't know your brother.'

Gates moved in.

'I just found him. Beyond that, I don't know anything.'

'You heard the boss,' Crichlow barked. 'Stand up!'

Before I could, he jerked the chair out from under me and
sent it clattering off into the distance. Gates yanked me up off
the ground and before I could say a word, he drove a fist into
my stomach. The impact moved something inside me and I wasn't
sure if I wanted to throw up or shit myself. I slithered through
Crichlow's grasp, collapsing on to my knees.

'Get him up.'

Crichlow lifted me back up on to my feet and held me up by bracing my arms behind me.

'Dawn is a long way off and I can keep this up all night, because I am a very angry and upset man. I don't think you can, so you need to talk. Someone killed my little brother and I want to know why.'

Gates underlined his point by slamming his fist into my stomach a second time. I dry-retched against the impact and sagged, but Crichlow kept me from collapsing.

'Did you kill my brother?'

'No. I tried to save him.'

'You did a shitty job,' Gates said and punched me again.

I anticipated the blow and tightened my stomach, but it didn't do me any good and I folded. This time, Crichlow released his hold on me and I dropped to the ground.

My stomach was red hot from the punishment.

'Talk to me while you still can,' Gates said.

He disappeared into the shadows and returned with a toolbox. Panic knifed through me. Tools could be used to build things but, in the right hands, Gates' hands, they could be used to destroy things.

He pulled out a five-pound mallet and smashed it against the concrete floor. Concrete chips flew into the air from the impact.

'Hands are important to a driver, aren't they?'

Crichlow pushed me forward and kept me pinned with his knee on my neck. He yanked one of my hands out and pressed it to the ground.

'Look, I don't know what you think happened, but I don't know anything!' I yelled.

Gates pressed down on my wrist and raised the mallet. 'Did you kill my brother?'

'No!' I injected every ounce of honesty and truth into that one word.

Gates froze as he tried to read me and I willed myself to be as transparent as possible so he could see the truth.

Then he brought the mallet down. It struck the concrete milli-metres from my outstretched fingers. The shockwave travelled through my hand and up into my shoulder.

'I'm going to ask you some questions. Answer truthfully and I won't hurt you. Lie and I'll make sure you're never able to pick up a spoon let alone hold a steering wheel. Am I clear?'

'Yes.'

'Get him up, Dominic.'

Crichlow helped me to my feet and had to support me. The emotional toll had robbed me of my strength.

Gates reclaimed the chair Crichlow had thrown aside and I fell into it. He found himself another and sat it down opposite me. Only Crichlow stood, like a hawk ready to take down its prey should it decide to run.

'How well did you know my brother?'

'I never met him.'

'You would have liked him. Everyone did, didn't they, Dominic?'

'They did,' Crichlow said.

'He was an honest, decent person. Everything I could never be.' Gates' eyes shone with tears and pride. This sign of his humanity failed to relax me. His brother's death had left him wounded. That made him dangerous.

'Tell me what happened.'

I replayed it for him the same way I had for the police. That I'd returned to the transporter to see my name. How I'd found his brother, how I'd tried to save his brother's life and how I'd heard footsteps of someone running away.

The details of Jason's death tore into Gates. I watched how my words blew holes in him. I understood the pain of losing a loved one. I'd been lucky in comparison. I was a child when my mum and dad died. I wasn't able to understand the enormity of that mammoth loss then. My loss was drip-fed to me as I reached the various milestones of my life – they weren't there at school sports day and PTA meetings, when my first girlfriend dumped me, when I passed my driving test, when I took part in my first race, or today when I stepped on to the stage for my interview. I'd suffered incremental awareness of what it was to be an orphan. The pain of losing them was cushioned by having my grandfather, Steve, raise me. Andrew Gates wasn't so lucky. His loss had been delivered both barrels full in the face. I pitied the poor sod. Almost.

'What did the cops say?'

'Not a lot. They asked the same questions as you.'

'You were in the cop shop a long time,' Crichlow said.

It was the first time Crichlow had gotten in on the questioning. Maybe he saw the cracks forming in his boss.

The cop shop question brought up a big point. They had to have been watching the police station to know that I was the one the police were questioning about Jason's murder. Maybe they had someone on the inside feeding them information. If so, it certainly wasn't Huston or O'Neal or anyone connected to the investigation or Gates would already know the answers to these questions.

'Are you a witness or something more?' Crichlow asked.

The question snapped Gates out of his sorrow. His body stiffened. I had to tread carefully around this point. The bloodlust was back in his eyes.

'They treated me like a suspect.'

Gates' words came out cold and hard. 'Are you still one?'

'You'll have to ask them.'

'I'm asking you.'

'They didn't hold me and they didn't tell me not to leave town.'

Gates and Crichlow exchanged a look and Crichlow nodded. I didn't know if it was one of approval or disapproval.

'Did they mention me?'

'No. Should they have?'

'Do they have any suspects?'

'Other than you,' Crichlow chipped in.

Snide remarks like that were going to get me killed. 'They didn't mention any, but I doubt they would.'

No one said anything for a long while. Gates stared through me while he thought. Crichlow stood in sentry-like silence. Nothing could be heard except the harsh splat of rain pouring through a hole in the roof and striking the concrete floor in the far distance.

'Someone from the racing world killed my brother.'

'How do you know?'

'He was killed next to one of your trucks, wasn't he? That's why you're going to find the killer for me.'

I groaned inside. I should have seen this coming. 'You don't know that this had anything to do with motor racing. You said yourself that you've got a shady past. Jason's murder could be the result of someone getting back at you.'

Gates ground his teeth. That possibility had to be tearing him up. 'Don't you worry about that. I'll be looking into that side of things myself. You look into your side of things.'

'I'm not the person for this. The cops are better equipped to look into this than I am.'

'I disagree. The cops will blunder their way through and we can't investigate this without causing waves, but you can. You can hide in plain sight.'

'I know nothing about your brother.'

'You'll learn. I'm not taking no for an answer. You will do this for me. And just as an incentive . . .' Gates let his words hang for me to pluck from the air.

'Incentive?'

Gates picked up the mallet. I flinched. He smiled.

'Calm yourself. Hurting you doesn't help me. Hurting someone important *to* you, that is a real incentive. Refuse to help and I'll take out my disappointment on that grandfather of yours.'

Gates knew a lot about me – that I raced, that Steve was my grandfather, that the police had held me – and he'd found it out in a hurry. He had connections that stretched further than just having Crichlow as his muscle. That scared me more than the five-pound mallet.

'Have I made myself clear?'

He had. I understood Gates' need for revenge and justice. His brother hadn't deserved to die. But fuck him for taking it out on me and now Steve. Gates might have been out of the bad-guy business for a decade, but he hadn't let any rust build on his skills for intimidation. 'Yes,' I forced out between gritted teeth.

'I see a little anger in those eyes. Don't waste your energy getting angry with me. Turn it into fuel for finding my brother's killer and no harm will come to your family. Even better, you'll have my undying appreciation.'

'What happens when I find the person responsible?'

'Hear that Dominic? "When". Not if, but when. I like that. It shows confidence and determination.' Gates examined the mallet in his hands and his mood changed from condescending to sullen. 'I expect to be updated regularly on your progress and when you find the bastard responsible, you just tell me where I can find him and I'll take things from there. Just make sure you don't tell the filth first.'

I could only imagine what Gates would do to the culprit if and when he got his hands on him. That thought left me queasy.

Jason's killer deserved to be brought to justice, but not this way. I'd be delivering him to his death. That made me no different than Gates. I'd be a killer. It was a role I wasn't sure I could play.

'So we have a deal?'

Gates had proved that he could easily get to me at any time. He'd do the same with Steve. I didn't have a choice. 'Yes.'

'Good. Get him out of here, Dominic.'

Crichlow grinned, then pulled the hood back over my head.

Lap Five

C richlow stuffed me back in the boot of his BMW and drove me back to my car, which he'd stashed on the service road to the Windsor Racecourse. My tyre was still flat. I drove home on it. I was definitely not in the mood to change it. Crichlow had let me go with the reminder: 'Not a word to anyone. We'll be in touch.'

No doubt, I'd thought.

I got as far as letting myself into the house before Steve appeared from the living room. He was still dressed, but his ruffled hair said that he'd fallen asleep waiting up for me.

'Where you been, son? I expected you home hours ago. You have responsibilities now. You can't go off partying when it suits you.' He stopped and looked at my clothes. 'What the hell happened to you? Are you OK?'

'No, not really.' It was nice not to have to pretend to someone that everything was normal and I was fine.

The lecture went out of Steve's tone. 'You'd better have a sit down then.'

I followed Steve into the living room. I held in a groan when I sat down on the sofa. My body wasn't quite bolted back together after its tazing and Andrew Gates' fists. I don't think the sofa had ever felt as comfortable as it did at that moment.

Steve sat in his armchair and put his feet up on the corner of the coffee table. 'What's happened?'

I told him about finding Jason, the police interview and picking up a flat tyre. He didn't need to know about Crichlow and the bargain I'd struck with Gates. Last year, I'd dragged Steve and Dylan into a situation that had almost gotten all three of us killed. I couldn't risk putting him through that again. This time, it was my burden.

'So how do you feel?' Steve asked.

'Shitty.'

'Why?'

'I was so caught up admiring my name painted on the side of a fucking truck that I missed that a man was bleeding to death at my feet. If I'd seen him straight away instead of having my head up my arse, I might have been able to save him.'

'You don't know that.'

A tremor started in my hands and crept up my arms. 'I should have done more.'

'You did your best. No one could ask more of you.'

Andrew Gates could and had. He had a noose around my neck now. 'That's easy for you to say. You weren't there.'

'OK. You're right. What do you think you could have done?'

'I could have chased after the killer. I heard him running away. But I stayed with Jason.'

'And get yourself killed? Don't be stupid.'

I was shaking all over now. 'I'm not being stupid. If I'd had the balls to leave Jason, I could have seen the killer's face or his car or something and the police would have the bastard right now.'

And I wouldn't have Gates' boot on my neck. I hadn't known where this night would lead, couldn't have known, but that simple act of identifying the killer would have sated Gates' bloodlust.

'Or you'd be dead. You did the right thing.'

I jumped to my feet and jabbed an accusing finger at Steve. 'You don't know that!' I shouted. I was shaking all over now.

Steve jumped up, grabbed me and pulled me to him. 'You're right. I don't know. I'm sorry.'

'Christ, you should have seen the blood. There was so much and I couldn't stop it.'

'It's OK, son. You did what you could. It's over.'

I burst into tears and my body rocked as I let the pain out. Steve just held me and, like always, he didn't let me fall. It took several minutes before I was cried out.

Steve made coffee and we talked. Jason's murder never made it back as a topic. We talked about my hopes and dreams, football, Mum and Dad and how much we missed them. I remembered the night's sky turning from black to blue as dawn approached, but at some point, fatigue must have gotten the better of me because the next thing I knew it was morning and I woke up stretched out on the sofa. Strictly, it wasn't morning. The clock on the satellite TV box said it was coming up on one in the afternoon. I sat up and a note rolled off my chest.

Gone to work. I put the spare on and took your wheel. I'll get the tyre changed.

Catch you later, kid.

Steve

I showered and made breakfast. I didn't know if my body clock was off or if my nerves had killed my appetite, but the sight of breakfast turned my stomach. I choked down half of it before tossing the rest in the bin.

I drove across town to Archway, Steve's classic-sports-car restoration business. I parked by the workshop entrance next to Steve's pride and joy, a 1972 Ford Capri RS2600. Never released in Britain, Steve owned one of a handful of right-hand-drive models.

I spent most days at Archway. Since picking up the ESCC drive meant I didn't have room for a day job, I'd handed my notice in last month. I could have made it work, but it wouldn't have been fair to the company. I missed the wages and access to the CAD design software I'd used to design parts for my racecar and for Steve's restoration jobs in my off hours. But when one door closed, another opened. Picking up the title of *Pit Lane*'s Young Driver of the Year put me in hot demand at the driving schools. Three times a week, I was instructing at tracks across the country.

The roar of a Ford Cosworth DFV-V8 engine greeted me as I let myself in. It was a glorious sound. An automotive symphony.

For the last two months, Steve, with a little help from Jack Brabham himself, had been restoring a Brabham BT/26A grand prix car that Jacky Ickx raced in 1969. Steve knew Lotuses inside out, but not Brabhams, so he'd been calling the Australian at home for advice. I'd been reduced to a total fanboy when I'd picked up the phone to find the oldest living Formula One world champion on the other end of the line. My dad had raced against his sons, David and Gary, and we'd talked about Dad until Steve got on the line.

Steve cut the engine. 'How you doing? You look like you've been hung out to dry.'

I felt it. 'You don't look much better. Did you sleep after I woke you?'

Steve shook his head. 'Wasn't much point after you nodded off. The alarm was about to go off.'

'Shit, I'm sorry for keeping you up.'

'Don't be daft. Someone died in front of you last night. A sleepless night comes with the territory.'

It was a territory I wished I knew nothing about.

'You eaten?'

'I made breakfast.'

'But you didn't eat it, if I know you. I've got something in the crow's-nest.'

We went upstairs into the office overlooking the workshop. The crow's-nest was more of a gallery for racing memorabilia than an office. Framed pictures of some of racing's greatest drivers and posters from some of the great events of the past fifty years hung from the curving walls. Amongst the bric-a-brac were pictures of my greatest hero, Jim Clark, and my dad. If someone looked closely, they'd find me amongst the ranks, standing on the shoulders of giants. Steve had hung a photo of me winning a heat at the Formula Ford Festival last October.

He opened the mini fridge that sat between our two desks and tossed me a sandwich he'd bought from Marks and Spencer. 'Eat that. You need something to give you some colour. You look like a ghost.'

I fell on to the sofa Steve kept for clients and peeled open the sandwich. I bit into it and while it tasted fine, it failed to ignite my appetite.

Steve put his feet up on his desk and broke open his sandwich. Before he took a bite, he picked up a padded envelope on his desk and tossed it to me.

'That came for you this morning.'

With just my name scrawled on the front and no stamps or address written on the envelope, it hadn't been posted. I tore it open and peered inside. It contained only a door key and a note.

The note was from Gates. It was Jason Gates' home address in Northampton and the simple message: You might find these useful.

I supposed I'd just been given my first task – to check out Jason's place, but the subtext to this message came written in big, bold letters a mile high. Gates hand-delivering an envelope to Archway said that he knew where to find Steve. It was a crude message, but got its point across. 'What's that?' Steve asked.

'Just something from a friend.'

'What's your plan for today?'

'I have to deliver the Van Diemen later this afternoon, so I need to get it ready.'

The Van Diemen was the Formula Ford I'd raced last season. There was no point holding on to the car. I wouldn't be racing Formula Ford again, so I'd put it up for sale and landed a buyer straight away. My third place finish in the Formula Ford Festival had put a premium on the car's valuation and helped lift the price by five hundred quid. It was certainly worth the extra money. Steve and I maintained a top-notch car and the price I'd offered it for was a fair one. I was glad I didn't have to haggle.

We spent the next hour on my Van Diemen. Steve went around the chassis, tightening all the joints while I made copies of my set-up notes and the gear ratios I'd used at different circuits. I boxed up the spare parts and bodywork I was throwing in with the deal. Together, we loaded the Van Diemen on to my trailer and hooked it up to Steve's Transit van.

'You want some company?' Steve asked.

'No, I'm good,' I answered and took off. I didn't have far to go. Selling a racecar isn't like selling an ordinary car. There aren't that many buyers, so I was lucky that my buyer lived just twenty miles away in Walton-on-Thames. I chose the scenic route instead of going on the motorway.

The guy who was buying it, Ryan Green, was new to racing. He was in his thirties and indulging a whim. His eyes had lit up when he'd come to Archway to see the car a few weeks earlier. My multi-generational racing bloodline had helped close the deal. Whatever got the job done, I thought.

I arrived at his house, a very nice four-bedroom affair with a double garage in an upscale neighbourhood. I doubted his neighbours would be very happy when he fired up the engine.

He helped me unload the car and we wheeled it into his garage. He'd done a nice job of setting up a workspace for the car. He was taking the pursuit seriously, which was the only way.

I spent an hour going over the car's operation, its idiosyncrasies and the best way of setting it up. At the end, he asked if he could hire Steve and me to work the pits during his first race. I said I'd take it up with Steve. The money would be nice, but I think he was looking forward to having his weekends back now that he didn't have to run my car. His girlfriend, Maggie, would certainly like having him back. Steve bore a passing resemblance to Steve McQueen, which made him popular with the ladies. It was a look that hadn't been passed down to my father and me.

By the time I got away, it was after four and I hit rush hour. My progress slowed to a crawl. As I inched along with all the other automotive rats in the trap, my thoughts turned to Jason Gates.

Ignoring who had killed him, what had been he doing next to the Ragged Racing transporter that night? Huston had floated the idea that I'd killed Jason because he was trying to nick my car. What if he'd been trying to break into the transporter and got caught? That seemed likely. But if Rags or any of the other Ragged Racing crew had caught Jason, they would have given him a slap or called the police. A lot more would have to be at stake for someone to cut his throat.

That thought turned everything on its head. What if Jason had witnessed something he shouldn't have or was trying to steal something so important or valuable that killing him was the only possible course of action?

That was a scary thought with plenty of implications. What was that valuable? Ragged Racing's cars. Rags' cars were wiping the floor with the competition. I was sure one or two of the team owners wouldn't mind getting their hands on them to understand Rags' alchemy. Townsend Motorsport stuck out as an obvious contender. They'd been the big loser when Honda had dropped them a year ago and put their backing behind Ragged. The team had struggled for results ever since. Now, I was sure they'd do almost anything to get their hands on Rags' tweaks or expose any technical infractions. But as much as that picture fit, it also didn't make sense. If Townsend Motorsport wanted to know what Rags was doing, they just had to throw money at a crew chief to make him defect. And the idea of Rags or anyone else at the team killing someone over it was beyond ridiculous.

My mobile rang. It was Claudia.

'Aidy, Rags told me what 'appened last night. Are you OK?'

'Shaken, but fine.'

'It's a terrible thing. I'm so glad you're OK. 'Ave the media been in touch?'

'No.'

'Good. Word is out at the show. I made a statement on behalf of the team.'

'What did you say?'

'I just stated the facts as we know them. A man was killed last night near the Ragged Racing transporter. You discovered the man and attempted to save 'im.'

'Did you know the victim is a mechanic for Townsend Motorsport?'

'No. I didn't know that. What do you think 'e was doing?'

I preferred to keep my thoughts to myself at this point and told her I didn't know.

'Maybe 'e tried to stop someone from breaking into the transporter,' she suggested.

That wasn't something I'd considered. I'd seen Jason as a potential thief, not a hero. That put a different complexion on everything.

I'd reached Staines and traffic was thickening up with vehicles pouring off the M25 ahead. I needed my full attention on the road with the trailer hanging off the back of the van.

'Look, I'm on the road at the moment. I have to go.'

'OK. I'll be in touch. Take care of yourself.'

I hung up on Claudia and descended into the crush at the Runnymede Roundabout. The multi-lane roundabout turned into a dogfight at rush hour. It was a direct feed on and off the M25 for anyone coming from or going to Staines, Ashford, Egham, Windsor and a half a dozen other London bedroom communities. Me driving Steve's Ford Transit with the attached trailer upset the natural balance of cars merging as they approached the roundabout. Combined, I was driving a forty-foot mobile road-block and everyone seemed eager to get in front of me. I wasn't in a hurry, so I played submissive and let people pass me until I reached the busy roundabout.

A thick tide of cars flowed around it and I needed a little cooperation to join the flow. It was hard to sneak my way in, especially when I had to go more than halfway around the roundabout to pick up the Windsor Road. I bided my time, much to the frustration of the cars behind me, and when I saw a gap, I went for it.

I slipped in behind a Vauxhall and guided the van and trailer around the roundabout. Despite the congestion, traffic moved fast. When my turnoff came into view, I indicated and eased over into the exit lane. Just as I did, a Renault hatchback darted out from behind me to squeeze by, but there was no squeezing by me. I was halfway between lanes with nowhere to go. The Renault driver and I both slammed on the brakes. The trailer wavered but it didn't jackknife. If it had, it would have wiped out cars like bowling pins. The Renault and I ground to a halt, inches from each other. Cars behind did the same as we managed to turn all the traffic on the Runnymede Roundabout into gridlock.

The woman behind the wheel of the Renault screamed muted obscenities from inside her car. I waved her on, but she continued to mouth off.

Horn blares made any chance of hearing her impossible. I imagined the traffic building up behind us.

I wound down the window. 'Go. If you want this exit so much, you take it.'

Still she didn't move.

'Go!' I yelled.

She powered down her window and leaned across her seat.

'You're in my way!' she yelled.

I pointed at the exit for Windsor Road. 'It's right there. Take it.'

'I'm trying to get on the M25. You're in my way, you dickhead.'

She was in the wrong lane for the exit she wanted and I was the dickhead. Typical. She might want to play games, but I wasn't in the mood. I eased the van and trailer forward. The Renault driver jumped on the horn as the trailer came within an inch of her front bumper. It was a tight manoeuvre, and to avoid tearing the front of her car off, I mounted the island on the Windsor Road exit. As soon as I was clear, I stepped on the accelerator and the van and trailer lurched forward.

I hadn't gone more than two hundred yards when a blaring car horn from behind caught my attention. I checked my mirrors and God help me, the Renault was behind me. After all her bitching and whining about wanting to get on the M25, she was following me, flashing her lights as well as leaning on her horn. She was waving her arms and mouthing words I couldn't hear. Obviously, she still wanted to give me a piece of her mind. Did she really think I was going to pull over just to get into an argument? If she wanted to burn her horn out, flash her lights and scream, so be it. I wasn't going to get involved.

Then a half-arsed sense of déjà vu hit me. Someone was trying to waylay me again. A ten-year-old Renault hatchback didn't quite fit Crichlow's image, but I looked beyond the Renault for Crichlow's BMW anyway. I didn't see it behind me or in front. Still, he seemed too smart to use the same car twice.

I didn't see any vehicles that caused my neck hairs to stand on end, but I wasn't taking any chances. I wasn't stopping for anyone, unless it was a police car, and I wasn't so sure about that.

I kept my foot planted on the accelerator until Miss Angry Renault's temper tantrum had run out of steam. She gave up by the time we reached Old Windsor.

Rags had told me to stay out of the limelight. I wasn't doing a great job.

Lap Six

The following Monday, I drove down to Snetterton in Norfolk for my first official test session with Ragged Racing. Weekday testing is when the circuits open their doors so that teams from all classes and divisions of motorsport can practice between races. It can be a real zoo out there because you can be sharing the track with anything.

Excitement and anxiety joined me on my drive to the circuit. I wasn't playing at being a racing driver anymore. I was the real thing now. That realization had kept me awake most of last night. I couldn't screw up this opportunity. I had to believe in myself. If I maintained my confidence, I'd do fine.

I tempered my excitement. I had an additional job to do today. This test session would also give me a chance to check out the transporter. I hoped it would provide some insight into why Jason Gates was killed and give me something to get Andrew Gates off my back.

I arrived to find the team already in place and working on the cars. They were the only team in the pits.

Rags shook my hand. 'Good. You're on time. I like that. Come with me. Driver briefing. How are you doing . . . since, you know?'

'OK.'

'Good. You witnessed a terrible thing. But you can't let it distract you. You ready for this?'

'Yes,' I said and meant it.

Rags took me into one of the unused garages where Kurt Haulk was already waiting with Barry Nevin. Nevin was the Ragged Racing crew chief. He was short, squat and built like an oil drum with Popeye-like forearms. He almost broke my hand when he shook it.

'Aidy, Barry will be running your car with his guys. He might look like he just escaped from Middle Earth, but he knows his stuff.'

Rags' joke got a laugh.

'I'll expect you to get the best out of each other as well as the car. I think you two will do well together.'

Nevin grinned at me. 'I watched you during the shootout. You have a good technical head on your shoulders, so we'll do great.'

Rags clapped his hands together. 'OK, chaps, with the arse kissing over, here's today's menu. I want to give these cars a thorough workout. The ESCC has a new tyre compound for this season, so I want to see how it compares to last year's tyres. Aidy's new and I want to see how well he slots in with Haulk. I also want to run some exercises. Finally, we're getting to play on the new track. That will be a great leveller, so I'll get to see how good Aidy is and how rusty Kurt is.'

Snetterton had gone through a major redevelopment. The track's profile had always looked like a slightly wonky exclamation mark, but the track's owner, Jonathon Palmer, had redesigned the layout and installed a fantastic in-field section that added a mile to the track's length, making it a very challenging three-mile circuit.

'OK, I think that's it. Everyone get suited up and let's get out there. We've got the track to ourselves.'

'Ourselves?' I said.

'Rags doesn't play well with others,' Haulk said. 'He always books exclusive test days.'

Exclusive test days were commonplace for Formula One teams with deep enough pockets to rent the track for themselves, but not teams in the ESCC. The sponsors had to be pumping in some serious cash for Rags to afford this. I reckoned I was going to like racing for Ragged.

'We can't keep a competitive edge if everyone gets to see what we're doing,' Rags said. 'Before you get out there and impress me, I have a quick announcement. Come with me.'

We followed Rags out to the pit lane.

'Can I have everyone's attention?' Rags called across the pit garages. 'Everyone gather around, please.'

The crew stopped what they were doing and crowded around him.

'As everybody is aware, Jason Gates was murdered last week.'

Several people looked my way.

'Most of you know Jason started out with us.'

I didn't. That put a fresh spin on events.

'He started out as a grease monkey and left us an accomplished technician. He deserved better. As a mark of respect, I'd like to have a moment's silence in Jason's honour.'

We bowed our heads. There'd been so much fervour in our preparation before hitting the track that the sudden silence was haunting. The only sound was the wind gusting down the pit lane.

'OK, guys, let's get back to it.'

'Lads, a moment,' Nevin said to his crew. 'Aidy, these reprobates will be running your car. Say hello to Jim McLeod, Dalton Mitchell, Roy Carroll and Stephen Price. They'll break their backs for you, but they'll expect you to do the same for them.'

I shook hands with all of them.

'OK, intros out the way, let's impress the boss,' Nevin said.

I jogged back to my car, grabbed my kit bag and changed into my race clothes. This consisted of flame retardant socks, long johns, a long-sleeved T-shirt, shoes and overalls. The clothing always seemed like overkill. Racecars rarely caught fire these days, but there was always the exception. I just hoped I'd never get to find out what it was like to be the exception. All dressed up, I jogged across the paddock back to the pits.

I stopped when I reached the team transporter. The doors were open, so I clambered up and stood inside. The transporter was a mobile workshop, all gleaming aluminium and polished steel. The cars sat on tracks inside. Storage compartments galore provided a home for replacement parts and tools. Everything that might be needed to strip and rebuild any of the cars was here. Jason had wanted something from here, but what? Nothing stood out at first glance. There was plenty worth stealing, but there'd be no point. Anything he'd find here he'd also find with his own team and certainly none of it was worth killing him over. If Jason had been breaking in to take something, it would be something very specific.

'Aidy, what are you doing?' Nevin asked from behind me.

I hadn't heard him walk up on me. 'Just looking. It's a bit more than I'm used to.'

'Well, you're in the big leagues now, son. C'mon, we've got work to do.'

I jumped down from the transporter and the two of us walked back to the garage.

'I know you've driven this car, but now you've got to race it. Remember, it's a lot different from your Formula Ford, OK?'

'Got it.'

'The telemetry will feed us everything you're doing, so don't think you can bullshit me on what's happening.'

I smiled. 'I won't.'

Nevin smiled back. 'Good lad. I want you to go out and give me twenty. Use ten to get a feel for the car and then give me ten flying laps to let me see how you put it all together.'

'No problem.'

'Questions?'

I frowned. 'More of a request.'

'Shoot.'

I had pre-race customs, although Dylan called them superstitions. I was used to prepping my own cars and knew every inch down to the nuts and bolts. Before I climbed behind the wheel, I always checked each joint and torqued my wheels. It served a technical purpose, but it also calmed and focused me. I explained this to Nevin and he and his crew laughed their heads off.

'We're going to get on well,' Nevin said. 'Aren't we, boys?' His crew responded with thumbs-up and yeses.

'You're in a different world now, Aidy. These lads have got your back. We'll forget nothing. You're in safe hands, but I like someone who crosses t's and dots i's.' Nevin handed me a checklist. 'I run through this with the boys before any of my drivers hit the track. You call it out and we'll do it.'

I liked Nevin's military precision. I called out the checks and my crew carried them out, making sure everything was tight, locked down and operating normally, even down to retorquing the wheels.

When the checklist was completed, Nevin handed me my helmet, which was mic'd up. This was the first time I'd be driving with a headset.

'I like drivers who talk to me,' Nevin said. 'I want your commentary. Your feedback is just as useful as the telemetry.'

I completed my final pre-race custom by kissing my mum's St Christopher that I'd been wearing since her death. I pulled on my helmet and climbed into the car. Nevin belted me in, plugged in my headset, then sent me out.

Haulk had already joined the circuit and I accelerated hard on the pit lane. The car shuddered over the concrete surface on its stiff springs until I hit the track's smooth asphalt. I wound the car up through the gears. With its interior stripped out, the roar of the engine echoed inside the cavernous cockpit.

As Nevin asked, I worked my way into the car, adjusting to its power and adapting to its idiosyncrasies. The extra weight and higher centre of gravity meant I couldn't corner as fast as in my Formula Ford. I had to work the brakes hard before I entered every corner, but I also had the power to compensate on the straights. As I racked up the laps, the car lost its unfamiliarity and I felt it respond to me.

'That's ten laps,' Nevin said through my headset. 'Now show me what you can do.'

I pushed the car, but I didn't go crazy. With each lap, I went a little deeper with the car, getting on the power earlier, braking later and refining my racing line. Nevin kept in contact the whole time. I liked having his voice in my ear, guiding and encouraging me. It reminded me of Steve, that voice of reason smoothing my reservations away.

At the end of my second set of laps, I came in. Nevin kept me in the car while the crew carried out checks and refuelled.

'I like your times. They aren't earth shattering, but you're chipping away at them. Keep it up.'

I put in another thirty laps under Nevin's tuition before Rags called in all the cars for lunch. I hated stopping for lunch. It meant losing the rhythm I was in, although it made sense to come in to refuel the body as well as the car. Most people would be amazed at how much energy a driver burns off during a race, considering he remains seated for all of it.

I came in to find the crew had converted two of the unused garages into a team canteen with tables and chairs. It was just one of the many perks of having the whole pit lane to yourself.

Nevin handed me a prepared lunch consisting of a pasta salad and roast chicken and I grabbed a bottle of water from an ice bucket. I took a seat at the table with everyone else and ate a forkful of the pasta salad.

'Hmm, that's weird,' Price said to me.

'What?'

'I'm surprised you didn't turn around three times before you sat down. You being a superstitious sod and everything.'

Everyone laughed.

'Ha-bloody-ha,' I said with a smile. I should have known I was going to take some ribbing over wanting to carry out my own spanner checks.

Haulk ruffled my hair as he passed by. 'So what else are you superstitious about? You don't sit down when you take a piss, do you?'

This got another laugh.

'Leave the lad alone,' Nevin said.

'I'm sure I'm not the only one who has superstitions.'

'Show him,' Rags said to Haulk.

Haulk frowned.

'Do it,' Rags insisted.

Haulk reached inside his overalls and pulled out a tiny teddy bear. It was frayed and manky looking. 'I never race without it.'

'What's everyone else got?' I asked.

Nevin slapped his groin. 'I've got my lucky underwear.'

'Not so lucky from where I'm sitting,' McLeod said.

'Hey, at least you can find me in the dark,' he said.

'I don't know why I have any of you working for me,' Rags said, grinning.

The crew spent the next twenty minutes taking pot shots at each other. I liked it. We felt like a family instead of a team and it was nice to be a part of the fun, but I had to get them talking about Jason.

'I didn't know Jason Gates worked for Ragged,' I said.

The life went out of the crowd and frowns replaced smiles.

'Yeah,' Rags said. 'He started with us four years ago, the year after Mike Whelan won his first championship for us.'

'Jason left us about a year ago,' Nevin said.

'Was he really still alive when you found him?' Mitchell asked.

I nodded.

'Christ, I can't imagine having my throat cut.'

That brought a fresh lull to the conversation and everyone focused on their food.

'Why do you want to know about Jason?' Carroll asked.

'Just wondering. I was with him when he died and I don't know a thing about him.'

'He was a good lad,' Nevin said.

'He didn't know a wing nut from a hand job when he started out with us,' Price said.

'But he was a fast learner,' Nevin said.

The crew shared half a dozen stories about how Jason had either screwed up or saved the day, but none of it helped me explain why he'd been killed and who would have done it.

'The thing that confuses me,' I said, 'is what he was doing hanging around our transporter.'

My remark brought the conversation to a screeching halt. Everyone looked to Rags for guidance.

'Time to wrap this up. We've still got a lot of road to cover and this conversation is getting a little morbid for my liking.'

And that was that. At least I had one answer. When it came to skeletons in the cupboard, Ragged Racing operated on a code of silence.

Rags sent Haulk and me out on drills for the afternoon session. We practised slipstreaming with the cars running nose to tail with no gap between us. The first car made a hole in the air, which reduced the wind resistance on the cars behind. We'd use this

practice when it came to setting qualifying times. Next, Rags had
me practise blocking. I drove ahead of Haulk and protected my
position by keeping to my lines and making myself as wide I
could to keep him behind me. Then we swapped. We finished off
the day with a dogfight. Rags told us to pull off the gloves and
go for it. The two of us went at each other for twenty-five laps
like we were in a real race. It was a serious affair. Haulk didn't
want to finish second to the new boy and I didn't want come off
second best. I deserved my spot on the team and I wanted to
prove it. And I did. For the most part, nothing separated us. I
rode Haulk's bumper for five laps before I blew by him. But my
lead didn't last. Haulk pulled an audacious move, out-braking me
on the back straight and muscling his way past. Naturally, I blew
it on the following lap and spun out on the hairpin trying to regain
my position.

'Don't prang that car on your first day,' Nevin said over my
headset.

'It's not a real racecar if it doesn't have some dents.'

A glint of something caught my eye. Off in the field, someone
was watching us with binoculars. It could be just a race fan, but
a spy wasn't out of the question. Rags was top dog and naturally
other teams would be interested in his progress.

'C'mon, get your arse in gear,' Nevin said.

I grabbed first and stamped on the accelerator. 'Hey, we've
got a spy out by the Bentley Straight.'

'What?'

'There's a guy with binoculars watching us.'

'Don't spook him. Keep driving.'

I did as I was told. I kept racing. Every time I came around,
I checked for the spy. He was there for the next two laps. On
the third time around, I saw three of my pit crew manhandling
him into Rags' Mercedes.

Rags called us in a lap later. I brought my car to a halt in
front of my pit garage. I couldn't park it inside because Rags
had the spy suspended from a mobile engine hoist with his hands
duct taped together. His feet dangled a clear six inches above
the ground.

'Boys, you've arrived just in time,' Rags said to Haulk and
me. 'Do you know who we have here? Nick Ronson, a grease
monkey from Townsend Motorsport.'

And a grease monkey from the same team as Jason Gates. Maybe I was looking at a motor-racing espionage angle here.

'I don't like spies,' Rags said, then drove a fist into Ronson's stomach. Ronson folded up and swung like a heavy bag. 'Tell Russell Townsend that if he wants to know what I do, come ask me and if he wants to know how to beat my cars, be more inventive. Am I clear?'

Ronson coughed, then nodded.

'I can't hear you,' Rags said and drew back his fist.

I grabbed his wrist. 'I think he got the message.'

Rags whirled around on me. 'This is my team. I'll decide when he's had enough. Not you. All right?'

'Yeah. I just don't want anyone getting hurt.'

'Listen, son, this tosser is getting off light. If the tables were turned, my guy would be coming back with broken fingers. Cut him down and everyone get the hell out of here.'

Rags walked off in disgust.

Nevin dragged me out of the garage by the bicep. 'Don't do that again,' he said. 'He makes the rules and we follow them.'

One of the techs tried handing Rags a pile of printouts, but Rags just knocked them away, sending them scattering to the ground.

'You're in the big leagues now, Aidy,' Nevin said. 'We play fair, but we play serious. Take that home as today's lesson.'

Lap Seven

The crew worked in silence as they loaded the racecars on to the transporter. I gave them the space they needed to work and went to change. As I wriggled out of my overalls, I watched Nick Ronson trudge across the paddock. Rags emerged from the pits and climbed into his Mercedes. He churned up mud as he pulled away.

'Oh, shit,' I murmured.

Rags was cutting across the paddock straight for Ronson. My heart skipped as I imagined him mowing Ronson down. Instead, he dropped two wheels off the paddock road and sprayed Ronson with dirt as he passed.

Rags had proved he wasn't someone to be messed with.

Considering the sombre mood that had descended over the team, I got into my car and left without saying my goodbyes. I followed the paddock road and crossed over the bridge that separated the paddock from the spectators. On the other side of the bridge, I found Ronson. If he and Jason had been working together, then he'd have a pretty good idea of what got Jason killed. I pulled up next to him and powered down my window.

'Need a lift?'

'Piss off.'

I frowned. I should have expected that reply. 'Do yourself a favour, swallow your pride and get in the sodding car.'

'Bollocks,' Ronson mumbled to himself and got in.

'Where are you parked?'

He pointed at a field used for spectator parking that ran along the newly renamed Bentley straight. A lone car, a Honda Civic hatchback, sat at the end. As a spy, my passenger was no genius at the art of concealment. I drove across the field, bumping over the damp, uneven surface.

'Nick, right?'

'Yeah.'

'Aidy Westlake. I hope Rags didn't hurt you too much.'

Ronson rubbed at his wrists where the tape had burned them. 'I've had worse.'

I pulled up next to his car. 'Who sent you – Russell Townsend?'

Ronson sneered at me. 'Thanks for the ride, but that's as far as my gratitude stretches.'

He reached for the door and I hit the central locking button, locking us in.

He whirled on me. 'You want to take your shot at me? Give it a go and we'll see how far you get.'

I raised my hands in surrender. 'I just want to know why you're here. It doesn't go any further.'

I unlocked the doors. Ronson made no move to leave.

'You found Jason?'

I nodded.

'Did you see who did it?'

'No, but I think I heard the killer running away.'

'Did Jason say anything to you?'

'Hey, I'm the one questioning you. Not the other way around. Now, who sent you?'

'No one sent me. I came on my own.'

'Why?'

'Why do you think? I want to know which one of you fuckers killed Jason.'

'You think one of us did it?'

'Stands to reason, doesn't it? Jason was killed next to your transporter.'

'Yeah, but what was he doing hanging around our truck in the first place – spying, stealing?'

'Fuck you. Jason wasn't like that. Not everyone is a cheat.'

'What's that supposed to mean?'

'Take a look at your team. There's something very wrong there.' Ronson pointed at the Ragged Racing fleet of transporters and support vehicles heading towards the exit. 'What's wrong with that picture?'

I shrugged.

'Sponsorship.'

'We've got sponsorship.'

'Not enough to explain the amount your team is spending.'

'How do you know?'

'You lot have just rented Snetterton to yourself for the day and you do it all the time. Every square inch of your cars should be covered with sponsors' logos to cover those running costs, so something bent is going on.'

Ronson had a point. The surface of a racecar was advertising real estate. Some locations were better than others and to get into those good neighbourhoods, you had to pay. Getting your company's name or product splashed down the side of the car cost more than it did on the back bumper.

I watched Ragged's transporters go by with the outline of the cars painted on the sides. Rags' major sponsor was a men's anti-perspirant. Their sponsorship cash got them the rear door and quarter panel, boot lid and bumper. *Pit Lane* magazine had the front bumper and the Honda symbol covered the bonnet. I guessed that there was around a hundred thousand pounds in unused ad space on each car. Compared to the rest of the field, Ragged Racing looked like the poor relation. Ronson was right. The team shouldn't have been in a position to be so lavish with its spending.

'But the team is factory backed now. Honda is giving us the cars for free and donating technical support, so the budget is low.'

'But Rags has been spending big money for years with no major sponsor underwriting him.'

'So what? He's spending big. What has that got to do with anything?

'It's a sign that Ragged Racing is bent.'

'Bent how?'

Ronson was silent. I took that to mean he didn't know.

'What did Jason suspect?'

'I don't know. He never gave me any details, but he thought something wasn't right. Our whole team does.'

'Because Honda switched support from you to us?'

'Hey, fuck you.'

'No, fuck you. You haven't told me anything that doesn't sound like petty, professional jealousy.'

'Yeah, believe what you want.'

Ronson jumped from the car and slammed the door.

I clambered from the car. 'I'm just trying to understand what's going on. You say someone from Ragged killed Jason, but you've got nothing to back it up.'

'Like I said, believe what you want. Just know that your team doesn't play fair and when it catches up to Rags, you'll suffer the consequences,' Ronson said.

'What's that supposed to mean?'

'When your team gets caught out, you'll all get painted with the same brush. You'd be wise to get out while you can.'

Ronson got behind the wheel of his Civic and churned up the field as he pulled away.

I slipped back into my car and pulled out the envelope Crichlow had left for me containing Jason Gates' door keys. I looked at the address written on the envelope. Northampton wasn't exactly on the way home, but it was close enough. I programmed the address into the sat nav and set off.

Just as I reached Cambridge, my mobile rang. It was Dylan.

'How did your first day as a hotshot racing driver go, matey?'

'Pretty good,' I answered, focusing on my track performance instead of Ronson's spying.

'You want to celebrate?'

'I can't. I'm tied up here.'

'Oh,' Dylan said. 'That's OK.'

Disappointment shaded his reply and I felt bad. As racing asked more and more of me, I'd be disappointing my friend more and more often.

'How about tomorrow?' I offered.

'Sure, I'm not working tomorrow. You want to do a pub for lunch?'

'Sounds good. Meet me at Archway.'

'See you at noon,' Dylan said and hung up.

I arrived in Northampton just before seven in the evening. The address led me to a housing development on the edge of town. It was a typical, modern development consisting of narrow streets and every type of housing option from flats to large, detached houses. Jason had lived on the top floor of a three-storey block of flats. I let myself into the building using the security code written on Gates' note.

Despite having the permission to enter – sort of – from the family, I felt like a thief. I raced up the stairs to the top-floor landing and quickly let myself in with the key.

The acrid tang of smoke, like a fireplace left to burn itself out, hit me before I flicked on the light.

'Not good,' I said to myself.

I followed the smell down the hallway and flung open the doors to the living room, bedroom and bathroom. The story was the same in each. Someone had ransacked them. Furniture was overturned. Drawers had been yanked out and the contents dumped. Cupboards and wardrobes had been flung open and cleared out. The smoke detector in the living room clung to the ceiling with its cover and battery missing. I guessed that the police didn't know about this carnage or there would have been crime-scene tape or something to mark their presence. That probably meant the ransacking was very recent.

The smell of burning was strongest in the bathroom. Flakes of ash and soot stained the sink. A half-arsed attempt to clean the sink had resulted in a grey-black swirl. The sink might have served as the makeshift fireplace, but the toilet bowl had served as the disposal for the ashes. Fortunately, not every fragment wanted to do as it had been told. Small pieces of singed paper floated on the water in the soot-stained bowl.

The smart move for me would be to call the police. That notion fell apart when I pictured myself trying to explain why I was in the home of a murder victim I'd discovered. Instead, I sighed, reached down and fished out the charred paper fragments with my hand. The biggest piece I recovered was a thumbnail-sized corner piece. I flicked on the strip light over the sink and peered at it. Even through the charring, it was easy to tell it was a photograph, but being a corner piece, it provided no useful detail. The other pieces were in worse shape. Two of them dissolved in my hand. The firebug might not have done the neatest of jobs, but he'd sufficiently destroyed whatever he needed to destroy. I scooped up the remaining pieces, dropped them in the toilet and flushed, sending them to a watery grave.

The evidence might have been destroyed, but it did leave behind one useful fact. The thumbnail-sized scrap had been a photo, but it had been printed on ordinary paper and not on photo stock. That meant it had come off a printer. So where was the computer? I searched the living room and found a printer in the wreckage, but there wasn't a computer attached.

Whatever was worth finding was probably gone, but continuing the search wasn't a waste of time. Jason Gates was a ghost to me, but you can learn a lot about a person from their belongings. I sifted through the mess in the living room and discovered that he had a subscription to *Pit Lane*. He didn't cook much, judging from all the ready meals in his fridge and freezer. He owned a very nice set of Snap-On tools that he kept in his bedroom and he had a number of framed motor-racing prints and action shots of Townsend Motorsport cars in action from the ESCC. I found a second toothbrush in the bathroom, but I didn't detect a girlfriend's presence. The place smacked too much of a man cave. It felt a little like my room at Steve's house.

I froze at the sound of a key slipping into the door lock. If this was the killer returning to clean up, I was buggered. There was only one way out of the flat – past the killer.

I stared at the twisting doorknob, raced into the kitchen and grabbed a knife, then stopped halfway down the hallway. The lock snapped back into place.

My plan was simple. The second this tosser made an aggressive move, I was charging him with the knife. I didn't care if I cut him, just as long as I broke free.

The door eased open and my grip on the knife tightened. I controlled my breathing by taking long and deep inhalations.

C'mon, you prick, I thought.

The door swung open and a blonde woman no older than twenty-three stood in the doorway. She froze at the sight of me, her key still outstretched.

I dropped my knife and raised my hands. Her gaze flicked past me to the mess in the living room.

'It's not what you think,' I blurted.

My words must have gotten lost in translation somewhere along the way. Her expression tightened, distorting her attractive face into something ugly, as if I'd promised to kill her and her family. She reached into her shoulder bag and charged at me.

I kept my hands up and retreated into the living room.

'Really, it's OK.'

I tripped on something and fell backward. In the time it took me to land on a CD player that caught me across my kidneys, the blonde was upon me. She sprayed me in the face with something that smelled floral but burned my eyes like acid. I yelled out and clutched my face as she delivered the *coup de grâce* by kicking me in the balls.

So much for my escape plan.

Lap Eight

My vision was in shreds, but I recognized the beeping sounds of buttons being pressed on a mobile phone.

'Stop,' I choked out. I palmed at my eyes, but it did nothing to clear my vision or stop the burning. 'I can explain.'

'Do you want another kick in the nuts?'

'Jason's brother, Andrew, sent me to check in on his place.'

She stopped dialling. 'What?'

I looked her way, but she remained a blur. I fished for the door key Gates had given me and held it out. 'I came by and found this place turned over. I heard the door and thought it was the burglar coming back.'

She was silent for a long moment. I hoped she was deciding not to call the cops and kick me in the balls again.

'You're a friend of Andrew's?' A heavy note of contempt edged the question.

'Not really, but he's not the kind of guy to take no for an answer if he asks you to do something.'

'That's for sure.'

'Look, can you help me up? That crap you sprayed me with is melting my eyes.'

I held out my hands and felt hers take hold. She guided me to the kitchen sink, where I doused my eyes. I groaned as the pain ebbed away and my vision returned.

'What was that crap?'

She held out a small can of extra hold hairspray. 'Pepper spray is considered an offensive weapon. Hairspray isn't and works just as well.'

'Good to know,' I said wiping my face with a paper towel. 'How'd you discover that nugget?'

This time she smiled. 'A cop told our self-defence class about it and how it wouldn't be classed as a weapon if we used it.'

'Who are you?'

'I'm Carrie Russell. Jason's girlfriend. Well, ex-girlfriend.'

'Ex?'

'We broke up three months ago. His idea. Not mine.'

The break-up hadn't been serious enough for him to take his door key back. That explained the second toothbrush in the bathroom.

'I'm Aidy Westlake,' I said and offered my hand.

She eyed it for a moment before taking it. I'd yet to fully earn her trust. I needed to give her something to win her over.

'I suppose you know about Jason.'

She nodded when the word yes wouldn't come.

'Could I talk to you for a minute? Please. I'd really appreciate your help.'

'With what?'

'With what happened to Jason. I was the one who found him that night.'

She paled and put her hand to her mouth.

'Let's sit down.' I righted the sofa and we sat on its slashed and shredded cushions.

'I talked to the police,' she said. 'They said someone from another team found him.'

I nodded. 'I drive for Ragged.'

'Did he say anything before . . . y'know?'

'No. I tried to save him. I didn't know what I was doing. I was just trying stuff I'd seen on TV. I felt so useless.'

'You aren't a doctor.'

'I know, but I should know the basics. We all should.'

'We should know a lot of things that we don't.'

Tears clouded my vision and I palmed them away in some lame attempt to hide the fact from Carrie.

'So why are you here? And more importantly, how are you involved with Andrew Gates?'

'He wants me to find out what happened to his brother.'

'Why? Did you know Jason?'

'No, but I found him next to the Ragged Racing team trans-porter. That and the fact that I drive for them was enough for Andrew to decide that I'm the person that can find something out. He doesn't trust the police.'

'Typical of him.'

No love lost between Carrie and Andrew. I thought that could help me. 'I think Jason was looking for something when he was killed.'

Carrie's eyes flashed recognition.

'What is it?' I said.

She said nothing.

'Obviously, Jason was on to something and whatever it was got him killed. Whatever he had or knew, he didn't give it up, so someone came here looking for it. I think they found it. Someone burned up printed pictures from a computer in the bathroom. Jason's printer is here, but I can't find a computer.'

Carrie jumped up and clambered over the wreckage to the corner of the room where the cheap office desk rested on its side. 'His laptop's gone?'

I followed her. 'What's going on? What was Jason up to, Carrie?'

'I don't know. He wouldn't tell me.'

She sifted through the cast-aside papers, books and belongings.

'It's gone, Carrie.'

'I know. I'm looking for a picture. Help me find it? It's a print of Nigel Mansell racing in the rain.'

I knew the picture. It depicted Mansell's second-place finish at the 1988 British Grand Prix in the vastly underpowered and temperamental Williams Judd. It has to be one of the top ten drives of the modern era. I found the framed print, or what was left of it, by the kitchen. The glass had been broken and the back ripped from the frame.

I held up the ruined picture. 'Found it.'

'No, no, no.' She scrabbled across the room and snatched the frame from me. 'It's gone. They've got it all.'

'What's gone? Who's got it all?'

She let the frame slip between her fingers and hit the ground. 'Jason wouldn't tell me what he was doing. I just know something happened with his team.'

'Townsend Motorsport?'

'No, Ragged Racing. It was why he left. He wouldn't talk about it, but he was very upset.'

Ronson thought Ragged was cheating. Had Jason caught Rags in the act a year ago? Gates claimed that Jason was straight. If that were true, he wouldn't have wanted anything to do with cheating. If Jason was trying to get evidence, it explained why he'd been trying to break into the transporter that night. If he'd gotten it, that would have been a problem for Rags. It's easy to deal with a spy or blackmailer. You slap one around and pay the other off. An honest man is different. There is no paying off that kind of person. Rags' reputation was massive. He couldn't risk seeing that destroyed. Jason's murder would make sense under those circumstances, which seemed like a stretch at this point.

'Jason has been digging into Ragged Racing for a year?'

'No. Only the last few months, I think.'

So, Jason walked out on the team a year ago, did nothing for months, then went on a private crusade. Why the time gap? I tried to make sense of that. Rags could have promised to be a good boy, then when Jason found out he wasn't, he made it his aim to expose the truth. It was a nice theory, but that was all it was – a theory. I needed something to back it up. If I told any of this to Gates, it would be Rags hanging from an engine hoist.

'And you don't know what set Jason off?'

'He wouldn't say. He cut me out of his life, saying it was for my own safety. I hated him for it, but it looks like he was right. Silly sod.'

'Jason had been gathering evidence. Did you ever see any of it?'

'Not really. I knew he took some pictures and hid them in the frame. I walked in on him and that was when he said it was over between us.'

'I didn't find a camera.'

'You wouldn't have. He didn't have one. He used the one on his phone.'

Jason should have had his mobile on him when I found him. 'Did the police give you Jason's belongings?'

'No. I'm not next of kin.'

But Andrew Gates was.

'OK, thanks for your help. I have to go, but do you want a hand tidying up?'

She reclaimed her purse and pulled out her mobile. 'I'm calling the cops.'

'Maybe we shouldn't. I'm sure Andrew wouldn't want that.'

'No. Andrew definitely wouldn't. Are you going to scurry back to him to tell him all you learned?'

'Yes. I don't have a choice.'

'Just leave my name out of this.'

'Why?'

'What did he tell you – that he sacrificed his life so Jason could live an honest one? Don't believe it. If he told you they were close, he's a bloody liar. They hadn't spoken in a year. Are you really going to find Jason's killer?'

'Yes. In spite of Andrew.'

Carrie smiled and raised her phone. 'I'm calling the cops, but I won't tell them you were here.'

I headed for the door.

'Word of advice, Aidy. Jason loved his brother, but he didn't trust him. And you shouldn't either.'

Lap Nine

I had Archway to myself the following morning since Steve had gone out on a parts run. The problem with maintaining cars thirty and forty years after production has ceased is that replacement parts are a rarity, but luckily Steve had Grant Smith. Grant was a classic-car parts dealer. He was the Indiana Jones of lost car parts. If he didn't have it, he'd make it his quest to track it down. He was worth his weight in gold to Steve.

The Brabham was finished and back in the loving arms of its collector, so I cleaned up the workshop, sweeping the floor and returning tools to their rightful places. The task helped me think and I had plenty to think about. Yesterday's revelations had served only to muddy my situation. I was wedged firmly between a rock and a nutcase. Rags could be dirty and so could Andrew. That left me in an ugly position. I had to watch myself with both of them. I could throw myself at DI Huston's feet and plead for mercy, but she didn't seem like the merciful type.

I had my back to the workshop door when it creaked on its old hinges. I turned expecting to see Steve, but a uniformed police officer stood in the doorway instead.

He smiled. 'Hello. I'm Sergeant David Lucas, Surrey Police. I'm looking for Mr Stephen Westlake. Is that you?'

I leaned the broom against a bench and picked up a rag to clean my hands. 'No, that's my grandfather. He's out at the moment. Can I help?'

'Maybe you can. Does he own a white Ford Transit van?' He flipped open a slim file folder and read off the number plate.

'Yes. Is there a problem?'

'I'm afraid so. The vehicle was involved in a traffic incident.' Sergeant Lucas studied me for a second then referred to his notes. 'The incident occurred last Friday evening at approximately four thirty p.m.'

Suddenly, I understood the meaning of the curious look. 'Where did the incident take place?'

'Staines.'

'With a Renault hatchback?'

Sergeant Lucas took a step closer. 'Yes.'

'Steve wasn't driving the van. I was.'

Sergeant Lucas smiled at my admission. I think my honesty passed his test. I didn't see the need for a test, since I couldn't see why my roundabout near miss warranted police intervention. I guessed that angry Renault woman must have been pissed off enough to report my number plate to the police. I supposed I deserved a slapped wrist for the inconvenience I'd caused.

'You were. Good. Then you're the man I need to talk to. What's your name?'

'Aidy Westlake.'

'Do you have somewhere we could talk, Aidy?'

I led Lucas up to the crow's-nest and we both took a seat.

He looked up at the memorabilia on the walls. 'You like motor racing, I see.'

'It's what we do. My grandfather was a grand prix mechanic in his day. He restores racecars and sports cars now.'

'Really? Wow. And you work for him?'

'I just help out.'

'So what do you do?'

'I'm a racing driver.' A blush followed my admission. I hadn't gotten used to the idea that I'd graduated from someone who raced cars to a full-time racing driver. My chosen career sounded so pretentious without a championship title under my belt.

'Really? That must be exciting.'

'It has its moments.'

Sergeant Lucas showed no sign of recognizing my name or a connection to my father's career. It made for a refreshing change.

'Obviously, you know why I'm here, yes?'

'Over the traffic jam we caused on the Runnymede roundabout.'

Lucas squeezed out a pained smile. 'I'm afraid it's a bit more than that, Aidy.'

'What do you mean?'

Lucas held up his hand and opened up a notebook. 'I just have to get this part out of the way before we go any further. You do not have to say anything. But it may harm your defence if you do not mention when questioned something which you later rely on in court. Anything you do say may be given in evidence.'

'Are you arresting me?'

'No, it's just a caution at this stage, but I do have to make you aware of your rights.'

'What's all this about? I want to know why you're cautioning me. What am I being accused of?'

'Whoa, slow down. One thing at a time. The victim alleges—'

'Victim?'

'Please, Aidy. Just calm yourself. You'll have all the time you need to respond, but let me get through the basics first. OK?'

What had Miss Angry Renault said that had brought the police to my door?

'The victim in question alleges you crashed into her at the roundabout then drove off. When you didn't stop, she pursued you and you proceeded to run her off the road.'

'Bullshit.'

'Mr Westlake, please.'

'I'm sorry, but nothing of the kind happened. She cut me off in traffic and I went around her. End of story. Do you think I'd drive off if I had clipped her, let alone run her off the road?'

'Mr Westlake, I don't know you.' Unlike me, Sergeant Lucas kept his tone level, but he'd switched to using my last name. We were no longer buddies.

'I'm a racing driver. I don't take chances on the road. If I lose my driver's licence, I lose my race licence. The risks are just too high.'

Lucas nodded thoughtfully.

'This woman – what's her name?'

'I can't divulge that information.'

'OK. Whoever she is, she's trying to get back at me over this roundabout thing. There's nothing to it.'

Lucas nodded. 'Maybe you should look at this.'

He removed a Polaroid from his folder and handed it to me. It was a driver's-side shot of the Renault hatchback sitting in a field. The front windscreen was split and the side windows were missing, but that was the least of the damage. The car looked as if it had been dropped from a great height. Every body panel was bent and buckled. The door mirror dangled from a trail of wires. My mouth dropped open in shock.

'What is this?'

'I have to warn you that a number of charges are being levelled at you which include failing to stop after an accident, failing to give particulars or report an accident within twenty-four hours, driving without due care and attention, dangerous driving, furious driving and offences not covered by other codes. These are serious charges.'

'I realize that. This is insane.'

Any two of these charges was enough to claim my driver's licence. I didn't have a clue how long I'd lose it for if all of them applied. My racing career was staring into an abyss.

'I don't get any of this,' I said. 'I swear to you that I didn't put a scratch on this car, let alone the damage pictured here.'

Lucas produced the pained smile again and took the Polaroid from me.

'Don't give me that look. This is bullshit. If I'd done that, my grandfather's van would be a mess and my trailer would be in pieces. But they're not. My grandfather's out in the van right now, but the trailer's right outside. Go look. You won't find a dent, scratch or repair.'

'There'll be time for that later. You're getting excited again.'

'Wouldn't you be?'

'Maybe I would. Let's calm down and just go through the facts. I think if we take things logically, one step at a time, there'll be less emotion and we'll have everything we need to be able to make a judgement. Sound like a plan?'

I exhaled. I appreciated what Lucas was doing. He was working with me. 'Yeah. Sounds like a good plan.'

'OK, I need to get a formal statement from you. I need the one-two-three of everything that occurred as you experienced it and nothing else. Just your viewpoint. OK?'

I liked Lucas and the way he went about his job. He was impartial and balanced, which made sense. He wasn't judge and jury. He just collected the information.

I nodded and proceeded to outline what happened from the moment I entered the roundabout until the woman in the Renault gave up on her chase. Lucas wrote down everything I said on a statement form, stopping me when he needed clarification on a point. Every time I tried to insert an assumption, Lucas reined me in and asked me to stick to the facts. At the end, he handed me three pages of paperwork.

'Read that over, initial each page and sign the last page. If you need to make changes, just make them and initial.'

I looked the pages over. Sergeant Lucas had captured my account as I'd described it. A couple of additional things occurred to me as I read the statement. Lucas stood next to me while I hand wrote in additions and initialled the changes.

'So, is this an accurate account, according to you?'

It was and it didn't look like much. I put my faith in the facts. They were probably the only thing that could save me. This woman could say I'd driven her off the road, but her story didn't hold water. Steve's van didn't have a scratch. Considering the damage to her car, she probably ran off the road all by herself in her rage, and was trying to squeeze some money out of Steve's insurance to pay for it. 'Yes, this is how it happened.'

'Then all I need is your signature.'

I picked up the pen to sign, but Sergeant Lucas put his hand over mine. 'Now you're sure you want to sign this?'

'Yes.'

'Once you sign this statement, it goes on record, so if there's anything you want to change, do it now. We can tear this up and start over. It doesn't matter to me how long this takes as long as we get the truth.'

I tapped my statement. 'This is the truth.'

He looked at me with disappointment. He didn't believe me. 'What are you trying to say?'

'All I'm saying is if your cars collided, I understand the situation. You're a racing driver who can't afford to lose your licence. Maybe you panicked and drove off. It's totally understandable. I could see myself doing the same in your position.'

'But I didn't. I did exactly what's written here. I don't know why the other driver is saying what she's saying, but it's not the truth.' I tapped the statement again. 'This is the truth.'

Sergeant Lucas stood back from me. 'If you sign that document, I can't help you further. Charges will likely be filed against you.'

'I don't need your help,' I said and signed the statement.

Lap Ten

Dylan poked his head through the door just after noon. 'Ready for lunch?'

I was more than ready. I'd been stewing in my own thoughts since Sergeant Lucas had left. I couldn't believe that Miss Angry Renault had lied. What did she want – revenge for the incident? No. She couldn't be that bent out of shape over it. Maybe she'd seen the Archway logo on the back of the van and thought she could squeeze some money out of the business. 'Let's get out of here,' I said.

'Rough morning?' Dylan asked.

'More than you know.'

I locked up Archway and Dylan drove us towards Ascot.

'You want to lose the scowl and tell me what happened this morning?'

I hadn't realized I'd been wearing my feelings for all to see. 'Sorry. When I dropped off the Van Diemen the other day, I had a near miss with a car on the way back. The police just came by to question me because they're investigating a claim that I ran a woman off the road.'

'Has she got anything to back this up?'

'Her word and her car. It's a write-off.'

'But you never made contact with her car?'

'No.'

'Then you're golden. Did you show them the van?'

'Couldn't. Steve was out in it. The cops are coming back to check it out in the next week or so.'

'Then you've got nothing to worry about, mate. The second they see the Transit hasn't got a scratch, this bird is screwed.'

It was nice to have someone believe in me. My recent run-ins with the police showed they had little faith in anything I said.

'Have you told Steve?'

'Not yet. I'm not looking forward to that.'

'Steve will have your back; you know that,' Dylan said. 'Let's forget that crap. How'd testing go yesterday? Tell me all about it. I want to hear.'

'It's amazing, mate. I have five guys working on my car alone. If something needs replacing, it gets replaced. No scrambling for loose change to pay for it. You wouldn't believe how many sets of tyres we burned through.'

Dylan beamed. 'You are in a different world. You're not trying to compete with the big boys – you are one of the big boys. I'm so proud of you.'

Dylan drove us out to one of his favourite haunts, The Coach and Horses. It was a pub restaurant where the local AC Cobra owners' club held their meetings. Drive by the last Sunday of the month and the car park would be chocka with the king of muscle cars.

We ordered food and drinks at the bar. We grabbed a table by the window and Dylan went quiet. He fiddled with the beer mats on the table, stacking a bunch together, shuffling them, turning them around in his hands, only to shuffle them again.

'You OK?'

'If I say no, is that a problem?'

'No. What's up?'

'It's a weekday and I'm not working, and I'm not likely to be any time soon.'

'What happened?'

'Can you say economic downturn and housing slump? The building trade has dried up.'

Dylan was a bricklayer and plasterer.

I felt bad. I'd been so wrapped up with my own life over the last few months that I hadn't kept up with Dylan's situation. 'I thought you were working on that housing development in Bracknell.'

'They've finished with me and there's little else going on right now. I'm trying to see if I can get on some plumbing or electrical crews, but that doesn't really matter. I don't want to be a bricky all my life.'

'What do you want?'

'To ask a favour.'

Last year, Dylan and Steve put their lives on the line to save me. Whatever he needed, I'd do my best to make it happen.

'Look, I'm done with the building trade. My heart isn't in it anymore. I want to work the pits. All I need is a break. Do you think you could ask Rags to give me a job?'

It seemed like a simple request, but it wasn't. The days were gone where you could just be a good mechanic to get into motorsport. Technology was so ingrained in the sport, you needed to be junior rocket scientist and that meant qualifications, which Dylan didn't have. He could claim that he'd worked alongside Steve, which carried some weight, but I doubted it was likely to sway Rags, especially since I'd pissed him off yesterday when I'd told him to leave Nick Ronson alone.

'I can ask, but I'm the new guy. I don't have any sway.'

'I know you can't make promises, but please do what you can. If I get on with a team, it'll be my break from the building trade.'

That bittersweet feeling that I'd felt at Earls Court returned. If my motor racing continued on the upswing, I'd be forced to leave my friends behind. There was only room for one person in the cockpit, literally and figuratively.

The barman called out a number and Dylan got our food. Despite my limp promise, his spirits had lifted and his smile was back.

Two office workers walked into the pub. They went straight to the barman and pointed outside. The barman nodded and rang the bell for calling time to grab everyone's attention.

'Who's got the Subaru WRX outside?'

'Me,' Dylan answered.

'You've got a flat tyre, mate.'

'Shit. That's all I need.'

We left our food and went outside to check the car. Dylan didn't have one flat tyre, he had two and neither were the product of bad luck. Someone had slit the sidewalls.

Dylan crouched in front of one of his ruined tyres. 'What prick did that?'

A prick like Crichlow. His BMW was parked across the street and he was behind the wheel watching us. A moment later, my mobile vibrated in my pocket. I had a text with the simple message: Lose the friend.

I glanced Crichlow's way and nodded.

'I'll call Steve,' I said.

Replacing one flat wouldn't have been a problem, but two turned our afternoon into a production. We jacked the car up and removed the wheels. When Steve arrived, he drove Dylan to a tyre shop for replacements. I stayed with the car to quell the pub manager's fears that we were dumping it.

The second Steve and Dylan were out of sight, I walked over to Crichlow. 'Was that really necessary?'

'Consider it a reminder that you should be devoting your energies to the task you've been assigned and not getting lashed up in the pub with your mate.'

'Duly noted,' I said sourly.

'Mr Gates wants to meet to discuss your progress,' Crichlow said.

'And so do I.'

'Good. Maybe I won't have to cut anything else.'

Lap Eleven

The next morning, I left for a Hertfordshire address Crichlow had texted me. Steve had already left for a meeting with a potential new client who was looking for someone to maintain his collection of classic British sports cars. It saved me the job of explaining where I was going.

The route took me into the countryside where the roads narrowed and the speed limits climbed. The address Crichlow had given me wasn't strictly an address, just a location. My X marks the spot was a wrought-iron gate. It wasn't hard to find. It was the only entrance on a long, winding road with nothing in between. I pulled over and stopped in front of the eight-foot-high gate. Brick columns on either side of it proclaimed: Private property. Keep out.

Another secluded spot. It failed to fill me with confidence after my last run-in with Andrew Gates.

I got out of the car. A thick chain and combination lock protected the gate and there wasn't a squawk box to announce my arrival, so I called Crichlow on my mobile.

'I'm here,' I said.

'Good,' Crichlow said. 'The combination to the lock is nine-nine-nine.'

I supposed that was meant to be funny.

'Follow the path to the end. You'll find me waiting. Lock the gate after you. This is a private meeting.'

I did as Crichlow told me. I followed a narrow gravel path,

made narrower by two walls of thick shrubbery. Eventually, it opened out on to a hillside. A hundred yards off, Crichlow leaned against the bonnet of his BMW. He looked very much the country gent in his Barbour jacket and corduroy trousers. He didn't acknowledge my arrival, instead staring out across the fields at the manor house off at the bottom of the hill. Andrew Gates wasn't on the scene. Did that mean I was in for another blindfolded ride in the boot of Crichlow's car? Not if I had anything to do with it. In case of that eventuality, I pulled up behind the BMW to block him in and climbed out.

'Where's Andrew?' I said, but the words lost their power when I saw the rifle in Crichlow's hands. He carried it low across his stomach with the barrel tilted towards the ground. I made no sudden movements.

He held the rifle up for me to see. The walnut stock gleamed and the black barrel seemed to stretch forever. 'The bolt action rifle. It's been around for donkeys.'

'What's going on?' I fought to keep my voice steady.

Crichlow removed a shell as long as his little finger from his jacket pocket, dropped it into the open breech, then drove the bolt home. He turned his back on me and sighted the rifle down the hillside towards the house.

'Rifle makers hit the development ceiling when some clever fucker came up with this simple design. You don't need a fancy scope to be accurate. If you know your trigonometry, you're as good as gold. As long as you've got the guts to pull the trigger, you'll hit your target every time.'

The display confused me, but there was a point to this. There always was with people who thought they held the power.

I walked over next to Crichlow and followed his aim. A row of sports cars sat in the spacious gravel driveway in front of the house. Steve's Ford Capri RS2600 was amongst them. Gates was Steve's morning client? I snatched the pair of binoculars off the bonnet of Crichlow's car. Steve and Gates were standing over a Jensen Interceptor. Steve had the bonnet up and was leaning over the engine compartment. He had his back square to Crichlow's aim.

'The wind is nice and steady.' Crichlow adjusted a knob on the scope. 'That makes it so much easier to predict the trajectory.'

I tossed the binoculars and lunged at him, striking the rifle with both hands, destroying his shot. I left my midsection exposed and he drove an elbow into my stomach just below my ribcage. I lost the ability to breathe and crumpled to my knees. He drove his heel into my chest and sent me sprawling on to my back, then he whipped the rifle around and aimed it at my face.

'This is a demonstration to remind you of how serious we are about finding Jason's killer and how easily we can follow through on our threat to hurt the people you care about.'

'The demonstration isn't necessary. I know what you can do.'

'Isn't it? It's been days and we haven't heard one damn word from you.'

My fear evaporated. I was sick of being pushed around. 'Do I look like a cop? No. I'm one person. If you were looking for instant results you should have asked a genie. Now get that sodding rifle out of my face.'

Crichlow slung the rifle over his shoulder and helped me to my feet. 'You know this isn't personal. It's business.'

'Like that makes a difference.'

Crichlow ejected the unspent round from the rifle and put it in his pocket. 'Get in the car.'

I picked up the binoculars and climbed into the BMW's passenger's seat alongside him.

'What have you found out?' he asked.

Being upfront with Andrew Gates and Crichlow was now an issue after talking to Carrie. I had to keep them at a distance until I knew one way or another how involved they were with Jason's death. That meant keeping some of what I knew to myself.

'Someone turned over Jason's flat. The place is a mess.'

'Shit. Anything taken?'

'Hard to tell. I don't know what he had beforehand. It wasn't a robbery, that's for certain. His TV and DVD player weren't taken.'

'So, someone was looking for something.'

'Yeah, I think they found what they were looking for. Jason's laptop is gone. You should probably have it cleared out just in case.'

'Yeah. Good point.'

Through the binoculars, I looked down the hillside. Steve and Gates stood in front of the assembled cars. They were laughing and joking like all was good with the world, except Gates knew

Crichlow was up here with his rifle. Gates claimed he'd gone straight, but he obviously hadn't lost his nasty side.

'Look, can I talk to you about Jason? I want an outsider's opinion and not one coloured by family devotion.'

'Are you saying Andrew can't be honest when it comes to Jason?'

'When it comes to family, who can?'

'Ask away.'

'Was Jason as honest as Andrew thinks he was?'

'Jason was a straight arrow.'

'He was trying to break into that transporter, so his arrow had a little kink to it.'

'Watch your mouth.'

'What was he up to that night?'

Crichlow was silent for a long moment. 'I don't know, but Jason would have had his reasons. Look, if you want to know more, you need to take this up with Andrew.'

But I couldn't. Gates was still wrapped up with Steve and Crichlow wouldn't let me spoil the surprise. Steve was in his element. Although I couldn't hear him from inside Crichlow's car, I knew what he was saying. He was regaling Gates with an insider's knowledge of every car, from who worked on the design and manufacture to their racing pedigree. It was there in Gates' rapt expression. I'd seen that look on many people's faces over the years when they brought cars to Steve. He always knew more about the vehicles than the owners did. He gave their car a historical context and sold them their place in it. Despite the situation, I smiled.

'What's that smile for?' Crichlow said.

'For Steve. Your boss is going to write him a blank cheque.'

'You think?'

'I know.'

It was an hour before Steve left in the RS2600, cheque in hand. I followed Crichlow back out to the road and to the main entrance of the property. Security consisted of a wrought-iron gate that Crichlow opened with a remote. I was half expecting to see a bevy of bouncer types on show, but there was no one except Crichlow. Maybe there was something to Gates' claims that he'd left the violent side of his past in the past. The lack of security said as much.

Gates emerged when we pulled up in front of the house. He stood with his hands in his pockets. 'I hope my demonstration made its point felt,' he said as Crichlow and I crossed the drive.

'I hope you're paying Steve well.'

'Consider it my payment for your services. I just hope Steve gets the chance to enjoy the money.'

'He will,' I said, and walked into his house without being invited.

Gates and Crichlow followed me inside and Crichlow closed the door. I followed Gates across the marble-floored foyer into the living room with an attached conservatory. There were a couple of family portraits hanging on the walls. One was of Gates with an attractive woman. The other was of a couple of kids, both girls, not quite teenagers. I hadn't thought of Gates as a family man. There was certainly no sign of them around at the moment. I was sure he didn't expose them to the ugly side of his business.

We took seats at a bar and Gates poured whiskies for all three of us without asking us what we wanted. I never drank and drove. My race licence relied on a clean driver's licence and it was already in jeopardy with the reckless-driving charges looming.

'What have you got for me?' Gates asked.

'Jason was breaking into our transporter when he was killed.'

Andrew Gates smacked his glass down on the bar top with a crack. Whisky slopped over the marble and on to his hand. 'Jason wasn't a thief.'

'I didn't say he was, but he must have been on to something. I don't know what, but it's connected to the Ragged team. I think he thought the proof was in that transporter and I think it got him killed.'

I was being vague with my information. I wanted to feed Gates enough to keep him satisfied, but after talking with Carrie, I was wary about what I shared with him. At the same time, I had to give him something to show him that I was making progress with the investigation.

'And you've got no idea who killed him?' Gates said.

'Not yet. It could be anyone at this point, but Jason spooked whoever killed him.'

'Someone turned over Jay's flat,' Crichlow said.

I let Gates digest that for a moment. 'I think Jason was collecting evidence against someone, but it's gone. His computer's been taken and his papers burned.'

'What was Jason playing at?' Gates said more to himself than to us. 'He shouldn't have been doing this alone. Why didn't he come to me for help?'

I dodged the question by shaking my head. Jason wouldn't have turned to his brother since there was a trust issue.

'So we've got nothing and they've got everything.'

'I wouldn't say that,' I said. 'The cops gave you back Jason's things, right?'

Gates capped the bottle and looked at me quizzically. 'Yeah.'

'Did they return his mobile?'

He was quiet for a moment. 'No.'

'Can I see what you got back?'

'Yeah. Wait here.'

Gates returned with an expandable paper envelope and I used it to push my unwanted whisky aside. The sight of Jason's possessions emptied out over the bar affected Gates. His features slackened and tears welled in his eyes. He was human, after all.

I picked through Jason's things. It was the usual collection of items we carry with us. There was nothing that actually defined him. Just keys, loose change, a pen, a handkerchief, a cheap digital watch, a signet ring, a cross on a chain and a wallet stained with his blood.

'Anything missing?' I asked.

'Besides the phone? No, I don't think so.'

'Did the cops keep anything back as evidence?'

'Not as far as I know. Not that anyone would have said if they did. The bastards wouldn't tell me. Straight for over a decade, but they still see a villain.'

After the treatment he'd given me, he didn't deserve the benefit of the doubt.

'Are you looking for something specific here?' Crichlow asked.

'Hard to say, but I thought there might be gloves or tools or something for breaking into the Ragged Racing transporter.'

Gates' grip tightened on his whisky glass. He looked disgustedly at it and tossed the contents down the sink. 'Tell me you've got ideas.'

If Jason hadn't brought any tools to break into the transporter, how was he planning to get inside? I picked up Jason's keys. In addition to the keys to his flat and car, I recognized the red anodized keys to the Ragged Racing workshop. As a former

employee, he shouldn't still possess them. So how had he come
by them?

'I do. Can I borrow these?'

'Yeah. Sure.'

I got up to leave. 'And just so that we're clear, I'm going to
find your brother's killer, not because you're threatening me, but
because your brother deserves justice, so don't ever pull a stunt
like this again. And just so you know, if you lay a finger on my
grandfather, I'll cut you off at the knees. Got me?'

Lap Twelve

I left Gates' house in one piece. He'd just smirked at my threat.
Crichlow hadn't. Maybe he recognized the dangers of dealing
with a cornered person.

As I drove back, I thought about Jason's mobile phone. That
phone held a lot of potential in its memory. Any pictures or video
could explain a lot of things. If there were ever any calls between
the killer and Jason, the phone log could also prove damaging.

I played over the possibilities as I drove back to Archway. The
noise of the road and existing in the limbo between places always
soothed me. No matter how big the problem, there was always
a big enough road to solve it.

So where was Jason's phone? Neither DI Huston nor Gates
had it. The killer might have taken it after he'd cut Jason's throat,
but I had my doubts. There hadn't been much time for searching
Jason between the time his throat was cut and I found him.
Another factor at play was the ransacking of Jason's flat. If the
killer had the phone, there would have been no reason to turn
the place over. Of course, this was all dependent on the phone
being valuable. Was that why his flat was ransacked? If Jason
knew he was going to be attacked, he could have ditched it before
the killer got to him. I thought about Jason pointing just before
he died. I thought he'd been pointing in the direction of his killer.
What if he was pointing at something else?

I left the car at Archway, then took the train into London and the tube over to Earls Court. While driving helped me think, driving into London didn't. It was a bottlenecked fortress.

The exhibition centre was between events, so the place was closed. Without the hubbub, the monolithic building resembled a forgotten ruin. I slipped unnoticed into the parking area. Despite not having the rows of vehicles from that night to guide me, I located the spot where Jason had died. I could have found the place with my eyes closed. Some moments in time are indelible.

I stared down at the ground where I'd done what I could to save a dying man. Blood no longer provided an epitaph. It had either been removed by the Earls Court staff or washed away by the rain. I dropped to one knee and touched the asphalt. It was cold and unfeeling, like the murder itself.

I stretched out on the ground, positioned myself like Jason and pointed in the same direction that he had. I looked beyond the end of my arm for my aim to strike something. I hit nothing but the street beyond. That wouldn't have been true the night of the murder. My aim would have struck vehicle after vehicle. I closed my eyes to bring that picture to my mind's eye. Cars, vans and transporters appeared, but the vision failed to take on a definite outline. I remembered some of the landscape that night, but I couldn't be certain about what had been parked where. If Jason had ditched his phone under someone's car or truck, I wouldn't know which one. Parking was first come first serve, so I couldn't rely on assigned parking.

'Bollocks,' I said and opened my eyes.

I realized I'd been wrong about my assumption. I was pointing at something – just not something above ground.

I jumped to my feet and jogged over to the drain cover. It was one of many unassuming grates littered across the car park. I peered into its depths. The drain ended in a sediment trap filled with silt, leaves, rubbish and something resembling a phone.

'Sorry it took me so long, Jason.'

I dropped to my knees and yanked on the grate, but the cast-iron cover failed to budge. It was welded in place with dirt and months of neglect. I heaved and felt muscles ping in my back. Each tear burned, but I kept pulling and received my reward. The grate slipped an inch, then another and another, finally popping up on its hinge.

I dropped on to my chest and reached down and pulled the phone from the soupy concoction of wet litter and dirt.

'What the bloody hell are you doing?' a voice said from behind me.

I turned to find a security guard standing over me. I held up the dirt-covered phone.

'I dropped my bloody phone, didn't I?' I said, getting to my feet. 'Couldn't drop it on the ground. No, I had to drop it down the drain.'

For an on-the-spot cover story, I thought it was inspired. So inspiring, it immediately disarmed the guard's suspicions. The crossed arms and stiff stance relaxed.

'You should have gotten one of the crew to pop the grate. Look at you. You're covered in crap.'

I didn't care. I had Jason's phone. 'These things are too expensive to leave down there.'

'If it's been down there in that cesspool, I doubt it works.'

That was my fear. I pressed the on button. Nothing happened. 'Shit.'

'No joy?'

I shook my head.

'Yeah, thought as much. Did you take the insurance option?'

'No. No insurance.'

'You should think about it. You wouldn't believe the number of people who end up dropping their phones down the bog at this place.'

'It could just be the battery. Any phone shops around?'

The guard named one.

I thanked him and headed for the street. I didn't get ten feet before he called me back.

'What were you doing here anyway?'

'Taking a shortcut to the tube.'

'Let that be an expensive lesson. In life, there are no shortcuts.'

Didn't I know it.

As soon as I was out of sight of the guard, I opened up the phone and removed the battery. The phone wasn't waterlogged, but droplets of water clung to the inside of the battery compartment. I did my best to dry it out with my shirt.

I found the phone shop and held up the component pieces to the guy behind the counter. 'Can you help?'

Obviously I wasn't the first person to drench a phone because

Mick, according to his nametag, knew exactly what to do. He produced a hairdryer and ran it over the phone's internals.

'This doesn't always work, but you never know. I suppose your life is in here.'

More than you know, I thought.

After five minutes of warming the phone into life, the shop guy installed a new battery. 'Moment of truth,' he said and pressed the on button.

The phone burst into life, but that was as far as it went. Either the keypad or the electronics were fried, because I couldn't access any of the phone's functions. I couldn't even make a call.

So much for technology. Just like paper, once it got wet, it was ruined. It held the answers to why Jason was killed. I was convinced of that, but it was all gone, washed away by the rain. I couldn't believe I was this close to the truth only to have Mother Nature destroy it for me.

'Sometimes you get lucky,' Mick said.

And sometimes you don't, I thought.

Lap Thirteen

The next morning, I was eating breakfast in the kitchen when Steve poked his head through the door.

'You got much on today?' he asked.

'No. Do you need a hand with something?'

'I have to take a run out and I could do with the company.'

'Sure. No worries.'

'Good. Be ready to go in half an hour.'

By the time I finished up breakfast and grabbed a shower, Steve was waiting for me in the Capri.

'Where we going?' I asked as I got into the car.

He smiled and reversed on to the street. 'I'm taking you to see someone I think you should meet.'

Steve had a surprise for me. It wasn't the first time he'd taken me on an excursion like this. He was so plugged into the motor-racing scene that a call from him opened doors. The week before my first go-kart race, he'd taken me to the Williams Formula

One factory for a personal tour. When I was growing up, I was forever getting to visit F1 teams at their factories or the circuit, and getting to hang out with drivers I admired. It had been a while since he'd set one of these up. While there hadn't been a special occasion to justify one of these jaunts, I guessed this one was meant to pep me up after Jason's murder.

Steve peeled off the M4 to take the clockwise loop of the M25. 'How'd your test session go?'

'Not bad. Nothing special. Still adapting to the car.'

'You'll get there. The key is not to expect instant results.'

'You want to tell the team that?'

Steve laughed. 'Gave you a hard time, did they?'

'No, not really. It's just a very serious environment.'

'They're used to winning.'

'I hope I will.'

Steve smiled again. 'On a different topic, the insurance company got in contact over the van. They're sending their claims adjuster to inspect it.'

I'd told Steve about the reckless-driving charges as soon as he'd returned to Archway that day.

'I'm really sorry about this,' I said.

'It's OK. The van's spotless. I know you didn't do anything and it'll get resolved.'

'Will it?'

'Hey, don't be like that. It's been a rough few days, but everything will turn out OK. Trust me.'

I wished I shared Steve's confidence.

'Just don't keep everything bottled up. I'm always here for you.'

'I know you are,' I said and felt bad for holding back my bargain with Gates.

Steve pulled off the motorway in Hertfordshire. I didn't have a clue where we were going. He couldn't be taking me to visit a team. None of the big names had their headquarters in Herts. As we left the towns for villages, I decided he had to be taking me to see a driver or team boss. I tried to remember who lived out this way and failed to come up with a name.

I was wrong on both counts. Steve stopped the Capri in front of a small church. At the sight of the hearse and mourners, I knew exactly who Steve had brought me to meet.

'Oh, God.'

'So you've worked out where you are?'

'Why didn't you tell me we were coming to Jason's funeral? I'm not dressed for something like this.'

'Don't you worry about the funeral just this second. We've got some things to discuss first.'

My stomach fluttered. I didn't like being scammed, especially by Steve. 'Like what, Steve? What's going on? Why have you brought me here?'

'I just want you to take this in. Look at these people. Look at their faces. Tell me what you see.'

Happy to do anything to avoid making eye contact with my grandfather, I looked over at the crowded churchyard. Dozens of people had come to pay their last respects to Jason. Gates was greeting people as they filed into the church. I recognized his wife and kids from the portraits back at his house. Gates had his arm around an elderly woman who I assumed was his mum. She was one person who knew what he was capable of. Naturally, Crichlow stood faithfully at his master's side, albeit at a respectful distance.

While most faces were strangers to me, I did recognize others. I watched Carrie Russell put her arms around Jason's mum before entering the church. I saw Russell Townsend, Nick Ronson and what looked to be everyone else from Townsend Motorsport. Barry Nevin followed them in as the lone contingent from Ragged Racing. I didn't see Rags or anyone else from the team. I thought it odd that for someone supposedly well loved by the team, Rags hadn't had the team attend. I guessed it could be viewed in poor taste considering where Jason had been murdered. So, was Nevin here without permission? I found that interesting. But my interest evaporated when Detective Inspector Joan Huston climbed from her car. She was the last person I wanted seeing me here.

'And look over there.' Steve pointed at Gates. 'There's Mr Lavery, who only yesterday wrote me a big cheque to maintain his cars. Why would he be at Jason Gates' funeral? Unless that name he gave me was bollocks. From the way he seems to be greeting everyone, I'd say he's family. Close family. Possibly a brother. Something's happened and I know you're involved so why don't you tell me about it?'

I felt my face redden. 'Nothing's going on. It's just the new drive. It's got me—'

Steve held up his hand. 'Don't lie to me, son. I'd rather you said nothing than listen to you lie to my face.'

I hated seeing his disappointment in me. He'd been there so many times for me. I wanted to tell him, but not with the risk of Andrew Gates following through on his threat.

'I saw the bruises,' he said after a long moment.

My throat tightened.

'The night you came home after the murder, you fell asleep on the sofa. I got a blanket. When I came back, your T-shirt had ridden up and I could see the bruises covering your stomach. I'm not stupid. I saw the condition you came home in that night. You weren't even in your own clothes and those were covered in dirt. I should have demanded answers from you, but you were still in shock. I was willing to wait, knowing you'd tell me when the time was right. Then three nights ago, you come home with red, raw eyes like something had burned them. Instead of getting better, the situation is getting worse. Something happened that night with Jason, didn't it? And that man is involved somehow. I don't care what because I'll help any way I can.'

Steve had put all the pieces together and had built something completely different. He thought I was involved with Jason's death. God, he had to be torn up inside. 'It's not what you think.'

'Then tell me.' His voice cracked. 'I've lost everyone I've ever loved in this world. You're all I've got left and I'll be damned if I'm going to lose you.'

I couldn't hold his gaze. It was too much. 'Please trust me when I say it's best I don't tell you.'

Steve slapped me across the face. 'No, it isn't.'

Steve had put no power behind the slap. He didn't have to. The slap itself was enough. He'd never raised a hand to me in the whole time he'd raised me. I'd pushed him too far.

'You tell me what's going on and you tell me now, or so help me God, I'll drag you up to that family and you can tell them what you're hiding. Have I made myself clear?'

More than clear. I couldn't keep this up any longer.

'I told you the truth about Jason. I didn't know him. But his brother had me hijacked right after the police released me. That's the man you know as Mr Lavery. He's an ex-loan shark. You know that flat I picked up? That was his neat way of snatching me. He wants me to find Jason's killer. If I don't, he's threatened to take it out on you.'

'Why didn't you tell me? Don't you think I had a right to know this?'

'Yes, but I didn't want to drag you into this mess.'

'Is that why you've been pushing Dylan and me away?'

'It's my problem to solve.'

'No, it's not. It's your problem, but it's down to your family to solve it. It's how these people prey on others. They make them feel like they don't have anyone to go to for help.'

'I'm sorry.'

Steve ran a hand through his greying hair. It used to be strawberry blond. Over the last few days, I had no doubt helped make room for more grey.

'I'm guessing the cops don't know about this arrangement.'

'Nope.'

'Jesus, Aidy. Why's he think you can help?'

'Because he thinks Ragged Racing is responsible for Jason's death.'

'Any truth to it?'

'Maybe, I don't know. Jason was up to something or someone thinks he was. His place was turned over.'

'You'd better start from the beginning.'

I laid it out for Steve, this time leaving nothing out. My revelations seemed to shift a weight from his shoulders.

'See that woman over there?' He pointed at the elderly woman Gates had his arm around. 'That's Jason's mum. She's burying her son today. I know the hell she's going through right now and so do you. She deserves justice. She deserves to know who killed her son.'

'I know. I was just trying to protect you.'

'Forget me. I know how to look after myself. I've been doing it all my life so I don't need you making decisions for me. Got that?'

I nodded.

'Good. If you know something or think you can find something out that can help ease her pain, you do it. Not because someone is threatening you. You do it because it's the right thing to do. Have I made myself clear?'

'Yes.'

'Good. And what happens when you serve the killer up to Jason's brother?'

'What do you think?'

'That makes you a killer too.'

This made me sick every time I thought about it. 'I know. If I find out who killed Jason, I'll tell him, but I'm telling the police first.'

Steve forced out a smile. 'Just see that you do. Now let's find this killer.'

Lap Fourteen

The ESCC championship kicked off the season at Spa-Francorchamps in Belgium. I set off for Spa on Thursday, a day ahead of the team. I drove alone, happy for the distance from my problems. I didn't want anything to do with murders and reckless-driving charges. I just wanted to race.

I reached Francorchamps just as night was falling on Thursday. I stopped the car at the roadside, giving me a panoramic view of Spa carved into the Ardennes. Twilight struck the circuit in all the right places, lighting up the black ribbon of tarmac. It was an amazing place to kick off my European racing career. The historic track is as frightening as it is exciting. It's a real driver's circuit, featuring the stomach-churning climb in Eau Rouge and the seemingly endless Kemmel Straight. Jim Clark was a master of this circuit, having won the Belgian Grand Prix four times in a row from 1962 to 1965. That was in the bad old days when the circuit was over eight and a half miles long and the weather could be different from one side of the track to the other. Even though safety standards had reduced it to half that length, it was still fearsome. It looked like paradise and I couldn't quite believe I was going to race here. I was frightened and ecstatic at the prospect of following in the wheel tracks of Jim Clark and my dad.

'I thought I was the only early bird,' Haulk said.

Lost in the moment, I hadn't heard him pull up behind me. 'I wanted to play tourist before the race.'

'Good. Our careers are short,' Haulk said. 'Enjoy these times, especially when someone is paying your way. Looking forward to the race?'

I took a big breath before answering yes.

Haulk cocked his head. 'Nervous?'

'A bit.'

'You've got nothing to be nervous about. You drove well at Snetterton.'

'Testing and racing are two different things, especially here.'

'Give yourself a break and don't overthink this. If you pile the pressure on yourself, you'll screw up. Forget the expectation, the results, lap times and qualifying positions. Just focus on your driving and the results will come. You can't let the other stuff get on top of you because it'll drag you down.'

'That's easy for you to say. You're at the top of your game.'

Haulk smiled. 'Do you think someone cracked an egg and out I rolled out a championship contender? No, I worked hard to understand the sport and conquer my doubts.' He snorted a laugh. 'You should have seen my Formula Ford career. I couldn't finish a sentence, let alone a race. I did so poorly that I switched from single seaters to saloon cars. I started over, focused on my driving and my results improved. In one season, I went from the back of the pack to winning races.'

I'd admired Haulk for what he'd achieved in the sport, but I now admired him for the way he went about his trade. At thirty-one, he was only ten years older than me, but he was a generation ahead of me in terms of experience. I thought the learning curve had been steep last season. It didn't look like it was going to flatten out any time soon, if ever.

'Let me ask you this,' Haulk said, 'what are you afraid of?'

'Making a tit of myself.'

Haulk smiled and nodded. 'I can't fault that, but if you focus on the negative, you'll never achieve the positive.'

'Thanks, Yoda.'

Haulk frowned. 'I'm trying to help you here.'

'I know. I know. I'm sorry. You just make it sound so simple.'

'That's because the solution is always simple. How you achieve it is the difficult part.'

My dad never had this problem. He was a natural. He could get into any car and make it fly and not have a clue why. How I wished I had a little more of that DNA in me right now.

'How much cash do you have on you?' Haulk asked.

'About a hundred euros.'

He grinned. 'That should be enough.'

'For what?'

'You'll see.' He held out a hand. 'Keys?'

Haulk drove me the short distance to the competitors' entrance at the circuit. The security guard approached us and Haulk powered down the window. He put on a white-toothed grin when the guard recognized him. He pumped the guard's hand two-handed while the guy showered him in praise.

Haulk belted out something to the guard in rapid-fire French that left my schoolboy French in the dust. He waved an arm in the direction of the track then at me. I waved. The guard and Haulk laughed, no doubt at my expense. Haulk continued to bombard the guard with perfect French. He stopped after a minute or two and then made a 'what do you say?' gesture with his hands. The guard teetered on the brink of a decision which I guessed wasn't leaning towards the positive, judging from his expression. Haulk put his hands together in prayer and bombarded the guard again. The guard smiled, shook his head, then nodded. Haulk took the man's hand two-handed again and pumped it hard. I noticed he had pressed the hundred euros I'd given him, along with a hundred of his own, into the handshake.

'Say thanks to René, Aidy.'

'*Merci, René.*'

René waved my thanks off and opened up the gates. Haulk put the Honda in gear and drove through, waving to René as we passed by.

'That was smooth.'

'Be good to everyone in the sport, not just the fans and organizers, because everyone holds the keys to something you want.'

Haulk guided my car through the paddock and stopped in the pits. 'OK, we don't have long. René says he can cover for us for about forty minutes.'

'I'm going on the track now? In this car?'

'A night drive isn't the best way to teach you, but it's better than being blindfolded.'

I swapped seats with Haulk and drove on to the track. I shouldn't be doing this, but I couldn't turn down the opportunity of a driving lesson. I accelerated hard on to the track and the climbing turn of Eau Rouge loomed ahead like a wall. This was going to be fun.

Haulk gave me minimum input on my first lap, letting me find my lines. Spa's biggest obstacle is its topography. There's not a flat section to it. You're either climbing or falling. The uphill portions give you grip, while the downhill ones steal it away. I had the better of the circuit climbing to the highest point, but I struggled on the long, seemingly endless downhill part. I either slithered or crashed through Revage, Pouhon and Fagnes where the corners are not only falling away, but have no camber to counterbalance with the lack of grip. Haulk stopped me after my first lap.

'Stop. Stop. Stop!' Haulk barked. 'You're fighting the car and you're braking too late. This isn't a Formula Ford. This car is heavy. You have to kill some of its momentum. The engine is in the front. The balance is all different. Understand the car. Then drive it.'

He talked me through a lap, telling me when to brake and when to hit the power. He taught me his lines around the track, including the little tricks that you only picked up from years of experience driving here. His inside knowledge was worth its weight in gold. I owed him big for this.

After five laps, I had a feel for the circuit. I swept through the bends, using the uphill sections to cut my braking distances and the downhills to carry the car along. Instead of fighting the continually changing topography, I took advantage of it. I was in control of this car now.

After eight laps, my brakes faded on me. When I pressed down on the pedal, it felt like a sponge under my foot. This wasn't my racecar. It didn't have high-temperature brake fluid and it was probably boiling at the callipers. But I didn't care. I worked around it for the next couple of laps, until Haulk made me call it quits.

'I think you have the measure of this place,' he said. 'Now let's get out of here.'

I thanked René on the way out, then drove back to the lookout spot where Haulk had left his car. We met back up at the hotel and I bought Haulk a drink in the bar.

'You drove really well out there tonight,' he said. 'I don't understand the nerves.'

'I'm out of my comfort zone.'

'Why?'

'This is the first time I'm racing without my grandfather and my best friend as my crew.'

The answer had come without thought and hearing it stopped me. I hadn't realized this was a problem until I said it. Steve and Dylan's presence always put me at ease and gave me confidence, but instead of looking to them for support, I'd almost gone out of my way to sideline them.

Haulk echoed my thoughts. 'Then involve them.'

'I was trying to grow up.'

'Forget that. What's grown up about motor racing? If you need to have a lucky rabbit's foot in the car with you, do it. Half of racing is psychological. You have to have a good mental grounding if you're going to do well. If you need your grandfather and best friend around, get them.'

'I swear, you are Yoda.'

Haulk smiled and kicked back his beer. 'Maybe I am. Using my Jedi powers I detect another problem.'

I shifted awkwardly on my stool. 'Like what?'

'Like Rags taking care of that spy the other day. It spooked you, didn't it? I saw it on your face.'

'It's not every day you see someone hanging off an engine hoist.' I turned my beer glass around in circles on the bar. 'How much of that was show? It seemed like overkill.'

'One thing you'll learn about Rags is that he doesn't do anything for show.'

The mix of adrenaline still coursing through me and the Belgian beer's high alcohol content hit me harder than normal, leaving me a little light-headed.

'There's a lot of money on the line here and he's worked damn hard to turn Ragged Racing into one of the premier saloon-car teams in Europe. He's not going to let anyone take that away from him. Talk to your grandfather. He knows the score and what some people will do to learn your secrets. You fight to protect what's yours. Plain and simple.'

I thought of Jason Gates lying on the ground with his throat cut. Would Rags go that far to protect what was his?

'Has he roughed up spies before?'

'Of course. It's not the first time we've found someone poking around the cars. The other year, this was before I began driving for Rags, a crew chief from Griffin Motorsport quit the team to join Rags. It was all a ploy to see what he was doing.'

'What did Rags do?'

'You don't see Griffin Motorsport around anymore, do you?'

I wondered how Rags had brought a whole team down. 'What do you think Rags will do about Townsend Motorsport? He caught one of their mechanics red-handed and Jason Gates was found dead by our transporter.'

'Are you saying Rags cut Jason's throat?'

'No, but he's not the person I thought he was.'

'You don't have to know a person well to know whether they're capable of murder.'

You'd be surprised, I thought. 'I'll be honest. Rags spooked me when he strung that guy up.'

'A few body blows are a million miles away from killing someone.'

A note of irritation was building in Haulk's voice. Time to switch gears.

'How well did you know Jason?'

'Pretty well. I liked him.'

'What do you think he was doing that night?'

Haulk frowned. 'Why all the questions?'

I shrugged. 'Just trying to know him, I suppose. I was with him for the last minutes of his life and I'm trying to make sense of it.'

The tension went out of Haulk's face. 'That's understandable. I hear the police gave you a hard time.'

I wondered where he'd heard that from. 'Yes, well, you know cops. Everyone's a suspect until proven otherwise.'

'And even then.'

Both of us smiled.

'So, Jason was a good guy?' I asked.

'Yeah.'

'Why'd he leave the team?'

'He said he had a better offer from Townsend.'

'Can't knock that. Did he stay friendly with the crew?'

'Yeah, particularly with Barry Nevin. Barry had taken him under his wing. They were close.'

Nevin had attended Jason's funeral. 'I'll talk to Barry about Jason.'

'Do that. I think Jason's death affected him as much as it's affected you.'

'What do you think Jason was doing with our transporter that night? Do you think he was breaking into it?'

The frown was back on Haulk's face. I didn't care. Right now, I needed answers more than I needed a teammate. 'Why do you think Jason was killed?'

The barman came over, breaking the moment by asking if we wanted another round. One Belgian beer was more than enough for me, but Haulk ordered another. Just as the barman turned to pour his drink, Haulk asked for an apple from a basket over the bar. The barman tossed one to him and he snatched it from the air.

Haulk reached into his jeans' pocket and brought out a flick knife. I jumped at the sound of the blade snapping open. It was long and thin with a fine edge from years of honing. DI Huston had said the weapon used to kill Jason had a fine edge, probably a cutthroat razor.

Haulk sliced off a section of apple and popped a slice into his mouth, then he noticed me staring at the blade.

'A product of a misspent youth,' he said, handing me the weapon. 'It's gotten me into a lot of trouble in its time, but just like a bad friend, I can't bear to let it go. So what was your question again?'

Lap Fifteen

Rags and Ragged Racing arrived in Spa-Francorchamps on Friday. I spent the afternoon going through car preparations with Barry Nevin. He talked me through what to expect from Saturday's qualifying session and how he'd manage me during the race for eventualities such as engine problems, tyre changes, weather reports and telemetry feedback. Nevin also outlined what to expect from the track. I didn't mention that I'd already driven the track the night before. I glanced over at Haulk in his pit garage next to mine. He winked at me.

We also practised a tyre change. The weather forecast was changeable. In some races, you could nurse your way through on slick tyres in the rain. Spa was different. Thanks to the ever-changing geography, water cascaded across the track in sheets in all the worst places. In those conditions, you had no choice. You had to switch to wet tyres.

In the evening, Rags outlined team tactics with the drivers and pit crew. I took notes. I knew it made me look a novice driver, but for the first time, I wasn't running the show. I'd called the shots in all my other races and Steve and Dylan followed my orders. Now that I was playing in someone else's playground, I needed to be au fait with their way of doing things. I kept up with Rags until my head swam from information overload.

My mechanic, Roy Carroll, was sitting next to me and he leaned over. 'Rags likes his prep work.'

So did I. I hated surprises on race days.

'Don't sweat the details. You can't. A race has a life of its own. You have to roll with the punches.'

After the team briefing, Rags dismissed us. Haulk and I chatted over coffee for an hour. Everyone was doing a nice job of making me feel like part of the team and their best to keep my nerves at bay. The more I got to know these guys the less I thought they could have any involvement with Jason's murder. I went to my room after that and called Steve. We chatted for a bit. He told me he was proud of me and not to overdo things on my first race. I promised I wouldn't. After the call, I went to bed. I wanted an early night, but was too anxious and excited about the race to sleep. I was frightened of failing, but I was more excited about succeeding. In the dark, I replayed my driving lesson with Haulk. I committed the braking points, gear changes, and every contour, twist, kink and curve of the track to memory before it put me to sleep.

Saturday was the sharp end of things. The season opener of the ESCC was a tough one – a double-header with rounds one and two of the championship over the same weekend. We had morning qualifying with the race in the afternoon. Those race positions determined the starting grid for round two on Sunday. Screw up in the Saturday race and not only did your team have to repair any damage for Sunday, but you were at the back of the field. I expected cagey performances from the drivers today. I planned on playing it conservatively, focusing on consistency with no fifty-fifty overtaking manoeuvres. I wanted to finish my first race. I could do without the embarrassment and the reputation as a loose cannon. That said,

racing conditions might throw the plan out the window. It was dry,
but for how long? A blanket of roiling grey covered the sky. I hoped
we'd get out before the weather changed.

A crowd was already filling the stands opposite the pits before
morning practice. People waved, cheered and called encouragement to anyone who'd listen. Just being in the pit lane at Spa
gave me a lift. There was something about being on the competi-
tor's side of the pit wall that gave me tingles. I was a racing
driver. This was what I did and where I belonged. I didn't feel
superior to the fans, just lucky in a way they'd never understand.
Whatever thrill they got from watching paled against the thrill I
got from being behind the wheel.

Nick Ronson stepped out of Townsend Racing's pit garage,
dampening my moment and blocking my path.

'How are you doing?' I asked. I didn't bother adding, 'after
your beating.'

'I'm OK.'

Nevin was looking down the pit lane at me. He shouted my
name and waved at me to get back to where I belonged.

'Look, I want to talk to you about Jason. I think you might
have a point. Can we meet after Sunday's race when things are
calmer?' I said.

'Sure. What's your mobile?'

I rattled off the number.

'I'll give you a bell.'

'Great. Thanks.'

I jogged up the pit lane to Nevin.

'Wasn't that the little tosser we caught spying last week?' he
asked.

'Yeah.'

'What'd he want?'

'He worked out that it was me who spotted him watching us.
He was giving me a little shit for it.'

Nevin slung an arm over my shoulders and guided me into
the garage. 'Forget him, Aidy. If he gets in your face again, I'll
take care of it. No one messes with my drivers. Anyway, I've
got something to show you.'

He pointed at my car. The crew stopped what they were doing
and grinned at me. A bath towel hung down over the driver's
door of my racecar, obscuring my number.

'We don't have time for the Queen and a bottle of champagne to christen this ship, so you'll have to do,' Rags said. 'Do us the honour, son.'

I grabbed the towel and yanked it away.

The number on my door was forty-three, my dad's number. I tried to say something, but the words didn't come.

'That's your official number. Now go out there and make it yours.'

Everyone clapped.

'I'll do my best,' I said.

'You'd better do more than your best,' Rags said and got a laugh.

Nevin shook my hand then handed me my inspection checklist. 'Let's get you out there for qualifying.'

I called off the inspection points and the crew checked them off as done, then I grabbed my helmet and Nevin fired up my car. It was a gorgeous sound. The garage's acoustics grabbed the exhaust's burble and transformed it into a roar. The symphony of sound intensified when Haulk's car fired up. There was no containing my smile.

I pulled on my helmet and kissed my mum's St Christopher before getting behind the wheel. Nevin got into the car where the front passenger seat should have been and belted me in.

'Stick behind Kurt. I want you guys joined at the hip. The slipstream will get us good times. He knows to take it easy during the first couple of laps. After that, he'll push for his own time. Got that?'

'Got it.'

'Show us what you've got and have fun doing it.'

Nevin clambered from the car and shut the doors. He was a good guy. I hoped he didn't have anything to do with Jason's murder.

A horn blared, signifying the start of the qualification period. The pits were open and the drivers had thirty minutes to set a time.

Nevin strode out into the pit lane. He waved Haulk, then me, out from our pit garages. On my way out, he flashed me a thumbs-up and I flashed one back. We exited the pit lane as a two-car train. Pride rose in my chest. I was part of a team and I knew how cool that looked.

I joined the track and boxed away Jason Gates' murder, Andrew Gates' threats, the reckless-driving charges and all the trouble that had glued itself to me. None of it mattered for the next thirty minutes. Setting a fast time was all that counted. I stamped down hard on the accelerator and worked my way up the gears.

As promised, Haulk maintained a pace I could match for the first four laps, then he steadily pulled away from me until he had a sizeable lead. I didn't let it worry me. I could still set a good time if I focused on my driving.

'You're doing good, Aidy,' Nevin's voice said over the headset. 'Your times are coming down.'

Nevin's words jinxed me a lap later. The car dropped power coming out of Blanchimont. Suddenly, I felt like I was dragging a weight behind me. A sick sounding note accompanied the power drop.

'We've got a problem,' I radioed in.

'What's wrong?' Nevin asked.

'I think I've dropped a cylinder from the sound of it.'

'Bring it in, Aidy,' Rags said. 'We'll see if we can get you back out.'

I heard the disappointment in Rags' voice and shared it. I'd gotten in enough laps to qualify for the race, but I was just finding my rhythm. More importantly to Rags, his showcase team had engine problems before the first race, which was hardly a good image for the number one ESCC team.

I nursed the car back to the pits. Rags and the team were ready to receive me. The second I stopped the car, the crew removed the bonnet and Rags descended on the engine.

'Keep the engine running, Aidy,' he barked over the din of cars racing by on the track. The sound of each car whipping by reminded me of the time I was losing. I willed Rags to find the problem and fast.

'Jesus Christ,' Rags said, then yanked his sleeve up and plunged his arm into the engine bay. A second later he pulled his arm back with a spark plug lead in his hand. It had come detached from the distributor. Rags pushed it back, then held it in place with a plastic cable tie.

'Let's get this lad back out while he's still got a chance of making a time,' he barked.

He stood back and let the crew bolt the bonnet back in place. As he rolled his sleeve back down, I saw three parallel scars on his forearm. Neat and straight, they reminded me of army stripes you see on a soldier's uniform. I was still trying to work out how Rags had gotten the scars when Nevin screamed at me over my headset to go and waved me out.

I got in another five laps before the chequered flag came out to signal the end of qualifying. I brought the car back to the pits to find Rags handing out a bollocking to the entire crew for dropping the ball. Someone had screwed up on my car and Rags was letting them know. There should have been cable ties holding my spark plug leads on. With all the vibration a racecar experiences, there's a good chance something will shake loose. Virtually every component is held in place with clips, ties, twist wire and bath sealant – anything to ensure it holds together.

Nevin broke from the group to help me from the car. 'By my reckoning, you got tenth. Well done.'

I turned that tenth-place qualifying spot into a fifth place finish in the race. It was wet and the rain proved to be a good friend to me and an enemy to others. Haulk won. Our collective results put Rags in a good mood after the morning's setback and he threw a big dinner for the team back at the hotel. Part way through the dinner, Rags stood.

'I'm very pleased with today's performance. We put a lot of points on the board and what do points mean?' He spread his arms wide and waited for the answer.

'Prizes!' the team answered in a collective roar.

'That's right. Prizes. We're in good shape for tomorrow. Be confident, but don't screw it up. All right?'

He made eye contact with everyone at the table.

And we didn't. The next day, we rewarded Rags with both of us on the podium. Haulk took the win and I claimed third. When I made it back to the pits, the crew dragged me from the car and pounded the top of my helmet with their hands.

Nevin grabbed me by the shoulders and put his face in mine. 'Fantastic. See, that's how it's done. Just keep it up, son.'

The second I had my helmet off, Rags swept me over to the podium where Haulk, second-place finisher, José Molina, Claudia, Easter and his camera crew were already waiting for the presentation. A cheer went up when the wreath was placed over my head. For the first time, I was experiencing the glory my dad experienced for most of his career. It killed me that Steve and Dylan weren't here to enjoy the moment with me.

George Easter moved in with his camera crew. He started with Haulk since he was the winner. Easter's question played out over the circuit's sound system and on the jumbo TV. His words bounced back over the PA system in the pits and spectator stands a moment after he asked them. Easter talked to Molina before turning his attention to me, while Claudia stood back and flashed me a smile.

'Aidy, you're proving to be a chip off the Westlake block. A podium position in your second saloon-car race. That's got to feel good.'

'It's more than good.'

'I bet it is. But do the finishes today and yesterday take the pressure off you?'

'Not really. Everybody is going to expect this performance every time. Now that's pressure.'

'Well said. I want to bring your boss in here.'

Rags joined me on the podium and slung an arm across my shoulders.

'Rags, how much has this young man impressed you this weekend?'

'Immensely. He grows in confidence and ability every time he gets in the car. Spa is no cakewalk as tracks go. Aidy has done something special this weekend.'

'No argument here,' Easter said. 'Aidy, before I let you go celebrate, I should ask you if there's any truth to the rumours that you've been charged with reckless driving. If so, how will that affect your season?'

Rags' hold around my shoulders tightened.

Lap Sixteen

Easter's question left me speechless. Who had talked to the press about the reckless driving and why the hell did George Easter have to bring it up now?

Rags jumped to my defence. 'You got proof of that, George?'

'Well, no,' Easter stammered. 'It's just something that was reported to me.'

'Well, I suggest you keep remarks like that to yourself, unless you've got proof to back them up. And for the record, we don't comment on unsubstantiated rumours.'

Claudia moved in swiftly to help end the interview and Rags pulled me off the podium. The second we reached the pits, he marched me into the back of the transporter and slammed the rollup door shut, sealing us in.

'What the fuck was that?' Rags barked. His question echoed off the walls, hitting me again and again. He paced back and forth like a caged animal as I filled him in on the details. 'Why the hell didn't you tell me about this?'

'I didn't think—'

'No, you bloody didn't. If you had, you would have come to me straight away.'

'It wasn't anyone's business.'

'You're wrong there, buddy boy. The day you signed for me, your business became my business.'

'The charges aren't going to stick.'

'It doesn't matter if they stick or not. What you do has an impact on me and this team. There's Honda to consider, sponsors, the ESCC and Ragged Racing's image just to name four. If you'd come to me with this the second it happened, I could have done something to protect you. I would have had an official statement in place as soon as this went public, instead of looking like a prize tit in front of a European audience.' Rags put his face in mine and tapped the side of my head with his index finger. 'Is any of this getting through?'

'Yes, it is. I'm sorry.'

'Sorry don't mean shit after the mess you've made today. Jesus Christ, the first double-podium finish of the season and all anyone will be talking about is your reckless-driving charge.' Rags finally drew breath. 'How bad are the charges?'

'Bad.'

'Bad enough to lose your licence?'

'Yes.'

'Jesus.'

'I'm sorry.'

'You've said that already.' Rags shook his head. 'I'm thinking I made a mistake with you.'

My heart dropped to the pit of my stomach. I'd gone from hero to villain at the flick of a switch.

'But I'm going to cover for you,' Rags said.

'Thanks.'

'Don't thank me. I'm not doing it for you. I'm doing it for everyone connected to this team. This ship is sinking because of you and I'm going to fix that leak. Got that?'

I nodded.

'In the meantime, I suggest you clear this mess up.'

'I will.'

'See that you do. Now, get out of here before you really piss me off.'

I let myself out and Rags slammed the door behind me. Claudia was standing a discreet distance from the transporter. She squeezed out a sympathetic and pained smile. I walked over to her.

'I pretty much 'eard everything.'

I groaned.

'We need to talk.'

'Can we get out of here? I'm feeling a little exposed at the moment. Hey, lock up your daughters, here comes that dangerous driver.'

Claudia smiled and her warmth helped soothe my angst. 'Where's your car?'

'Back at the hotel.'

'OK, I'll drive you.'

I grabbed my kit bag from the pit garage where everyone universally ignored me. I decided that was marginally better than getting a bollocking from them.

I skipped changing out of my racing overalls. At this point, I just wanted to get the hell out of there, so I climbed into Claudia's Peugeot.

Relief washed over me as she put distance between us and Spa.

'I just want to know one thing,' Claudia said. 'Are the claims true?'

'No.'

Claudia nodded. 'Then that's good enough for me. I'll do what I can to defend you to the press.'

I could have hugged Claudia at that moment. For once, someone believed in me.

'Now, there are going to be questions from the sports media. I will 'andle them. I'll work with Rags to ensure that the ESCC, Ragged Racing and you are all singing off the same hymn sheet.'

Singing off the same hymn sheet? Claudia had been hanging around far too many English people.

'OK. Thanks.'

She pulled up in front of my hotel. 'I'm 'ere to make you look good.'

'You have your work cut out for you.'

She laughed. 'No doubt, Aidy. As soon as you 'ave anything, please call me. From what you've told me, these claims won't stand up. When they don't, I'll make you look like an 'ero.'

'I'd like to see you do that. Thanks for the ride.'

I climbed from the car and she flashed me her million-euro smile.

'There's one thing you can do to help me,' I said.

'What's that?'

'Find out who leaked the news to George Easter.'

'I'll do that. *Au revoir*, Aidy.'

I left her, then showered and changed before checking out. I still had the room for the night but I didn't want to play black sheep for everyone at Ragged Racing.

I pulled out my mobile to call Steve and found I had a text from Nick Ronson. I'd forgotten all about meeting him. I opened the text. He wanted to meet in his hotel room at seven p.m., but I wasn't hanging around for another four hours. I called Ronson's number and told him to meet me in thirty minutes.

Ronson wanted to meet in Liege. It was a good place. It was far enough away from Spa that we wouldn't be spotted by anyone leaving the circuit and not too out of the way from my drive back to England. I plugged the address into my car's sat nav and pointed the car north.

As soon as I hit the road, the adrenaline high I'd been riding since the race petered out and fatigue set in. Maybe driving three hundred and fifty miles back to England tonight wasn't such a good idea. I set the cruise control and let the car carry me along.

I didn't want this meeting with Ronson anymore. It could wait until we were back in England. I was more interested in how George Easter knew about the reckless-driving charges. Obviously, someone had leaked the details, but I couldn't see Sergeant Lucas being the culprit. Smearing my name didn't help his case one way or another, but it did help Miss Angry Renault. The bigger issue here was how the hell had she worked out my identity?

My thoughts were broken by the wailing siren and flashing lights of a police car climbing all over my rear bumper.

'Shit,' I murmured. Just what I needed. A ticket on top of everything else.

I knew they couldn't be pulling me for speeding. I'd set the cruise control for the limit. I pulled the car over.

Two highway officers approached the car, one on each side. I powered down the window for the one coming up on my door.

The policeman rattled something off in French.

'*Je ne comprends pas*,' I said. It was one of those key phrases I'd never forgotten from French class: 'I don't understand.' If I was going to race in Europe, I needed to possess a tourist's understanding of a couple of key languages.

The policeman huffed in disgust and shared something with his colleague. I'm sure it wasn't complimentary.

'Do you speak English?' I asked and got a brusque headshake.

I smiled in an attempt to break the ice, which brought out a sneer. The cop snapped his fingers and rattled off more impatient French.

I still didn't know what he wanted or why I'd been pulled over, but I knew the preliminaries. I handed over my driver's licence, insurance and lease for the car. It was all in English, so I wasn't sure how much help it was to him.

Torchlight smacked into the back of my neck. I turned to see the other cop waving his torch over the car's interior.

The cop with my paperwork snapped his fingers at me and I turned back to him. He hit me with more French that I didn't understand.

'I'm sorry, but I don't know what you're saying and I don't know why you've pulled me over.'

I hoped the language barrier would play to my advantage. If I was too much of a bother to waste time on, maybe they'd wave me on with a warning. If they didn't go for that, I could call Claudia to play interpreter.

The cop shook his head at me and handed me my paperwork and licence back.

'Thanks and sorry.'

Before I could put the paperwork away, the second cop yanked open the rear passenger door, dived across the back seat and grabbed something off the floor mat.

'Jesus, what the hell?'

The cop fixed me with a disgusted glare and yelled something to his partner.

I didn't get to see what the second cop had found before my door was thrown open and the first cop wrenched me from my seat. I released the seat belt before it throttled me. The cop slammed me against the side of my wet car. Rain soaked through my T-shirt and I shuddered from the sudden damp.

'What's going on?'

I didn't get an answer, but my heart ratcheted up at the feel of handcuffs biting into my wrists. I was alone in a foreign country where I didn't understand the language. I could just imagine what Rags was going to say when I dropped this bombshell on him – whatever it was.

The cops bantered back and forth. Their conversation totally excluded me despite the fact that it was about me.

'Hey, hey!' I barked.

It silenced the cops.

'What the hell is going on? And if you don't know what I'm saying, get a sodding phrase book.'

The cops shared a glance before the one who'd dived across my back seat smiled. That smile chilled me more than the rain soaking through my clothes. He tossed what he'd found in the back of my car on the roof. It was a clear plastic bag filled with a white powder. No phrase book was required to explain what it was and how much trouble I was in.

Lap Seventeen

The cops put me in the back of their car and drove me to a police station in Liege. I was booked, printed, stripped of my possessions and dumped in an interview room. Thirty minutes later, two plain-clothes detectives blew in. One of them spoke to me in French. I shook my head and told them I didn't speak French. They frowned as if my inability to speak their language was an affront on my part and continued to bark at me. One of them opened a file and stabbed a finger at a handwritten form. I assumed it was the arrest report. The other detective dangled the bag of white powder now contained in a plastic evidence bag, then tossed it in my face.

Didn't anyone speak English in Belgium or was this a tactic to break me down? If this was their intention, it was working. My hands were slick with sweat and I didn't have enough saliva to unglue my tongue from the roof of my mouth. I was scared and isolated, but I'd had enough.

'Look, find me someone who speaks bloody English or give me my sodding phone back so I can bring in an interpreter.'

One of the detectives put his face in mine and butchered the word 'asshole'. He said something to his colleague and they gathered up their paperwork and the evidence and left.

The interview room seemed cavernous without the detectives.

'It's going to be OK,' I told myself, but the promise was brittle and it broke on my tongue as I said the words.

The door opened and a tall, angular-looking man walked in. He was in his fifties with thinning brown hair, swept back in a poor attempt to hide the fact. One strong breeze and it would be all over the place. He smiled at me, showing a neat row of teeth that seemed too small for his mouth.

'Adrian Westlake?' he asked.

'Thank God, someone who speaks English.'

'I might speak English, but I'm not your friend.'

'I don't need friends. I just need someone to listen.'

'That, I can do. I'm John Barrington, by the way.'

Barrington closed the door, took a seat in front of me and placed the file and the evidence bag the two Belgian detectives had been brandishing on the table.

'Despite the language barrier, I'm assuming you know why you've been arrested.'

'Drugs.'

'Yes, drugs.' Barrington held up the evidence bag. 'Not a huge amount, but enough to exceed what can be considered for personal use. So, this bumps the charge up to intent to distribute and if you brought it from the UK, then we're adding trafficking to this soup. Do you know the kind of time that carries in this country?'

'What's in the bag?'

Barrington laughed and leaned back in his chair. 'Really? Ignorance is your defence? You know that isn't going to fly.'

I wasn't in the mood to dance with this guy. 'Please just tell me.'

'Cocaine.'

'It's not mine.'

Barrington laughed again.

'Test my blood. Examine me. You won't find any drugs in my system.'

Barrington shrugged. 'That just confirms you're a dealer or mule and not a user. It's probably better you cough to a possession charge and hope for a lenient judge.'

'If it was mine, you'd have a really good point, but it's not.'

Barrington picked up the evidence bag and peered through it at the coke inside. 'Hmm, your car, but not your drugs.'

'Yes.'

Barrington flicked the baggie and wrinkled his nose. 'Then riddle me this, Aidy. How did the drugs end up in your car?'

'Someone put them there.'

Barrington dropped the evidence bag in mock shock. 'Who'd do that? Got any suspects? Who's been in your car? Tell me and I'll run them in.'

Haulk had been the only person in my car lately. I didn't see him as a cokehead.

'C'mon, Aidy. Name a miscreant.'

'No one I know.'

'Aidy, Aidy, Aidy, you can't give me that. Do you know how much trouble you're in?'

'I do, but I can't change the truth.'

'OK, let me get this straight. The drugs aren't yours and no one you know put them there, so what are you saying?' Barrington slapped his forehead. 'Don't tell me, someone planted them in the car. Am I right?'

Barrington was toying with me and it was beginning to irritate me. 'You said it, not me.'

'OK, I'll bite. If someone planted them, then who?' He spread his arms and waved them as if he was conducting a chorus. 'All together now.'

'The cops who brought me in?'

Barrington mimicked a rim shot. 'I served that one up for you. Seriously, Aidy, bent cops? Is that the best you've got?'

'They were the last ones in the back of my car.'

'C'mon, son, you're just wasting my time.'

'I don't think so. Why did I get pulled over in the first place? I wasn't speeding.'

Barrington flicked through the arrest report, as if he didn't know. 'Faulty brake light.'

'John, John, John, you can't give me that. The faulty brake light line, really? You're going to go with that?' I more than enjoyed using Barrington's mocking words back on him.

Barrington leaned back in his seat and crossed his arms. 'Why would Belgian cops want to set you up?'

That was a bloody good question and for a second, I didn't have an answer, but only for a second. The traffic stop, drug bust and Barrington all rang false.

'I don't know, but something isn't right here.'

Barrington's smile broadened to the point where he exposed all his perfect little teeth. 'What makes you say that?'

'There's nothing wrong with my car. It's brand new. A faulty brake light is possible, but unlikely, especially when you consider traffic was flowing and I had no reason to use the brakes before the cops pulled me over. And how bloody dumb would I have to be to leave a bag of coke out in the open?'

'Interesting.'

'And what's more interesting is you.'

'Me?'

I nodded. 'Who are you? You haven't produced any identification. You could be some twat off the street for all I know.'

'Don't be coarse. It doesn't suit you.'

'And how would you know? It's the first time we've met, but you know me well enough to call me Aidy and not Adrian, like it says on my licence.'

'Lucky guess.'

'I don't think so. I also find it weird that you haven't asked me what I'm doing in Belgium or what I do for a living. But you already know, don't you?'

'OK, you got me.'

'I'm not sure I want you.'

He reached inside the back pocket of his trousers. 'I'm Her Majesty's Revenue and Customs. I reach the parts that British police officers cannot reach. Some of the rules that tie the hands of your average bobby do not bind me. That makes me your best friend and your worst enemy.'

'And what do you want with me?'

'Your cooperation in an ongoing investigation.' Barrington opened the evidence bag and tipped the bag of cocaine into his hand. 'Someone is smuggling major quantities of this poison into Britain and I believe a team from the ESCC is responsible.'

'You're joking.'

'And you want to hear the biggest joke of all? I think Ragged Racing is that team. How's that for funny?'

I wasn't laughing. Suddenly Jason's death took on a different meaning. 'Is Jason Gates' murder connected to this?'

'Possibly.'

It seemed more than possible. If Jason had stumbled upon a major drug-smuggling operation, the smugglers would kill to protect it.

'Are you looking into it?'

'The police are. If their investigation is connected to mine, it gives me another wedge to split this operation open. So, have I got your attention?'

I had a nasty feeling where this was going. The cat had stopped toying with its prey. It was time to kill the mouse. 'You had me at a trumped-up possession charge. What do you want?'

'I need an inside man to tell me if my suspicions are correct.'

'I haven't seen anything remotely connected to drug trafficking.'

'Then I'm wrong, but I still need an inside man to prove that.'

I sighed. 'What if I say no?'

'Then I'll make it my job to see that these drug charges stick and when I take down your team and mark my words, I will, I'll take you down with them.' Barrington leered. 'Treat me badly, and I'll be your worst enemy.'

I was well and truly buggered. I should be scared, but I just couldn't summon up the emotion. Since finding Jason Gates' body, I'd taken too many body blows from too many quarters to feel much of anything.

'You're pretty proud of yourself, aren't you?' I said.

Barrington grinned. 'Just a humble civil servant doing his job.'

'Nice. Why me?'

'Ragged Racing is a tight unit. Everyone there has been part of the team for years. You're the new boy. That makes you the only one I can trust.'

'You could have just asked for my help.'

'And would you have agreed?'

I was a second too slow to answer.

'That's why I needed a little leverage. I know it doesn't seem fair, but it's for the greater good and all that tosh.'

Cornered with no escape route, I conceded. 'What do you want me to do?'

'I have an undercover officer operating within the ESCC as we speak. Your instructions will come from that person. You won't see me again if you do your job correctly.'

'That's something to be thankful for.'

Barrington belted out a laugh and gathered up everything he'd brought in with him. 'So can I assume you're on board?'

'Do I have a choice?'

'Not really.'

Lap Eighteen

B arrington watched me get back into my car from the steps of the police station. My hands shook on the wheel. I was running on empty. I blamed that on a heady cocktail of fatigue and fear. The smart thing would be to find a hotel and crash for the night, but I didn't feel safe here. I needed to get home.

I drove as far as the next town and pulled into a petrol station. Barrington had planted something on me once. Would he do it a second time? I wouldn't put it past him. While I refuelled the Honda, I searched it, but didn't find any other surprises. That gave me the confidence to keep going.

I crossed into France without any problems. In some ways, I hoped for problems. I'd take anything to get me out of this situation. Life was difficult enough with Andrew Gates cracking the whip for his aims. Now I had Barrington doing the same. Both demanded results and I got the feeling they didn't care what happened to me in the process. Neither seemed like a good guy, despite one of them being on the right side of the law. I didn't see how their investigations were connected, but Ragged Racing was the common denominator in both. I realized that getting to the truth meant I would have to go over the same ground as Jason had. Considering his fate, I needed an escape route. Maybe I should plead guilty to Lucas' reckless-driving charges. I'd be no good to anyone locked up in jail, but it seemed to be the lesser of many evils.

It was late by the time I reached the terminal for the Channel Tunnel, but that meant no wait. Less than an hour later, I was back in Britain and it never felt so good to be on home soil.

The morning rush hour slowed my return to Windsor, so it was eight by the time I reached Archway. I was very shaky and needed sleep, but I needed help more. Steve and Dylan were already at work on Andrew Gates' car collection. Dylan had his head under the bonnet of an MGA and Steve was up in the crow's-nest.

'Hey, it's podium boy back from his travels!' Dylan yelled across the workshop, more to Steve than to me.

Steve leaned on the crow's-nest's railing. 'Good job, son. We were expecting you back later.'

'Hey, you OK? You look like crap,' Dylan said.

'I'm in trouble.'

'Yeah, we saw the interview,' Dylan said. 'It'll blow over. We know there's no case.'

'No, that's the least of my problems. I'm in real trouble and I don't see a way out without your help.'

'You'd better get yourself up here,' Steve said.

Dylan followed me up into the crow's-nest. He sat at my desk and I took the sofa. Steve handed me a mug of coffee. I let its warmth soak into my hands.

'Talk, son,' Steve said.

'Jason's death has taken on a new wrinkle,' I said and told them about fun and games with Barrington.

'This Customs guy sounds like a nasty piece of work.'

As bad as Gates, I thought, but I supposed you needed nasty men to fight nasty men.

'Do you think Barrington will make good on his threat?' Steve asked.

'I do.'

'Shit,' Dylan said. 'This crap keeps getting deeper and deeper.'

'Then we deal with it,' Steve said.

'So Jason's death is connected to drugs?' Dylan asked.

I shrugged. 'I don't know. Maybe. But his murder isn't big on Barrington's radar as far as I can tell.'

'Did he mention Andrew?' Steve said.

'No.'

'Who's Andrew?' Dylan asked.

'Jason's brother. He's press-ganged me into service to find Jason's murderer.'

'What? Why didn't you tell us earlier?' Dylan watched the look I exchanged with Steve. 'Oh, it seems that I'm suffering from Last To Know Syndrome. Maybe I should change that to why didn't you tell *me* earlier?'

'I'm sorry,' I said.

'Bollocks to sorry. Can someone please tell me what's going on?'

'Hey, that's enough,' Steve said.

'Like fuck it is. How could you two keep me in the dark about something like this? I thought we were family.'

In my attempt to protect the people who meant the most to me, I'd made everything worse. 'We are family,' I stammered.

'Well, it doesn't fucking feel like it.'

'That's enough,' Steve said. 'You're right. We're family. And family doesn't turn on itself. Not when it counts and it counts now. Got me?'

The fight went out of Dylan. With all sincerity, he said, 'Yes. I'm sorry.'

'This whole thing feels completely out of control,' I said.

'Then we need to dial it back in,' Steve said. 'Go home, Aidy. Get some sleep. Get some food. Clean yourself up. I'll fill Dylan in. Then get back here and we can work out what to do next.'

I loved the sound of the word 'we'. Disaster got averted and tyrants got defeated with the word 'we'.

I made it home in minutes. I didn't realize how close I was to sleep until I stretched out on the sofa. This was the first time I'd stopped moving since yesterday's race and my body wasn't used to it. It tingled as my every molecule fought to keep moving. My desire overwhelmed my body and I was asleep in moments. I'd planned to doze for an hour, but it was late afternoon before I awoke. I stood in the shower for longer than I needed to, then cobbled together breakfast, lunch and early dinner with what I found in the fridge. It was after five before I was driving back to Archway.

I walked into the workshop to find the contents of the storage room filling the hallway out to the front entrance. Dylan emerged from inside. 'Hey, you're back.'

He came over and slung an arm around my shoulders. 'Sorry about earlier.'

'It's OK.'

'You're a twat for not telling me.'

Name calling. The universal sign that all is good between two friends. I smiled. 'I know. I'm sorry.'

'Join us in the situation room.'

I followed Dylan into the storage room-cum-situation room. The storage room was actually an unused office filled with spare parts, but now it was an office again – sort of. Steve and Dylan had been busy while I slept. They'd removed everything that wasn't nailed down and pushed the storage racks to one end of the room to open up the space. On one wall, they'd mounted two classroom-sized whiteboards next to each other, pretty much covering the wall.

'What's all this?' I asked.

'Our murder board,' Dylan answered. 'There are so many players in this game, we need something to keep all the information straight. This way we can jot things down as we discover them. Cops do it all the time.'

With a black marker, the board on the left-hand side had been divided up into columns with the heading, *People of Interest*. The names Jason Gates, Andrew Gates, Ragged Racing and HM Customs topped each of the columns. The right-hand board was, as yet, untouched.

'Who came up with this?' I asked.

'Your man there,' Steve said pointing a thumb at Dylan.

'It's cool, right?' Dylan said.

It was. I liked this. With so much happening, the murder board helped put the chaos in order.

'And it's not staying,' Steve said. 'Because I want this room back.'

Dylan waved Steve's objection away. 'He's got a thorn up his arse because he didn't think of it.'

'Thorn or no thorn, can we get on with this?' Steve said. He tossed a marker at me. 'You want to take us through this? We've been waiting for you to come back.'

I pulled a red pen from the pack and wrote *Victim* under Jason's name. That stopped the banter flying around the room.

Now that I had their attention, I talked as I wrote. 'Jason worked for Ragged Racing for three years, then left the team a year ago to join Townsend Motorsport. He then digs into Ragged's affairs, but not straight away. Whatever he was investigating was dangerous enough for him to dump his girlfriend, Carrie Russell, three months ago. After his death, someone ransacked his place, destroying everything he'd gotten on Ragged.'

'Why was Jason investigating the team?' Dylan asked.

I wrote a question mark. 'Customs says it's drugs and Townsend Motorsport says it's cheating.'

'Maybe one led to the other?' Steve suggested.

Under Ragged Racing, I wrote: *Suspect*.

'Who?' Dylan asked. 'Rags or the whole team?'

I wrote another question mark. 'I don't know. It could just be Rags or it could be all or none of them. But here are a few items of interest. The whole team was at a restaurant just a few streets from where Jason was killed, which gives everyone access. Jason was killed with a fine-edged blade and Kurt Haulk carries a flick knife, which he says is a product of a misspent youth. And Jason had a set of Ragged Racing keys on him when he was killed. Someone gave them to him.'

'But you don't know who?' Steve said.

I shook my head.

'Which means you can't trust any of them. That's not a good situation. You could be working with a killer, or working for one.'

It was a thought I'd already had and one I was trying to ignore. 'So what are you saying – I should quit the team?'

Steve shrugged.

Steve's point was a good one, but it needled me. Ragged Racing was my big break. How could I contemplate giving it up, despite the dangers? I tried diluting that bitter pill with the fact I was involved in a sport where getting killed was always a potential outcome. There was danger on the track and off it. I could live with both eventualities. For now.

'What you need is someone watching your back,' Steve said.

'How can he when any one of them could be the killer?' Dylan asked.

I saw the answer immediately. 'So we go with an inside man.'

Steve smiled and turned to Dylan.

Dylan pointed to himself. 'Me?'

'You said you wanted a job at Ragged,' I said.

'That's before I knew it was a den of potential thieves and killers.'

'It's a tough economy. Beggars can't be choosers.'

'Nice.' Dylan was silent for a long moment. 'Do you think you can get me in?'

'I think I can sell it. Put it this way, I have a really big incentive to sell it.'

'Woohoo. Lucky me. Can we move on to someone else, like the wanker who slashed my tyres?'

I wrote: *Dominic Crichlow. Heavy for Andrew Gates and wanker who slashed Dylan's tyres.*

'The more interesting person here is this guy,' I said and tapped the Andrew Gates heading with my pen, then wrote: *Jason's brother and loan shark.*

'Shouldn't that be ex-loan shark?' Dylan suggested.

I shrugged. 'We've only got his word for that.'

'I know someone who we can talk to on that front,' Steve said. 'Give me a day to look into that.'

Steve and loan sharks? I waited for him to explain, but he just stared at me.

'Move on, son. It's been a long day.'

In the column for Customs, I wrote Barrington's name with the suffix: *also a wanker.* 'Barrington says he has someone working undercover in the ESCC. I'm hoping this person can help us, although I get the feeling that relationship is supposed to be reversed.'

I added entries for Townsend Motorsport and Carrie Russell, under the classification of useful sources. The three of us then drew links between the various pieces of information we'd learned.

Dylan took a pen from the pack and added an additional column. At the top, he wrote: *Woman in the Renault.* He tapped the title with his pen. 'How's this woman feature in all this? I find it curious that your problems with her started up just after Jason's murder.'

I frowned. 'For what purpose?'

'It's a distraction. It gets you out of the way.'

I wasn't sure if I bought that story, but Miss Angry Renault was staying on the board for now.

'That's a whole lot of stuff up there, but I'm not sure what it all means,' Steve said.

'We have a handful of pieces to the puzzle, possibly to a number of puzzles,' I said. 'We need to be aware of them and focus on what we do know.'

'Which is what?' Steve said.

'Jason was murdered. Motives and reasons will reveal themselves if we can establish why Jason was poking around Ragged's transporter that night.'

I shifted over to the second board and drew a horizontal line. At the top of the board I wrote: *Timeline*.

'Where was everyone when Jason was killed?' I said.

At the centre of the line, I wrote the time and date Jason was killed. Working backward from Jason's time of death, I added a milestone for the approximate time the team had left the restaurant. Then I added milestones for three months ago and twelve months ago and wrote: *Breaks off his relationship with Carrie and leaves Ragged Racing*. I drew a separate line connecting these two times and wrote: *Somewhere Jason starts investigating Ragged's affairs*. And close to the start of the timeline, I wrote: *Four years ago, Jason starts working for Ragged Racing*.

'Now, there are things that will need to be added to the timeline, but the questions right now are: why did Jason leave the team and when and why did he start digging into their activities? If we start adding everyone else's activities to this timeline, we'll know who killed Jason and why.'

'And how do you suggest we do that?' Steve asked.

'By asking some questions that are bound to annoy quite a few of these people,' I said, pointing to the people listed on the murder board.

'I've got a lot of time on my hands at the moment,' Dylan said. 'I'll Google Ragged Racing, its history and its drivers and see if anything interesting falls out.'

'I think we've got a plan, gents,' I said.

Music from the Jumping Bean Mexican Cantina next door was

filtering through the thick brick wall that separated it from Archway. The happy hour crowd had moved in.

'Dinner's on me.'

While we waited to be shown to our table, Dylan said, 'You realize that you're following in Jason's footsteps, don't you?'

'I know.'

'And that ended with his murder.'

Driving back from Belgium, I'd come to the same conclusion, but my situation wasn't the same. 'I'm much better off than Jason.'

'Why?' Steve asked.

'Jason didn't have you two watching his back.'

Lap Nineteen

The next morning, I drove Dylan up to Ragged Racing's home in Banbury. A number of teams, covering the gambit of motorsport from circuit racing to rallying, called the Oxfordshire town home. With convenient motorway access, close proximity to a handful of tracks and reasonable rents, it made sense to establish a home there instead of anchoring a team to one particular circuit.

My reason for going to Rags wasn't just to get Dylan a job and make him my inside man. I needed to make peace with Rags. I hoped that the couple of days since Spa would have mellowed him and he would have gotten over the shock of my police problems. It didn't sound like he'd mellowed all that much when I'd called him to let him know I was coming. I definitely wasn't going to mention being picked up for drug possession.

I parked in one of the Ragged Racing-only spots in front of the warehouse that served as all things Ragged Racing. We got out of the car and walked over to the entrance.

'Do you think this is going to work?' Dylan asked.

'God knows with the way my luck is going.'

'Defeatism. That's the attitude.'

I glanced over at Dylan. He grinned and banged me on the back.

'Snap out of this, mate. You know you can do this. Am I right?'

Dylan was right, but I never liked to overestimate my chances. Chance always had the upper hand.

'I can't hear you,' Dylan mocked.

'This one is in the bag,' I answered as I opened the door.

'Hmm, I love it when you're forceful.'

My crew was poring over my racecar. I should say what was left of my car. Various body panels had been removed and all four wheels were off. Nevin was hunched over the engine bay when he spotted us. He left the carcass of my car and jogged over.

'I didn't know you were dropping by, Aidy.'

'I'm just here to see Rags.'

Nevin nodded. 'Yeah, I thought as much. Look, I don't know the details and I don't need to. You're a good driver and the boys like you, despite the black cloud you brought with you last weekend. Just be honest with Rags and it'll be sunshine again.'

'Thanks, Barry.'

'Who's your friend?'

Dylan introduced himself.

'Do you mind showing Dylan around while I talk to Rags?'

'No probs.'

I left Dylan with Nevin and went in search of Rags. The last time I'd been in his office was when he called me in to sign my one-year contract. It had been the best day of my life. Today could be the polar opposite.

The door was open and Rags was on the phone. I knocked on the door. He pointed to the chair in front of his desk and I took my place in the hot seat.

'Have I let you down before? No, that's right, I haven't. I'll get it to you. OK? Good. Talk to you soon.' Rags hung up and dropped his mobile on his desk.

'Problems?' I asked, wondering if the call had been about me.

'Not as big as yours.'

Ouch.

'You said you wanted to talk.'

'Yeah, I just wanted to say sorry again. I talked it out with my grandfather and you were right. I should have gone to you straight away about the police issue.'

'Damn right, you should have.'

'I know. Lesson learned.'

'I bloody hope so.' Rags leaned forward and put his elbows on his desk. 'I won't say I took a risk picking you for this drive, but there were more qualified drivers in the shootout. In fact, you were the least accomplished in the pack.'

Great, I thought and sighed.

'But I saw something in you. You deserved a shot and were worth the gamble. Now, that gamble doesn't look like it's paying off.'

Was I out? I didn't dare ask the question and risk putting the idea in Rag's head.

'How bad is this driving charge against you? And don't fucking sugar-coat it. I don't want another surprise.'

'The police have half a dozen charges lined up, but they haven't followed through and I don't think they will.'

Rags sat forward in his seat and rested his elbows on his desk. 'Why?'

'The woman who started this is lying and has nothing to back it up. When the police examine the evidence, they'll find she made the whole thing up.'

Rags was silent for a long moment. He stared at me, mulling over what I'd said. It seemed to meet with his approval. I saw the doubt leave his expression.

'How sure are you of this?'

'One hundred per cent.'

Rags flashed a flicker of a smile. I wanted to cheer. I was winning my drive back.

'How long is this going to take to resolve?'

'A month? I'm not sure.'

'Well, I don't want this hanging around our necks. I want it resolved as soon as possible. I'm guessing this bird wants something. Find out what it is and sort it. If she wants money, pay her. If she wants a new car, get her one. Whatever it is, do it and make her go away before this becomes a long-term issue.'

'Sure,' I said, with no idea how I was going to do any of that.

'Do you need me to get involved?'

The offer surprised me, but delighted me too. I liked that he'd support me, although he was more than likely offering to protect his own interests.

'No, I think I've got it covered.'

'Make sure you do. Just don't let her take your licence. If she does, you're finished with me. Is that clear?'

'Crystal.'

Rags glanced out his office window into the workshop. He jerked a thumb at Dylan talking to Nevin.

'Who's that?'

'That's my friend, Dylan. Can I ask a favour?'

'Oh, I don't like the sound of this.'

'He was part of my team last year.'

Rags held up a hand to stop me. 'Let me guess. He wants a job.'

'Yeah.'

'Jesus, Aidy. You don't want much, do you? You've hardly covered yourself in glory since being here and now you want me to add your mate to the payroll? He might be a good grease monkey, but that isn't enough. Those guys out there are highly skilled technicians.'

'I know. I'm just asking.' Under normal circumstances, I would have stopped pushing here, but I needed Dylan on the inside. 'He wants to works the pits and he's just after a chance. He's talented and I'm not just saying that. He's been helping my granddad since he was a teenager. Even a trial would be good.'

Rags looked at me, granite-faced, then shook his head. 'You've got some front on you, Aidy. Really, you do. But luckily for you, I like that.'

I was glad Rags liked *something* about me.

He got up from his desk. 'C'mon, let's have a chat with your boy.'

In the workshop, Nevin and Dylan were working on a brake disc assembly. It looked as if Dylan had been working his own angle while I'd been working mine. Dylan was doing the work and Nevin was telling him what to do. They stopped working when Rags and I walked up on them.

'Dylan, right?' Rags asked.

'Yes, Mr Ragsdale.'

'Call me Rags. Not even the bank manager calls me Mr Ragsdale. Your friend here says you want a job.'

Dylan glanced at me before turning back to Rags. 'Yes, I do.'

'Everyone here is a class act and I don't have room for passengers.'

'I'm no passenger, Rags.'

'I'm glad to hear it. You good enough to swing a spanner with these guys?'

'Given time, yes.'

'This ain't a nursery, son. Drivers rely on you being sharp. I'll ask you again. You good enough to swing a spanner with these guys?'

'Absolutely.'

'That's more like it. I'm going to have Barry put you through your paces. If he gives you the stamp of approval, then I'll give you a trial.'

'Already have,' Nevin said. 'And he's got good hands.'

'Really? People work fast around here when they want to.' Rags made a pretence of looking Dylan up and down. 'OK, I'm going to give you a trial run. If you keep your screw-ups to a minimum, I'll think about putting you on the books.'

Dylan, grinning like a kid on Christmas day, grabbed Rags' hand and pumped it.

'Don't get too excited. I'll cover your expenses when we travel, but there's no money in it until you prove yourself.'

'Great,' Dylan said.

'You room with Aidy too.'

'Not a problem.'

'Good. And part of your job is keeping this idiot' – Rags pointed at me – 'out of trouble. Other than that, welcome to the team.'

A cheer went up. Nevin shook Dylan's hand and the crew followed in turn.

Mission accomplished. Dylan had gotten his big break and I had my inside man.

Rags grabbed me by the arm and pulled me away from the crowd around Dylan. 'You owe me.'

'I know. Thanks so much for doing this.'

'I want more than thanks. I've got a job for you this weekend.'

He walked me over to a black Honda Accord. It was the road version of our ESCC cars.

'This car belongs to the person I was talking to on the phone. He's a sponsor. The boys here have been breathing on the car. By the time they're finished with it, it'll be no different than one of the ESCC cars. As a representative of Ragged Racing, I think it would be nice if you delivered it. Sponsors love that shit.'

'Sure. No problem. Where and when?'

'I want it there on Saturday. Munich, Germany.'

Lap Twenty

I was on the clock the next day instructing at Brands Hatch's racing school. Since landing a drive in the ESCC, I was something of a hot ticket and I'd picked up instructing work at several racing schools around the country because of it.

Track days consisted of teaching the basics of driving around a track to wannabe drivers who were getting their feet wet and at corporate events for entertaining clients. I liked instructing. The pay wasn't great, but it was easy work.

The racing schools liked to use drivers with rising reputations. I arrived for the drivers' briefing to see a number of stars from the single-seater and tin-top ranks, including Chloe Mercer. The schools also liked to use a few old hands, but I was surprised to see Tim Reid. I sat down next to Reid while Chloe did her best to ignore me.

After the briefing, the chief instructor assigned me a car. The school used BMW M3s, which was plenty of car for anyone to throw around a track, especially one as challenging as Brands. I sat behind the wheel. Before the student got to drive, I spent three laps showing them the lines around the track. Then they got fifteen laps to put what they'd learned in the classroom and from my demonstration into practice. To finish off, they got ten laps alone in the car to break a set lap time.

Punters spilled out from the briefing room underneath the race control tower and headed towards us. My passenger door opened and Detective Inspector Joan Huston climbed inside. It was a shock as I hadn't seen her since the night of the murder.

She smiled at my stunned expression. 'They tell me you're good, so I thought I'd see for myself.'

I didn't believe that for a second. 'Great.'

I helped belt her into her four-point harness. 'I'm going to show you the lines before I let you loose on the track.'

'You're in charge,' she said.

I didn't think so.

I put the car in gear and eased on to the track with the rest of the school cars. Brands is a fun track. It's challenging, because unlike most tracks, it's not flat. It undulates. Combine that with short straights and plenty of curves, and it's a tough track to get right.

I wound the BMW up through the gears and into the Druids hairpin. Cones at the edge of the track showed where to brake, turn in, the apex and the exit point. I talked my way through the bend, explaining to the detective how I applied the power as I put the car through the corner and demonstrating how I approached each corner the same, but adapted for the speed of the corner and the approach. After the three demonstration laps, I brought the car in so that Huston could take over.

'Did that make sense?' I asked her as I strapped her into the driver's seat.

'Yes, you're very good at this.'

'Thanks. Now take it easy on the first lap. Get a feel for the car and the track. Most importantly, just have fun.'

The second we hit the track it was obvious this wasn't Huston's first rodeo. She took the BMW by the scruff of the neck and dragged it around the track kicking and screaming. She hit all the marks with precision. She drifted the car through the bends, clipping the apex every time. She had to be a veteran of a police driving course. I didn't bother correcting her driving. There was nothing to correct.

Huston clocked a hundred miles an hour as she crossed the start-finish line to complete her first lap. 'No suggestions?' she said.

'None needed.'

She smiled at me. 'Good. Then we can have a little chat. You keep cropping up in my investigation. Did you know that?'

I felt myself sweating. 'No.'

'Yes. I found out that you questioned Jason Gates' girlfriend. I had to twist her arm to get that nugget of truth from her.'

Huston let the statement hang in the air for the next two corners. She was looking to me to fill the gap. I wasn't about to indulge her. I didn't know what Carrie Russell had told her. I liked to think Carrie had told the police as little as possible, but that was wishful thinking. She didn't owe me anything. Regardless, I wasn't about to say anything that could screw me. Let Huston drag the answers from me. It would give me an idea of what she knew.

'Nothing to say?'

'We talked, that was all.'

My answer seemed to irritate Huston, because she pushed the BMW hard through Graham Hill Bend. The car skittered through the sweeping lefthander.

'Feed the power in,' I said. 'Don't floor it.'

'What did you need to talk to her about? You said you didn't know Jason Gates.'

'I didn't. I just thought if I talked to someone who knew him, it might help jog my memory about that night.'

'What crap.'

Huston ignored my advice and went into the Surtees-McLaren-Clark curve complex too hard and fast. She missed the apex by a mile and lost a ton of speed.

'You're still getting on the power too early and too hard. Dial it back,' I said.

Finally, Huston listened to me and was perfect through Paddock Hill Bend and Druids.

'Did you know Jason Gates' flat was turned over?'

This question was a potential trapdoor. If Carrie had told Huston she'd found me there, then I was screwed, but I was sticking to the rule – deny everything. 'No. What was taken?'

Huston frowned.

Yep, she was testing me.

'And why did you return to the crime scene? Before you deny it, the security guard identified you from a photo.'

No wriggle room there.

'I remembered something from the night of the murder. When Jason was lying on the ground, just before he died, he pointed at something or someone. I went back to see if I could work out what it was.'

'You should have called me,' she snapped. 'You don't keep information like that from the police.'

'I didn't want to bother you if it was nothing.'

'And was it nothing?'

'I don't know. I think he was pointing in the direction of the killer's escape.'

Huston was silent for a moment as she powered the car smoothly through the Surtees-McLaren-Clark curve complex again. 'The security guard says he helped you recover your phone from a drain.'

'Yeah, I dropped it.'

'Because you were about to call me?'

'Something like that.'

'Let's cut the crap, Aidy. I don't like finding you shadowing my investigation and I especially don't like finding you one step ahead of me. Your interference slows my investigation down and helps the killer get away. You need to come clean with me or I'm taking you in. Am I clear?'

I got the feeling that she didn't know I'd been inside Jason's flat or about my association with Andrew. I wasn't about to admit to either of these things, but I had to give her something. I decided on the phone. It wasn't any good to me anyway.

'I found Jason's mobile phone at the murder site.'

'You what?' The temperature inside the car dropped ten degrees. 'Don't tell me you touched it.'

'Yes.'

'What the hell is wrong with you? Were you dropped on your head as a child? That's tampering with evidence. I should haul you in right now.'

'The phone was useless. It had shorted out.'

'I don't bloody care. You destroyed a vital piece of evidence. The second you found it, you should have called me.'

'I know. I'm sorry.'

'Screw sorry. Where's the phone now?'

'I've got it in my car. It's fried. I put a new battery in it, but I still couldn't get it to work.'

'You're going to give it to me.'

'OK.'

Huston jerked the wheel and pulled into the pits.

'You've still got another five laps.'

'I just want that phone.'

'OK. Stop here.'

Huston parked the car at the start of the pit garages, away from the line of school cars. She followed me to the parking area behind the pit lane where the instructors parked. I pulled the phone from the glove box where I'd left it after unsuccessfully attempting to breathe life into it. She took it from me and wrapped it in a handkerchief.

'I really should throw you in the cells. Maybe it would smarten you up.'

'I really am sorry.'

She waved my apology away. 'You've said that. What the hell did you think you'd get from it?'

'I thought I could check for messages or see who Jason called that night, but we'll never know.'

'I don't need the phone for that, love. I have the phone records. I've known for days who Jason spoke to the night he died.'

'Who was the last person Jason talked to?'

Huston patted my cheek. 'Stick to something you're good at, like racing, because you're a crappy detective.'

My mobile rang. It was Claudia.

'Hey, Claudia.'

'Aidy, I know who told George Easter about your reckless-driving charges. It was Chloe Mercer.'

'That backstabbing cow,' I said. 'I'm instructing at Brands and she's here.'

'Aidy, don't do anything stupid.'

'I won't,' I said and hung up.

'Problems?' Huston asked.

'Not if I've got anything to do with it.'

I raced back to the pits. I went from car to car looking for Chloe, ignoring the punters climbing in and out of the BMWs, but I didn't see her. A handful of cars trickled into the pits. Chloe emerged from the second of these cars with her student. She was all smiles as she talked up her student's performance. To the world, she was the consummate professional. Unfortunately, I knew differently.

'You drive like that,' she said to the student, 'and you'll do fine in the timed session.'

Chloe dropped the smile at the sight of me. I walked up on her just as her student headed back to race control.

'That was a classy move leaking my private business to George Easter.'

'People should know that you're a dangerous driver.' Chloe

grabbed her helmet off the roof of the BMW and walked by me.

I snatched her wrist. 'You should know the facts before you mouth off.'

She shook her hand free. 'I do. Reckless driving. Driving without due care and attention. Leaving the scene of an accident. Those are the charges, aren't they?'

Chloe was very well informed. 'Where'd you get your information?'

'From a fan. I received a very nice email via my website.'

I didn't have to ask the fan's name. Other than the police and me, only one person knew about the charges – Miss Angry Renault. She was the only person that would be interested in sharing the information. Why she'd go to Chloe was beyond me.

'You can't trust anything you read on the internet. No formal charges have been made. So you don't know the facts and you should remember that before you mess with someone's livelihood.'

Chloe smiled. 'Rags giving you shit? Good.'

Seeing the disgust and resentment chewing up her expression saddened me and deflated my anger. 'Does me having this drive piss you off that much?'

'You don't deserve it. You only got it on the back of your dad's reputation.'

'Why do you care? You have a Formula Three drive now, which is better than the ESCC.'

'It's the principle.'

'The principle of being a bad loser.'

Tim Reid appeared between us. 'You two cut it out,' he whispered. 'Everyone is watching. No one needs to see you two squabbling. If you've got dirty laundry, wash it elsewhere. Understood?'

Chloe snorted in disgust and stormed back towards race control.

'Thanks for that,' I said.

He looked back at Chloe as she was disappearing into race control. 'She giving you a hard time?'

'Yeah. She's still bent out of shape over not winning the *Pit Lane* shootout.'

'Well, she was the hot favourite.'

'And I was the long shot.'

'It's over. You won. She lost. Move on.'

'It's hard to do that with her trying to ruin it for me. She's the one who leaked the story about my reckless-driving case to George Easter.'

'Really? You think she's trying to disgrace you so that she can claim the title?'

I hadn't thought of that, but it was an interesting point. No wonder she was trying to ruin my name. 'Possibly, but who says she was in line after me?'

'Rags does. You were his first choice. She was second. Remember I was part of Rags' assessment panel.'

The PA paged Reid to race control.

'They're playing my song. We'll talk more at lunch. Have a good one, Aidy, and don't get any nutters.'

'Thanks. You too.'

I turned around and found Huston standing by the pit garages, well within earshot. I groaned inside. She smiled.

'I was starting to get a complex, but apparently you have a talent for annoying everyone. I see that I need to keep an eye on you from now on.'

Lap Twenty-One

I finished up at Brands at around four and drove up to Northamptonshire to meet with Nick Ronson. He'd left me a number of less-than-complimentary messages after I'd missed our meeting in Belgium. I arrived at the pub just before seven. As I climbed from my car, Ronson got out of his. He wasn't alone. Russell Townsend of Townsend Motorsport got out with him. His presence added a new dimension to Ronson's interest in Jason's death. It seemed Ronson had management approval. I crossed the pub car park.

'You didn't mention you were bringing anyone else, Nick.'

'I didn't know I had to. Get in.'

'I thought we were going in the pub.'

'Too noisy. Too crowded,' Townsend said. 'We should go somewhere private.'

'I'll follow you.'

'Just get in, Aidy, and stop pissing around,' Townsend said. 'You've already stood us up once.'

I cast a look back at my car.

'It'll be OK,' Ronson said.

I guessed changing the meeting location and separating me from my car was an attempt to unsettle me. Unfortunately for them, it didn't work. After Andrew Gates and HM Customs, it took a lot more to spook me these days.

I got into the back of the car and Ronson started driving.

Townsend turned around in his seat to face me. 'Are you going to play ball, Aidy?'

'Play ball?'

'Rags is a cheat. You know it and I know it. It needs to be brought out into the open.'

Even if there were suspicions surrounding Rags, Townsend's quest for truth and justice rang slightly hollow. The sound of sour grapes was thick in his voice. It was understandable. He'd lost his factory backing and all the cash and support that came with it.

'I'm here to find out why one of your guys was killed. And before you start pointing fingers, let's just remember where I found Jason. His dying next to Ragged Racing's transporter doesn't look good for you.'

'Or Rags. The last thing he'd want was someone exposing his secrets.'

I still struggled with the idea that Rags or anyone connected to Ragged Racing would kill someone over a racing indiscretion. The punishment for being exposed paled against the one for murder. The risk didn't match the reward.

'Did you send Jason to scope out the transporter?'

'No. He was working without my knowledge. He knew how I felt about Rags and what I suspected, but I didn't send him.'

'But you're involved now,' I said.

Townsend shot me a disgusted look. 'Only since Rags gave Nick a going over. That should tell you about the kind of man you're working for and what he's capable of.'

I let that one bounce off me. 'If you didn't send Jason, then why was he trying to find dirt on Rags?'

'Jason didn't like cheaters,' Ronson said. 'He believed in doing things the right way without exception.'

'He was a dying breed – an idealist,' Townsend added.

I didn't bother pointing out Townsend's unfortunate wording. I wondered if Jason's sense of right and wrong had anything to do with growing up around his brother.

'What do you think he was doing that night?' I asked.

'I think he wanted to look at one of the cars. If he found something bent, then he had Rags.'

'Or he was meeting someone from Ragged,' Ronson added. 'He knew most of the crew.'

It would explain how Jason had gotten a set of Ragged's keys. If he was such a straight arrow, he wouldn't break the law to find justice. He'd ask someone to help him open the transporter. I thought of the sound of feet running away when I'd been calling for help. They could have belonged to Jason's helper. Maybe Jason had asked someone to turn a blind eye for a few minutes and disappear while he searched the transporter, and when he came back, he found me crouched over Jason's body and ran.

'Like who?' I asked.

'Don't know. Like I said, he knew most of the crew.'

I wondered who Jason would turn to for help. Someone he was close to at Ragged? Or would he go straight to the top and confront Rags? I knew so little about Jason that I didn't know how he would act. His brother would though.

We arrived at our destination – the Townsend Motorsport workshop located within arm's reach of Silverstone circuit. Instead of a faceless unit on an industrial park, a farmhouse and a barn was home to the team.

Ronson parked in front of the farmhouse and we walked through the house into the barn. The agricultural motif ended with the exterior. Inside, the farmhouse had been converted into a modern office space and the barn was a well-equipped and organized workshop, just as you'd expect with a professional motor-racing outfit. The mismatch gave Townsend's operation charm. I bet it had won over a lot of sponsors in its time.

'Impressed?' Townsend asked.

I nodded.

'You should be. I'm the best in this business and so are my cars. That's how I know Rags is cheating.'

I looked from Townsend to Ronson and back. 'You keep saying Rags is cheating, but you haven't said how.'

Townsend slapped a roll of paper towels off a workbench next to him, sending it flying. 'I don't know how, but he has to be.'

'Why?'

'Because he's wiping the floor with us,' Townsend barked.

Sour grapes really were at the heart of this and I resisted the urge to point out that just because you're losing doesn't mean the other bloke is cheating. Half of winning was confidence and Rags was eating away at Townsend's confidence every time he took to the track. I picked up the roll of paper towels and handed it back to Townsend.

'I don't see how Rags is cheating.'

'Well, you wouldn't, would you?' Ronson said.

I sighed. 'I haven't been with the team long, but I haven't seen anything dodgy going on and it's pretty hard to get away with something major in the ESCC. The engines are sealed and there are only two tyre choices.'

'Then explain how he's getting that performance out of his cars.'

I shrugged. 'It's in the gear ratios he's selecting and the suspension setup. It's the only place where he's got room to play.'

'If he's on the up and up.'

'Yes, if he's on the up and up, and you haven't proven otherwise.'

'You disappoint me,' Townsend said. 'I didn't take you for a dirty driver. Then again, there is that reckless-driving charge pending against you.'

If Townsend hoped to needle me with that remark, he failed. I was tiring of his anaemic pressuring. 'What is it you want from me?'

'Your help in proving Rags is a cheat.'

Here we go again. Why did everyone think I could solve their problems at my own expense? 'And exactly why would I want to help you do that?'

'You seem like the kind of driver who wants to win and win clean. Now, I intend to prove Rags is a cheat one way or another, with or without you. If I do it without your help, the tar brush is going to splash you too.'

Townsend's intimidation play wasn't going to work. I could see how he thought it would. My twenty-second birthday was a couple of months away and I was still green in this sport. But,

life had put me on the fast track for growing up. I'd seen more
than my fair share of life already and while I didn't consider
myself the sharpest of the sharp, I wasn't a child who could be
pushed around with idle threats.

'So far, you haven't proved anything except your own
bitterness.'

'You little shit.'

Townsend's hands balled into fists and he lunged for me.
Ronson grabbed him and kept him from throwing a punch.

'See,' I said, 'we can both be rude to each other, but it doesn't
solve anything.'

'You really are an arsehole,' Ronson said.

'No, I'm just tired of your petty threats. You're looking for
my help. So, how can I help?'

Townsend stepped back and Ronson released his hold.
Townsend's fists disappeared.

'I want one of Rags' cars.'

'What?'

'Just for the night. You drop it off and I'll examine it. We'll
document everything we find and then you return the car. No
one need know.'

I was already shaking my head. 'You've got to be joking. Car
theft is not what I need at the moment.'

'It's not theft if we prove he's cheating.'

'It's theft regardless of what we find.'

Townsend and Ronson shared a look. I'd made a verbal blunder
and said we.

'I'll protect you.'

'I'd like to know how.'

Townsend's lack of a response gave me all the answer I needed
when it came to his protection.

An alarm bell went off in the back of my brain. Townsend
might be on a quest for truth and justice just the way Jason Gates
had supposedly been. But who was to say Townsend was
interested in proving Rags was a cheat? Motor racing was a
competitive sport with a capital C. When one team fell upon an
idea, all the others wanted it and they weren't backward in coming
forward when it came to discovering how. Rags had proved over
the last five seasons that his kung fu was the best in Europe and
it had cost Townsend his factory backing. My stealing one of

Rags' cars could be some scam to get me to hand over a car so that they could reverse engineer the answer to Rags' performance or worse, so they could cripple it. I'd have to be mentally deficient to buy into this scheme regardless of the motives.

'Why turn to me to help you?'

'Because you were there when Jason died,' Townsend said.

'And you stepped in when Rags had me,' Ronson said.

'So you'll help us,' Townsend said.

'I didn't say that.'

'I thought you Westlakes had a reputation for honesty.'

I held up a hand and Townsend stopped. 'What's in it for me?'

'The satisfaction that a cheat is exposed and a killer found.'

'And that you'll get your Honda factory backing back and a shot at the title for the first time in years?'

'Hey, that's not fair.'

'Nor is the fact that if Ragged Racing gets disqualified, I'll lose my drive and my reputation.'

'So you won't help?'

'I'm not going to screw myself over to benefit everyone else,' I said.

'That's self-serving of you,' Ronson said.

'I guess my family's reputation has been exaggerated.'

'Look, Aidy, you're right,' Townsend said. 'You didn't create this situation. You're just caught in the middle, so I'll make you a deal. You help me and I'll do my best to run a third car.'

'You'll do your best?'

'OK, I'll talk Honda and *Pit Lane* into putting you up as our third driver. It's not your fault they've hitched their carts to the wrong ponies, now is it?'

'No, it's not.'

'So you'll bring me one of Rags' cars?'

'No. I'll help you, but I'm not stealing a car for you.'

'Then what are you going to do?'

'You have the specs on the cars – wheelbase dimensions, the layout for the suspension pickups, power curves – yes?'

'Naturally.'

'Good. I want them.'

'Why?' Ronson asked with a note of suspicion in his voice.

'Because I will personally check every square inch of Rags'

cars down to the nuts and bolts and if they don't match specs, then we have our cheater.'

Lap Twenty-Two

The next morning, I went into Archway with Steve. There was a message on the answering machine from the editor-in-chief of *Pit Lane* magazine. He was calling to let me know how disappointed he was in me over the reckless-driving charges. I called him back and spent forty minutes explaining myself, which went some way to smoothing the choppy waters between me and the man who'd recommended me for the driver shootout.

When I hung up, Steve appeared at the top of the stairs to the crow's-nest. 'You ready for this?'

'Yeah.'

'Then let's go.'

Breakfast would have been nice.

We rode in Steve's Capri. He drove through Old Windsor to pick up the M25. Passing the spot where I'd had the run-in on the Runnymede roundabout brought a sour taste to the back of my mouth.

I didn't like how quiet Steve was. Normally, he'd be the voice of reason talking me through my problems. His hands were tight on the wheel and his knuckles shone white against his skin.

'Where are we going?'

'The east end. I want you to meet someone. We need to get a feel for Andrew Gates. He's no angel and we need to know who we're dealing with. I think this person can help us.'

'Who is this person?'

Steve's grip on the wheel tightened until the leather squeaked. 'A loan shark.'

'How do you know him?'

Steve said nothing.

I didn't like how much this meeting was getting to him. 'Steve?'

'Money is always an issue in motor racing. You can never have enough even when you have a lot. Another ten thousand can change everything. When you don't have enough, it's like you're starving and no one will give you the scraps off their plates. You'll do anything to get that money. Racing drivers and team owners aren't the best credit risks. Banks will only follow you so far down the rabbit hole. Family will go a little deeper. But everyone will stop short of supporting your dream. You'll take the money from whoever is willing to give it.'

A dream was an optimist's view of motor racing. There was no middle ground in this sport. It either granted your dreams or crushed you under its heel. I remember Steve once likening racing to a drug habit and habits needed dealers.

Steve had kept his gaze rigidly ahead to avoid looking me in the eye when he was telling me all this. I knew that he'd made sacrifices to keep my dad in the game and even greater sacrifices after his death to cover his debts, but I'd never asked him how he'd come up with the money.

'Steve, did you go to this loan shark?'

'Your dad died owing a lot of money to a lot of people. I used every penny your grandmother and I had and we were still short, so I sharked the rest. I never told your nan about it, but I did what had to be done. I wish circumstances had been different.'

Hearing Steve's anguish tore me up. I thought I'd known the extents to which he'd gone after my parents died, but I was wrong.

'It wasn't hard to get the money. You'll find loan sharks hanging around races, especially at the club level. There are a ton of drivers who need a grand quick.'

'Do you still owe?'

'No. I paid off this fucker years ago. Your dad's debts are clear.'

For what he'd done, I didn't think I could love my grandfather more.

We didn't speak for the rest of the drive. Steve cut his way through London until we ended up in an upscale part of Limehouse. Thirty years ago, the whole area had been in decline as the docks closed, but subsequent redevelopment had saved the place. Steve stopped the Capri in front of a warehouse conversion overlooking the marina and we walked up to the entrance. He pressed a button on the intercom.

'Yeah,' a gruff voice grunted.

'Steve Westlake for Eddie Stores.'

'Top floor.'

A buzz was followed by the snap of the door unlocking.

Bare brick and a faux industrial-steel staircase greeted us. We climbed the stairs to the top floor. At the top, a man in his fifties grinned at us. To call him heavyset was an understatement. He was a rhino in a leather jacket. The three-quarter-length coat, stretched to the limit, creaked when he moved. He smacked of Limehouse's past, not its rejuvenated present.

Neither man made any attempt to shake the other's hand. No, these men weren't friends.

'It's been a long time, Steve,' Stores said with a grin. 'I see you're still driving that RS. Christ, I love that car. You wouldn't sell it. I still have that Mark I RS2000 you *restored* for me.'

Stores leaned hard on the word restored. I guessed that meant something to Steve.

'C'mon in.'

We went inside. The place had simple laminated flooring and plain white walls. The fifty-year-old office furniture looked dated against the space's modern, clean lines.

Stores sat behind a long office desk. A computer took up one side while a tower of file trays took up the other. Instead of a phone, a neat line of six mobiles sat by his right hand. Front and centre on the desk sat a receipt spike. It was the old-fashioned kind with a wooden base and stiletto-like spike sticking out of it.

'Take a seat, gents. *Mi casa es su casa.* I picked up a little bit of Spanish since I bought a villa in the Canaries in the nineties. It's a gorgeous part of the world, but hot as fuck in the summer. It's great for when this country goes through five months of winter. So is this your lad, Steve?'

Stores' fake affability failed to win me over and didn't put a scratch on the casehardened shell Steve had put up.

'He's my grandson.'

'Your boy died, didn't he? I remember now. That's how we met – it was over your boy.'

Steve was a statue.

'What's your name, son?'

'Aidy,' I answered.

'You follow in the family business?'

'I race.'

'Good for you. I like legacies.'

'I'm sure you're busy, Eddie. We just have a few questions for you,' Steve said.

Stores' smile remained in place, but his gaze hardened.

'You want to know about Andrew Gates. Is that right?' Stores said to me.

'Yeah.'

'Why?'

'We've got our reasons,' Steve said, 'and we'd like those reasons to remain private.'

Stores dropped the weight of his gaze on Steve. Steve's lack of reaction seemed to satisfy him and he nodded to himself. 'Understood. I can't say I like the prick, so nothing leaves this room. You have my word on it.'

'Thanks,' I said. 'Andrew Gates was in your line of work, wasn't he?'

Stores' grin intensified until he exposed two rows of expensive dentistry that looked out of place on his melon-sized head. 'I like your tact, son, but we don't need to be polite. I'm a loan shark, and so was Andrew. We got started at the same time, back in the early eighties. With two-plus million unemployed, it was a good time to be in the lending business.'

'He moved into the property business, though,' I said.

'Kind of. Andy got lucky in eighty-nine when his dad pegged out. His old man didn't approve of what he did, but he left him a share of the house. Eighty-nine was at the end of the Thatcher boom years when house prices were at their peak. He bought out his mum, sold the house and used the cash to stick a zero on the end of the amounts he sharked.'

It was interesting that, to Stores, a death constituted luck.

'From there, Andy started lending to small businesses and as the interest payment grew, he took slices of the businesses, usually in the form of property. Before these fuckers knew what was happening, Andy owned the whole shooting match, leaving them out in the cold. That's how he got into the *property business*. Not my kind of thing, though. Property is like shifting sand. One minute it's up, the next, it's down. I stick with money. That doesn't change. I like to keep things on a smaller and more personal level. Don't I, Steve?'

The jibe bounced off Steve, but I saw the cracks appearing. A vein at his temple pulsed. It was time to end this before it hurt Steve any more than it had already.

'So Andrew doesn't shark anymore?'

'I wouldn't say that. When you conduct your business with a baseball bat over a few hundred, you're a loan shark. When you use lawyers for a couple of million, you're a corporate raider. It's all about the packaging.'

It was an interesting philosophical outlook. 'What about business ventures? Does Andrew have any sidelines?'

'Like what?'

'I don't know – drugs, illegal exports, prostitution. You tell me.'

At this point, I was open to anything that would explain what was going on.

'He's a money man, son, not Don-fucking-Corleone. Andy is like me. He likes things simple and without complication. He stuck to sharking. I know he didn't like drugs. He once hammered one of his blokes who did a little dealing on the side.'

'Do you know who?'

'Nah.'

'What about enemies?'

'When you've fucked over as many people as Andy and I have, all you have are enemies.'

Stores shot me a wink. I couldn't make out if his bravado was an act to make Steve squirm or if he honestly thought he was a loveable rogue.

'Someone killed Andrew's brother two weeks ago. Do you think that could be in retaliation for something he did?'

'You've seen too many movies, Aidy. We don't cut the noses off our debtor's faces to spite our own. Dead clients don't pay. We only provide motivation.' Stores picked up the dangerous-looking receipt spike.

Steve went rigid.

'I'm old fashioned. All my money has a hole in it because I make my punters put it on this nail. And when they don't pay, I make them put something else on the nail.'

Stores bounced his palm on the top of the spike.

Steve jumped up from his chair. 'Thanks for your time, Eddie. I think we've got everything we need.'

I chased after Steve. When he reached for the doorknob, I saw the scar that marred the palm of his left hand. The pencil-wide disfigurement had been there for as long as I could remember. Steve yanked the door open and was gone.

Stores belted out an ugly laugh. He rounded his desk and sidled up to me.

'Today's been a bit of a revelation for you, hasn't it, son?'

'Yeah and you've had your fun.'

Stores slapped me on the back. It felt like a shovel striking my spine. 'You've got balls, just like Steve.'

I bit back the urge to tell Stores to go fuck himself. I was here for something bigger than a petty thug. 'You liked your cash on the nail trick. What was Andy's way of keeping his punters in line for failure to pay?

'Knives. Andrew liked to cut his delinquent payers.' Stores drew a line across his forearm with his finger. 'He'd cut you every time you were late. He called them stripes. Only bad payers earned their stripes.'

I knew where I'd seen those stripes.

Lap Twenty-Three

I called Gates as soon as I was outside and free of Eddie Stores' corruption. As the phone rang, I watched my grandfather storm back to his Capri. His head was down and his fists balled. I'd never seen Steve angry from shame. The sight only served to boil me up inside.

The clamour of kids shrieking and laughing spilled down the phone line when Gates answered. 'Morning, Aidy,' he said over the din.

'We need to talk. Now.'

'I'm a little tied up with business at the moment. I'll call you later.'

'Not acceptable. I said now.'

Gates chuckled. 'That can't happen if I don't tell you where I am.'

'You lied to me. Where are you? Don't make me track you down.'

The cocky note went out of Gates' voice. 'What have you found out?'

'Not over the phone.'

'OK,' he said and gave me an address in Watford before ending the call.

I found Steve in the passenger seat with the keys dangling from the ignition. 'You drive,' he said.

I didn't argue or ask him if he was OK. He wasn't. It couldn't have been easy for him to reveal a side of himself he'd kept secret from Nan and me.

'I need to talk to Gates,' I said.

'You need me?'

'No. I'll be OK.'

I drove Steve back to Archway and left him to his work.

Again, I was meeting Gates alone on his turf. I was sure the address he gave me would be another secluded spot where he had the upper hand, but I was wrong. It turned out to be the home of a kids' community and play centre called Open Gates. The place looked to be a converted business unit with the car park turned into a play centre. Banners plastered the side of the building claiming 'Grand Opening' and 'Welcome'. Dozens of cars lined the street, including the mayor's Bentley, forcing me to park on the next street.

Inside, close to a hundred kids under twelve ran riot from the climbing frames outside to the video games inside. Parents and play centre staff did their best to corral their enthusiasm by handing out cake and soft drinks. A photographer snapped shots of the mayor with Gates. What the hell was going on?

Crichlow sidled up to me without me noticing. He'd kept in my blind spot so I hadn't seen him.

'Wait until Andrew finishes with the mayor,' he said, ever the faithful pit bull.

It was several minutes before Gates made his excuses and slalomed between the kids shooting back and forth. A little boy no more than seven ran straight into him. He ruffled the kid's hair and sent him on his way.

When he got to me, he swung his arms out wide. 'Impressed? This is the sixth place I've opened up. It might look like it's all games, but we've got a library and an after-school homework program here. We'll be starting up under-tens football and netball teams. If we keep the kids engaged and occupied, they won't grow up to be like Crichlow and me.'

I couldn't make Gates out. One minute he was threatening to hurt Steve and the next he was building community centres for kids. This was either a front for something or his attempt to atone for his ugly past.

'I think we should take our business outside,' I said.

Gates guided me across the street with Crichlow in tow, then glanced back at the community centre. 'I bet you're wondering how I came by this property. Well, not in a good way. I have a bunch of places that I own at someone else's expense. I'm making use of them now for something worthwhile.'

'Excuse me for not sharing in your special day after what you've put me and my family through.'

Crichlow took a step forward, but Gates blocked his path.

'You want to get down to this? OK. Let's get down to it. You said I lied to you. Got anything to back that up?'

'Why didn't you tell me Rags was a client?'

The colour drained from Gates' face. 'Who told you that – Rags?'

'It doesn't matter who. And don't tell me he wasn't. I've seen the scars on his forearm. That means he was behind on his payments to you three times. So what happened? Did you have Jason working teams from the inside so when he found one in trouble, he could let them know his big brother could bridge the shortfall? Is that how it worked?'

Before I could say another word, Gates grabbed me by the throat and slammed me against the wall of the building behind me. 'Jason had nothing to do with it. I told you he was never part of my business.'

Crichlow stepped in and peeled Gates off me. 'Remember where you are, Andy.'

Gates shrugged Crichlow off. 'Yes, I lent money to Rags. He got behind so I had to leave my mark. He knew the risks.'

I didn't care how many raw nerves I grazed. I wouldn't be intimidated by Gates. I pushed myself away from the wall. 'When did he start taking money from you?'

'Five years ago.'

That coincided with the start of Rags' on-track success. 'And he paid you back?'

'Yeah. Eventually.'

'Eventually? I don't get the feeling you do eventually.'

'You're right. I don't. After about a year, he was in over his head. The interest was killing him. He made me an offer. He knew Jason wanted to get into the sport and he said he'd let him apprentice at Ragged in exchange for wiping out his debt.'

Suddenly, two pieces of the puzzle fell into place. 'But you never told Jason how he got the job. He thought he'd gotten it on merit and when he found out, he walked out on the team.'

Gates nodded. 'Not my finest hour.'

'Why didn't you tell him?'

'He wouldn't have taken it. He wanted to get in on his own, not because of his brother's arm twisting.' Gates smiled weakly. 'He had integrity.'

'How'd he find out?'

'Rags let it slip.'

'Is that why Jason wasn't talking to you?'

Gates nodded. 'Yes. The second he found out, he left me a message telling me what he thought of me and that I was dead to him.'

That explained why he'd left the team, but it didn't explain why he'd started snooping around Ragged Racing. 'Do you own a piece of Ragged Racing?'

'No. I had no interest in being an owner. The property is leased and cars have no substantial value.'

'Did you lend Rags money just the once?'

'About a year ago he tapped me up again, but I told him to sling his hook. He burned me once. I wasn't about to make it twice.'

'Three months ago Jason dumped his girlfriend. She got the feeling it was because he wanted to protect her from something. Is that date significant in any way?'

Gates shook his head.

'Got any theories?' Crichlow asked.

Instead of feigning ignorance, I wanted to gauge their reactions. 'There's a couple of prevailing theories. Either Ragged Racing is cheating or mixed up with drugs, and Jason was on to them.'

Gates shared a confused look with Crichlow. 'Cheating I get, but drugs?'

'Didn't you have a problem with drugs within your organization?' I knew I was on risky ground here.

'And it was taken care of,' Crichlow snapped.

'How'd you come across that nugget of information? Gates asked.

'I'm not giving you names. You've lied to me and threatened me. I don't trust you.'

'Don't forget, we have a deal, Aidy.'

'We have nothing. I'll find Jason's killer, but I don't have to tell you how I'm doing it.'

Gates grabbed my wrist and yanked me to him. 'Remember your place.'

I nodded over at the mayor and her husband, who had appeared on the steps of the centre and Gates released his grip. 'Remember your reputation. You wouldn't want to tarnish it. When you feel like telling me the truth, let me know,' I said and walked back to the Capri.

I arrived back at Archway to find the place deserted. With Dylan spending his time at Ragged, Steve was working alone now. He'd left a note on my desk saying he'd gone out to pick up parts.

I let myself into the situation room and updated the murder board. I now had a direct link between Gates and Rags with Jason caught in the crossfire. I looked at the milestones I now had on the timeline. I had an explanation for why Jason left Ragged. I had a date when Rags started taking money from Gates. I still didn't have an explanation for what had sparked Jason's interest in Ragged. If I knew that, I'd have the corner piece to solve this puzzle.

'Tell me what happened, Jason.'

The doorbell rang before Jason's ghost could answer.

I locked the situation room and jogged through the workshop to the rear entrance. I opened the door to find Sergeant Lucas standing there.

'What can I do for you, Sergeant?'

'I've come to examine the van.'

I glanced over at the empty space where it usually sat. 'My grandfather is out in it at the moment. You should have made an appointment.'

'I did.'

'Oh. He didn't mention it. He shouldn't be long then. Do you want to come in?'

'No, I need to examine the trailer. But can you call your grandfather and tell him to hurry it along? I don't have all day.'

I retreated back into the workshop and called Steve. 'Sergeant Lucas is here.'

'Shit, let me finish up and I'll be back in half an hour.'

I hung up and rejoined Lucas outside. He was crouched over the trailer with a camera in hand.

'Steve says he'll be back in thirty minutes.'

Lucas frowned.

'Sorry.'

'I'll give him thirty minutes. I'll let you know when I'm through.'

I didn't like leaving Lucas unsupervised. He didn't exactly have my best interests at heart. 'I'll stick around if that's OK.'

Lucas went back to taking photos. 'Suit yourself.'

He spent the next fifteen minutes taking pictures and making notes. When he was finished, he stood and checked his watch, then looked at me.

'Find anything?' I asked. 'Any signs of recent repairs?'

'No. The trailer is clean.'

'So I couldn't have run her off the road.'

'I haven't seen the van yet.'

'You won't find anything there either.'

'The victim could have overreacted to an aggressive manoeuvre you made.'

The word victim grated against my skin. 'I thought you said she claims I crashed into her.'

'She may have thought that, but after the bang on the head she took and crash she endured, I doubt she was aware of a lot that happened.'

'It looks as if you've made up your mind regardless of the evidence and my statement.' I put my hands together and held them out. 'You'd better take me in.'

Lucas looked at my outstretched hands and frowned. 'If there's an arrest to be made, I'll decide when it'll be made.'

'We pissed off a lot of people that day. They should remember the incident. Have you asked for witnesses?'

'If that proves necessary, it will be done. You know what the shame of this is? It was her new car.'

'New?'

Lucas jerked a thumb at my Accord. 'OK, it wasn't new-new like yours, but not everyone is as lucky as you. It was new to her. She'd had the car just two days before the crash.'

I found that interesting. Another milestone to be added to the timeline.

My mobile rang. It was Steve.

'You need to pick me up, son. Some prick nicked the Transit.'

'Shit,' I murmured. This looked bad. Actually, worse than bad. 'I'll get over there as soon as I can,' I said and hung up.

Lucas crossed his arms across his chest. 'Problem?' he asked.

'I'd like to file a police report on a stolen van.'

Lucas' look of disapproval said everything.

Lap Twenty-Four

'It's going to be OK,' Dylan said for the third time.

We were driving to Ragged Racing. Today was the day I had to deliver the sponsor's tuned-up Honda Accord to Germany. We'd spent the drive to Banbury discussing the significance of someone stealing Steve's van. Dylan saw the theft as a potentially good thing.

'Without the van, the cops can't prove the case one way or the other.'

While that was true, the van's disappearance didn't look good to Sergeant Lucas. It appeared as if we'd stage-managed the van's theft to prevent it from being examined. Without it, there was nothing left to investigate and it was put up or shut up time for the police. I had the feeling I'd be returning home from this trip to find charges filed against me.

We arrived at Ragged at six a.m. as instructed and found Rags stooped over the engine bay of the car I was to deliver. He had the engine plugged into his laptop.

'Everything OK?' I asked.

Rags unplugged the laptop and dropped the bonnet. 'Just making sure everything is perfect.'

I hoped that was all he was doing. After Barrington's revelations of drug smuggling, I wasn't sure what I thought of Rags now.

He looked me over. 'I like that you remembered to dress up.'

I'd put on a Ragged Racing polo shirt. If I was meeting a sponsor, then I had to make a good impression.

Rags jerked a thumb at Dylan. 'He dropping you off?'

I wasn't sure if I should read anything into that reaction. Did Rags want me to do this delivery alone for a reason? God, I was getting paranoid. It wasn't surprising with all the puppet masters pulling my strings.

'Germany is a long way. I thought it would be good to have a co-pilot,' I said.

This wasn't strictly true. Yes, the drive would take all day, but I was a little tired of getting ambushed by everyone and their brother so I wanted someone as a witness and backup. Dylan had seen the situation a little differently when I mentioned my logic. He'd said, 'Great, I get to be your red shirt.' It was a joke that cut to the quick. I had put Dylan in harm's way before, and his unquestioning loyalty had saved my life.

'Good thinking,' Rags said, although he didn't sound convinced. 'But those five hundred euros will have to cover expenses for the both of you. Just be back by Monday. Your mate's got a new job to start.'

'No worries,' I said, knowing the money was unlikely to stretch to two airline tickets. We'd more than likely be returning by rail.

'All right, then. Get on with it and for God's sake, don't pick up any speeding tickets.'

'Hey, I'm a professional,' I said with a good amount of bravado.

That got me an eye roll and the flicker of a smile from Rags. Maybe I was winning him over.

He walked in the direction of his office and tossed a parting comment over his shoulder. 'Let me know when you get there.'

I elected to drive the first leg and got behind the wheel. Dylan fed the sponsor's address in the sat nav. At this time of morning, traffic was light and I kept my foot down. I wanted this car delivered and out of my life as soon as possible.

As soon as we were on the road, I called Barrington. My call didn't seem to have awakened him. Maybe he didn't sleep.

I'd clued Barrington in on this run to Germany the second after Rags had assigned it to me at the workshop earlier in the week. I'd felt Barrington's excitement over the line. He had a plan in place, but Barrington being Barrington, he hadn't bothered to share any of the details other than I'd be meeting his under-cover officer en route.

'We're on the move,' I said. 'What do you want me to do?'

'Drive to Dover and take the nine o'clock ferry.'

'We were going to take to the Channel Tunnel.'

'Not anymore you're not. Take the ferry and my undercover agent will brief you.'

'That'll slow us down.'

'Aidy, please do as you're told. Be on that boat and wait in the restaurant. Your handler will contact you.'

I really was bought and paid for. 'Is there a password?'

'Cute,' he said and hung up.

We arrived in Dover just in time to catch the nine o'clock ferry. I got in line for passport control.

'I'm actually enjoying this. Foreign travel. Fresh opportunities,' Dylan said.

I felt the opposite way. As we inched closer to the head of the line, my stomach churned. I'd put both of us at the mercy of others. I was operating on the assumption that everyone was playing straight with me. I was going on Rags' word that this delivery run was on the up and up and I wasn't playing mule in some drug trafficking scheme. I was going on Barrington's word that he wanted me to deliver the car to Germany. This ferry ride could all be part of some elaborate portside arrest. I'd be a fool to believe Barrington was my friend in all this. The tosser had already tried to fit me up once. There was nothing to say he wouldn't do it again, especially if this car was packed with drugs. I was at the wheel of a ticking time bomb and I couldn't see the clock.

'Just remember why we're doing this,' I said.

Dylan had been smiling, but that killed it. 'Do you hear that? That's the sound of you pissing on my fireworks.'

'I'm just saying we don't know what we're involved in.'

'No, you don't know what you're involved in, but you've dragged Steve and me into it.'

It was an unfair remark. Mainly because it was totally fair.

'You don't have to come,' I said sincerely.

'Sod it. I wasn't busy today.'

I smiled. 'Thanks,'

'I realize how bad this might get, so let's just get through it, whatever it turns out to be.'

I held my breath when we pulled up to passport control. Armed police didn't explode from unseen quarters and we weren't ripped from the car. The immigration officer just asked the purpose of our visit and waved us through.

We boarded and grabbed a table in the restaurant. I sat with my back to a bulkhead. I didn't want anyone sneaking up on me, especially my Customs handler. Any colleague of Barrington's wasn't a friend of mine.

As the ferry eased out of port, people migrated to the restaurant. Dylan and I watched for our undercover contact. No one stood out, but they shouldn't. It was the first rule of undercover work.

'Crap,' Dylan said. 'We've got a problem.'

I followed Dylan's gaze across the restaurant to Claudia. She looked sharp in jeans, knee-length boots and a leather biker's jacket over a form-fitting turtleneck jumper. How did she manage to look so good all the time regardless of the time of day? She smiled at me and cut through the human traffic to our table.

Crap was right. All I needed was Claudia hanging around with Barrington's man trying to make contact. Some days it wasn't good being me.

'Bonjour, Aidy. It's lovely to run into you like this. Who's this?'

'Hi, Claudia. This is my friend, Dylan.'

'Do you 'ave a minute? I need to talk to you about your problem.'

'I'm a little tied up at the moment.'

'Aidy, you're on a ferryboat. You're not going anywhere. You 'ave some time to chat.'

I opened my mouth to lob another brush-off, but then I got it. Claudia was Barrington's undercover contact. She read my expression and nodded.

'You're right. I've got a few minutes.'

'That's wonderful,' she said.

Dylan picked up on his third wheel status and got up. 'I'll go get us some breakfast.'

'Take your time,' Claudia said and slid into Dylan's seat.

'You must be good, because I would have never guessed. Did Barrington press gang you into service or are you a willing volunteer?'

'I'm a British Customs officer.'

'But you're French.'

Claudia grinned. 'You British will take anyone.'

I felt I deserved that. 'What happens now?'

'I will give you tasks. You will carry them out.'

She looked over at Dylan who was in line getting two plates piled with food. He was shooting furtive glances our way. 'You shouldn't 'ave involved anyone else.'

'You have your people and I have mine. After what your boss has done to me, I need someone with my interests at heart. So what's the plan?'

'Deliver the car as arranged. 'Ave you looked it over?'

'No, I didn't know I was supposed to. I have to get the car to Munich by seven tonight. That doesn't leave much time to play detective.'

'*Merde.* I was 'oping to 'and the car over to our people in France.' She held out her hand. 'Give me your keys.'

I handed them over and she slipped from her seat, which Dylan filled a minute later after planting two breakfasts on the table.

'Oh, she leaves a warm seat.'

'You need a girlfriend.'

'We both do. It might keep us out of trouble.'

When it came to lady love, Steve was the big winner amongst us. In the years since Gran had died, he'd put himself out there and was rarely without a lady on his arm.

Dylan shrugged and started in on his breakfast. He'd bought us both the full English – scrambled eggs, sausage, bacon, tomatoes, baked beans and toast. I had no problems whipping a car around a track at triple-digit speeds, but the slow roll of a ferry cutting across the English Channel left me feeling queasy. I forced the food down since I'd need the energy for the long drive ahead.

Claudia returned as we were finishing our meals. There was no smile on display. She put my keys down on the table. 'We need to talk. Alone.'

Dylan shrugged.

'Don't wait up,' I said.

Dylan smiled.

We walked out on to the deck. We were certainly alone out here. The wind coming off the sea was biting. Claudia leaned against the safety rail with her back to the water.

'We 'ave a problem. I found a GPS tracking device on the car. If you deviate from your route, someone will know.'

'It could be an anti-theft device.'

She frowned at me.

'OK. What happens now?'

'Keep to the schedule. We 'ave the advantage of knowing your destination.'

'As does whoever placed the tracker,' I added.

'This will be an information-gathering exercise. Get names, places, whatever you can.'

'If I'm going to do this, then I want something from you.'

'Like what?'

'Barrington says you have powers the cops don't have. I want to take advantage of that. Get me the name of the woman who's made the accusation that I wrecked her car.'

'I can do that.'

I expected to haggle. Maybe Customs did have some special skills. 'Good.'

Claudia looked towards France, now large on the horizon. 'We'll be arriving soon. Do you 'ave questions?'

'So how did you end up working for Her Majesty's government?'

'There was a joint taskforce between French and British authorities. After the case, Barrington put in a request to borrow me for this operation. I accepted. This investigation will be good for my career.'

'You want to be France's number one cop?'

'Or 'igher.'

I grinned. It was so damn hard to dislike Claudia.

A horn blared and an announcement followed telling all passengers to return to their vehicles. We followed the crush of people back down to the car decks. Claudia held the door open to my deck and followed me out. On the car deck, the roar of the ferry's diesel engines was deafening. She escorted me back to my car, where Dylan stood waiting.

'Where are you parked?'

She pointed to her Peugeot four cars back. I shook my head. I hadn't even noticed her when we'd parked. God, I wasn't the man for Barrington's job, or even Andrew Gates'.

'Don't let it get to you. You were tired and your mind was on your problems.'

She kissed me on the cheek and walked back to her car. Watching her go, something occurred to me.

I called after her: 'Is Claudia your real name?'

She turned and shook her head.

'Then what is it?'

She said something, but I couldn't hear it over the roar of the boat's engines.

Daylight flooded the car deck when the bow doors opened and the roar of dozens of car engines bursting into life filled the air. I guided the car off the ferry, fully aware that a satellite was beaming our position to some nameless, faceless person.

Dylan and I passed through French Customs and passport control without incident and picked up the road heading to Reims. I wound up the speed and found a nice groove that ate away at our arrival time display on the sat nav.

'You looking to pick up a ticket?' Dylan asked.

'The faster we get there, the faster we're rid of this car and whatever we're carrying.'

'Good point. Keep your foot down.'

The French countryside whipped past our windows as we ate up the miles. The weather was cool and overcast, but it didn't ruin the view.

'So Claudia is an undercover British Customs agent,' Dylan said. 'I didn't see that coming.'

'That's the point.'

'I feel like we're the last ones to laugh at a poorly told joke. Do you think we can trust her?'

'About as much as anyone at this point.'

'In other words, we can't. Shit, we're really in a hole.'

But I thought if anyone would throw us a lifeline, it would be Claudia. Barrington cared about the win at any cost and Claudia was ambitious, but I felt she was principled. She wouldn't burn us for the success of the case. I hoped for once that I was reading her correctly.

We raced by places I'd only ever seen on a map, eventually stopping in Reims to refuel. I didn't realize how stiff I'd gotten at the wheel until I got out and I was glad of the decision to bring Dylan with me. I tossed him the keys so he could take over driving duties. He didn't get into the car.

'You know where we are, don't you?' Dylan said.

'Reims.'

'And that means we're a short distance from the old grand prix track. We have to see it.'

'We're on the clock, if you haven't forgotten.'

'Mate, I know we're under a lot of thumbs, but when are we going to be out this way again?'

'I don't know.'

'There you go then. We're ahead of schedule and we can afford to play tourist. We have to go.'

'You're forgetting that we're being tracked.'

'And we're not supposed to know that. We're supposed to be on a jolly. If we don't act like it, then someone is going to suspect us.'

Dylan made a good case. Then again, I got the feeling Dylan was going to make any case he needed to get his way.

'OK, let's go.'

'Good man.'

Dylan parked the Honda on the start-finish line and we got out. Not much remained of the historic circuit – just the pits and the grandstand. It wasn't surprising, really. Reims wasn't a traditional racetrack. Triangular in shape, it ran on public roads connecting three villages. It had been home to the French Grand Prix in the fifties and sixties. The circuit had been closed for forty years and the rot had set in. Now it was nothing more than a motor-racing ruin. Stonehenge for racers.

Traffic whipped past us as we wandered through the pits. Not all was lost at Reims. Restoration was in progress. The pits had been cleaned up. Names of old sponsors had been repainted on the control tower and all along the pit garages.

'I want a picture of this,' Dylan said.

We jogged across the road and climbed the grandstand. I sat while Dylan snapped photos with his mobile.

I watched a lorry disappear into the distance and imagined what it would be like to go barrelling down these narrow French roads. Driving on commercial roads must have been dangerous in its day, but it would be lethal in today's cars that need a mirror-flat surface.

Dylan pocketed his phone and sat next to me.

'This was a good idea,' I said.

'I have them from time to time.' He smiled at me, then the smile disappeared. 'You shouldn't have shut me out. I get why you did it, but you still shouldn't have done it.'

'I know. I'm sorry. It won't happen again.'

'That's all I needed to hear.'

And it was. I wouldn't have to apologize to him again and he would never raise the subject again. Something bigger than my stupidity had to come between us for it to become a friendship-breaking issue.

'Do you think drugs is what got Jason killed?'

'Probably. I do wonder if he was aware of it, though. He could have been following up on this cheating angle and walked into something much worse.'

'Shit. I'm so glad we've got Customs looking out for us.'

I wasn't so sure.

'I know I've only been working at Ragged for a week, but I'm having a hard time believing that they're drug traffickers,' Dylan said. 'Nobody is acting like they're hiding something and no one's excluding me.'

I was having a hard time with it too. Barrington liked to tar everybody with the same brush, which was the easy way out. I pulled out the set of keys that Jason had had on him when he died. 'Anyone asked for their keys yet?'

'Not yet, they haven't. I'm keeping my eyes open.'

'Good.' I checked my watch. 'C'mon, play time is over.'

We hit the road. We kept talking about our situation without coming up with a solid theory, but the conversation carried us all the way into Strasbourg where we stopped for a fuel and food stop. We'd been on the road six hours since driving off the ferry and the car wasn't the only one in need of fuel. We gassed it up and drove around until we found a restaurant that looked interesting. The menu seemed to have more in common with German cuisine than French. Then again, with the German border in spitting distance, we were in that twilight zone where nationalities blended.

We half-arsed ordering a meal in English and bad French, laughing as we went, but we got what we were after – something filling in the form of *Alsatian Choucroute*. It was a heavy meat and potatoes thing consisting of sausages, sauerkraut and lots of root vegetables which made Dylan very happy. Seeing as I was resuming the driving after our meal, Dylan ordered a beer.

Our clumsy attempt at ordering dinner drew a few odd looks from our fellow diners, but I didn't care. It had been a long time since I'd enjoyed myself. Life had gotten so serious since Alex Fanning's murder at the end of last season. I'd gone from that investigation to testifying in multiple trials, then into the driver shootout, which led to my professional driving contract and the fallout from Jason Gates' murder. The simple act of hanging out with my friend as we drove a car across three countries was something I hadn't gotten to do. In the process of all this seriousness, I'd forgotten how to have fun.

After we'd finished, we walked out to the car park, where everything changed. The fun of the day evaporated in an instant as my stomach clenched and the seriousness returned to my life.

'Oh, shit,' Dylan said.

He couldn't have summed up the situation any more succinctly. The car was gone.

Lap Twenty-Five

With Mathieu Schöenberger, the restaurant's owner, acting as interpreter, I reported the car's theft to the police. He poured us free coffee while we waited for the cops to arrive. He was very kind under the circumstances, but I think it had a lot to do with the car being hijacked from his car park. There was nothing for us to do but wait.

'The police will be here within the hour,' Mathieu said.

I checked my watch. That meant in twenty minutes. 'Thanks.'

Dylan and I stared at my mobile phone on the table in front of me.

'You're going to have to call Rags,' Dylan said.

I was clinging to the vain hope that the cops would pick up the car thieves in a blink of an eye and Rags wouldn't have to know. It was a delusion I couldn't commit to with any great faith.

I sighed and picked up the phone. I scrolled through my directory and was just about to select Rags' number when I stopped. An alternative hit me.

'Please let it be so.'

'What?' Dylan said.

'Stay here a minute.'

I went outside and punched in Claudia's number. She answered on the second ring.

'The car's been stolen. Did you do it?'

'What car? The car you're delivering?'

Claudia sounded genuinely surprised, but I couldn't tell for sure. She'd already proved to be an expert liar. I only had Claudia's word there was a GPS tracker on the car. In fact, she could have been the one who'd planted it. I had no idea who to trust anymore.

'Yes, the car I'm delivering. The one with the tracker you found today. If you took it, just tell me, because if you didn't, I have to call Rags.'

'Aidy, I didn't take the car.'

'Don't lie to me. If the theft is your way of getting some time with the car to check it out, I get it. Just don't keep me in the dark.'

'Aidy, I swear I'm not lying.'

I could hear the truth in her voice. A flicker of panic singed her words.

'Shit,' I murmured under my breath.

'Where are you?' Claudia asked.

'Strasbourg.'

'When was the car taken?' Claudia asked.

'We stopped to eat, so I don't know for sure, but it can't be more than thirty minutes ago. I've called the police.'

'OK, let me take it from 'ere. I'll get back to you. Stay put for now. Call Rags with the news.'

She hung up on me before I could say anything else and left me out in the cold with an unenviable job to do. I dialled Rags. The phone rang and rang and I thought I was going to receive a stay of execution, but he finally picked up.

'What is it, boy?' he said, sounding jovial. That wasn't going to last.

'Rags, the car's been stolen.'

'What?' The word came out as hard as flint.

'I stopped to eat and when I came out, the car was gone.'

'You are fucking joking, right?' Rags' voice rose from a growl to a bark.

'No. I'm so sorry, Rags. The car was locked and we just stopped for a few minutes. I called the police. Hopefully, they can—'

'Do you like fucking up?'

'No, Rags.'

'Do you like screwing me over?'

'No.'

'No?'

'No.'

'Well, you do a fucking outstanding job of it. You have a fantastic talent for calamity. I give you the simple job of delivering a car to impress a new sponsor and you turn it into the balls-up of the century. That's a talent. I'm sure the UN could use you in the Middle East, because you'd give all the factions a single source of irritation and take the pressure off the rest of the world.'

I listened to the tirade. There was no point interrupting to apologize. I'd just be pouring petrol on the firestorm. I closed my eyes and let him burn himself out while the evening breeze cooled the heat of my shame.

'You know what's bad about this, don't you? It isn't the loss of the car, which is a pain in the arse all by itself, but that the car belonged to a new sponsor. First impressions count and this is one impression no one is going to forget in a hurry. Is any of this getting through to you?'

'Yes, it is.'

Rags was silent for a long moment. All I could hear was his exhausted breathing. When he spoke again, resignation replaced the rage. 'You really have fucked up this time.'

'I know.'

'You're damn lucky you're not here in front of me.'

I thought of Nick Ronson dangling by his duct-taped hands from an engine hoist.

'I'm going to take care of this mess with the sponsor. You could try and impress me by handling things from where you are.' Rags underlined his point by hanging up.

'I'm in Strasbourg, by the way,' I said to a dead line.

A police car pulled into the car park. I introduced myself in French and took them into the restaurant. One of the officers spoke pretty good English, certainly better than my French, but Mathieu took over the translating duties and it helped speed up proceedings.

But that all ended when we reached the ownership issue. I didn't need Mathieu to translate the shift in body language from sympathetic to suspicious. I didn't have any documentation on the car since everything I had was in the glove box. Driving from England to Germany to deliver a car to a man I didn't know sounded distinctly suspect. Suddenly, I faced a sticky situation. The cops would have to take it on faith that everything I was telling them was on the up and up. I saw that I was talking myself into another jail cell and this time I was dragging Dylan with me.

I gave them the phone numbers for Rags and the sponsor in Germany. I explained that we were delivering the car and nothing more.

The cops retreated to their patrol car and Mathieu returned to his customers.

Dylan waggled his phone at me. 'I clued Steve in just in case this goes sideways on us and we need someone to find us.'

'Good thinking.'

'What was the great revelation that sent you scurrying out the door?' Dylan asked.

I looked over Dylan's shoulder at the cops in their car talking on the phone. 'I wondered if Claudia had the car lifted.'

'Did she?'

I shook my head.

'That would be too convenient,' he said. 'Some tosser is going to be a very happy boy if they find something is hidden in that car. Can you believe our dumb sodding luck?'

I couldn't. What were the chances of a car under surveillance getting stolen on route to its potentially dubious destination? I stood more chance of winning the lottery. The improbability snagged my thoughts and I couldn't shake it loose. Before I could make any more of it, the police officers returned. Both men looked grim-faced.

'This doesn't look good. It could be handcuff time,' Dylan

said, watching the cops approach. Then he grinned. 'I haven't spent a night in a French police cell before. Possibly another first picked up from hanging out with you.'

'Never a dull moment.'

The second the cops returned, Mathieu rejoined us to offer his translation skills and support.

'Monsieur Westlake, we have spoken to the vehicle's owner and he has confirmed your story,' the English-speaking cop said in such a heavy accent it squashed every word. It made me long for Claudia's crisp tone. 'Monsieur Schöenberger has also confirmed your account and has asked that you act as his representative here in France. OK with you?'

'*Oui.*'

'*Bon.* We have a report of a car fire. Can you come see?'

I nodded. That was the icing on the cake.

The cops drove us a short distance across town to a scrap of wasteland by the canal that fed into the Rhine. Firemen stood over the smoking husk of a car. We pulled up next to a fire engine and got out.

The acrid stink of burnt plastic, oil and petrol stained the air. Not even the soap powder scent of the suffocating foam used to extinguish the fire did anything to mask the stench.

The policemen conferred with the firemen as we approached the burnt-out husk. The firemen shot Dylan and me commiserating looks. As a people, we loved our cars and seeing one destroyed was never a fun sight.

We stopped a safe distance from the wreck. It was easy to tell it was a black Honda Accord under the blanket of foam sliding drunkenly off the carcass. The number plates were missing, but what were the chances of there being another black Honda Accord stolen this close to ours? The thieves had stripped the car before torching it. It sat lopsidedly on bricks, missing its wheels. The front seats were gone. The windscreen was split, but that could have been from the heat of the fire.

I circled the car. One circuit told the story of how the vandals had done their work. They'd doused the car in petrol, stuck a rag in the open petrol tank fill spout and let the flames do the rest. The fire had been total in its devastation.

A fireman popped the boot with a crowbar. Cinders replaced

our overnight bags. We'd be walking about in the clothes we had on as we left France tonight.

The bonnet had been opened at some point. I peered into the engine bay. The engine was intact, although anything non-metallic wasn't. That would include the GPS tracker if it hadn't been removed beforehand. At least the cops would be able to identify the wreck from the chassis number.

'Is this your car, Monsieur Westlake?' the cop asked.

'Right make and model. It looks like it.'

The cop nodded gravely.

Dylan wandered over to me. 'What a mess.'

'Give me a sec, OK?' I pulled out my mobile and moved away from Dylan and the wreck.

'You calling Rags?'

'No, Claudia.'

I found myself a quiet spot and dialled her number. John Barrington answered the phone instead.

'Is that the idiot I put my faith in?'

'You didn't put your faith in me. You put the success and failure of your case on someone you thought you could push around.'

'Listen to you with your big balls swaying in the air. I don't remember you being so tough the last time we shared face time. I suppose a few hundred miles' separation gives you that swagger. That's if I am that far away. I could be around the corner.'

Barrington couldn't help himself. He had to assert himself to show who was boss.

'So you've heard about the car,' I said when he finished grandstanding.

'You mean that you let the hottest lead we've had in months get stolen out from under you? Yeah, I've heard about that and the fact that the French police have found a burned-up wreck matching your car's description.'

Barrington was well informed. 'News travels fast.'

'Bad news always does. It's a universal constant, like morons.'

I rolled my eyes and was sad that Barrington wasn't around to see me do it. 'I'm standing in front of the wreckage.'

'I'd rather you were standing in front of a car packed with

drugs delivering it to a connection. Then I could spend my Sunday celebrating a trans-European drug bust. But that won't be happening, thanks to you.'

'Look, I'm not a hotshot Customs officer trying to rid the UK of the drug scourge. You are. If you wanted this car, you should have done something about it.'

'I bet you're loving this, aren't you?'

'No. I want you out of my life and the longer it takes for you to get your result, the longer I'm stuck with you. So let's stop bitching at each other and figure out how we got sucker punched.'

'Sucker punched? What do you mean?' No sarcasm tinged his words.

'The car was never meant to make it to Munich. Someone wanted all of us looking one way while they picked our pockets.'

Barrington was silent for a moment. 'What makes you think that?'

'They were either following or tracking the car. Claudia found a GPS tracker on it. The second we left it unattended it was swiped and none of us is the wiser as to who took it. Fate is never that cruel. The odds were too high for this to happen.' Then the penny dropped. 'But you already know that, don't you?'

'Yeah, I do, but if I'm being honest, I knew only what happened after it happened. At least you're not as dumb as I thought you were.'

That was as close to a compliment as I was going to get. 'You wouldn't have turned to me if you thought I was that dumb.'

I thought I could feel him grinning from his end of the phone line.

'So what else can you tell me about this failed escapade?'

'I don't think the guy in Munich has anything to do with it.'

'Why do you say that?'

'Plausible deniability. I was a patsy and so was the sponsor.'

'And Rags? Is he a member of the dumb club?'

It was my turn to be silent.

'C'mon, Aidy. What's in that mind of yours?'

'In spite of our suspicions, there's no proof that there was anything in the car.'

'Don't disappoint me, Aidy. You have to believe he's involved now. I'll do better than that. You know he's involved.'

I did. Rags was up to his neck in something. I didn't know what, but I'd find out.

'By the way,' Barrington said. 'Claudia wants to speak to you. She says she's got the name and address of some woman for you.'

Lap Twenty-Six

Miss Angry Renault's name was Jenni Oglesby and she lived in a small complex of flats in Harrow, which was nowhere in the vicinity of our supposed hit and run. I wondered what tale she'd spun for Sergeant Lucas to explain her presence so far from home.

I drove out to her place on Monday afternoon. Dylan and I hadn't gotten back from Strasbourg until Sunday night. By the time we'd finished up with the police, it was too late to catch a flight or train home. We'd stayed the night in a hotel and first thing in the morning, we grabbed a train to Paris, then took the Eurostar into London.

Since Dylan had to go back to work at Ragged, Steve came with me for backup and to be a witness. I didn't want Jenni claiming I'd done something else to her. We arrived outside her place at two p.m. I tried her doorbell, but didn't get a reply, so we parked across the street and bedded in until she came home.

'Are you sure you want to do this?' Steve said. 'You're not meant to have any contact with her. If she tells the plod, you're buggered. Everything that's happened will be small beer by comparison.'

'She won't,' I said, although it was more wishful thinking than a certainty.

'How do you know?'

'She lied about me running her off the road. That makes her moral compass a little distorted. She wants something.'

'How do you know?'

'She grassed me up to Chloe Mercer and Chloe spilled the

beans to George Easter. It was unnecessary. The police are all over me and your insurance is likely to pay her out. Ruining my name doesn't get her anything more.'

'Other than making you desperate. And coming here is the mark of a desperate man.'

I knew coming here was a risk, but it was one worth taking, especially if I could expose Jenni as a fraud. I thought Steve would understand. 'Are you saying we should go?'

Steve nodded. 'Yeah, I am. This can do you more harm than good. She might still have something up her sleeve and there's no upside from you confronting her. If she runs to the plod, then you really are screwed.'

Steve made a lot of sense, but I couldn't listen to him. It still stuck in my throat that Jenni had the upper hand. I couldn't let her get away with screwing me.

'I have the element of surprise working for me right now. If I wait for her to do whatever she's planning, I'll be on the back foot. At least by confronting her today, I'll rob her of any control.'

'Aidy, drive away.'

'I can't. You can go, but I'm staying.'

Steve sighed. 'If you stay, I stay.'

'Thanks.'

'Just thank me by keeping yourself out of a jail cell.'

It was something I hadn't managed to do in the past.

Jenni arrived home just before five o'clock. She was driving a very new, shiny Ford Fiesta. The Fiesta, while not earth shattering, was a bump up from the clapped-out Renault I'd seen her driving before.

'That's her,' I said.

The flats came with a small parking area in the rear, but she had to walk back to the street to let herself into her place. The second she drove towards the parking area, I jumped from my car and Steve climbed out after me.

'No, you stay here,' I said. 'She might look at you and think I've brought a heavy along with me.'

'Am I that scary to look at?'

'No, but I want to look vulnerable.' I held out my arms. 'I'm desperate, right?'

Steve brought out his mobile. 'I'm getting your meeting down on video. She said you wrecked her car last time. I don't want her saying you wrecked her face this time.'

My stomach clenched at that thought.

I jogged across the street and waited for her by her front door.

When she emerged from the parking area, her jaw dropped at the sight of me standing on her doorstep. I smiled when I saw the look of shock on her face.

A large sticking plaster covered a purple bruise on her right temple.

'Hi, Jenni. Remember me?'

'Get out of my way.'

I held up my hands to say I wasn't here to hurt her. 'I just want to talk.'

'How did you find me?'

'No doubt, the same way you found me.'

She crossed her arms over her chest. 'Well, you are a public figure.'

'I think that's a little bit of an exaggeration.'

She shrugged.

'Nice car,' I said.

'Well, I needed a replacement after what you did to my previous one.'

'Come off it. We both know I didn't crash into you.'

Another shrug.

'What happened? Did you run off the road after you chased me? Or did you write it off on purpose?'

'Are you a little dense? You crashed into me and left me at the side of the road.'

She was keeping to a script. She couldn't afford to make a slip.

'Why are you doing this?' I asked.

'You're a menace to society.'

I thought my turning up on her doorstep would scare her into some admission, but it wasn't working. I had nothing to shake her belief, but maybe I could force her into incriminating herself.

'You know I'm not. You made the whole thing up. Why did you tell Chloe Mercer about this? It had nothing to do with her.'

'I like motor racing and I'm a big fan of hers. I've been following her since she started. I thought the information would be helpful to her.'

And it was. It had put a serious dent in my reputation. But what were the chances that a race fan just happened to get into a near traffic accident with a racing driver she doesn't like just so she can orchestrate a story to ruin him? The logical answer was it was almost impossible. I knew all about cruel luck from my parents' untimely deaths. But my run-in with Jenni was different. Bad luck was never that organized. People were, though. Someone had wanted this crash to happen.

'Big fan, huh?'

'The biggest.'

'What's your favourite race of Chloe's?'

Her arrogant confidence evaporated in a split second. She stared at me like I'd handed her a nuclear bomb to diffuse. That wasn't the reaction I expected from Chloe Mercer's number one fan.

'Well . . . I . . . I . . . I don't . . . there's so many to choose from. They're all my favourites, especially the races she won.'

Jenni Oglesby was full of crap. She was no fan of Chloe Mercer's or anyone else's or she would have known that despite coming close a few times, Chloe had never won a race.

Jenni recovered her composure. 'You're going to pay for what you did and it's going to cost you more than the damage to my car. You'll be finished by the time I'm through with you.'

I could see where Jenni was coming from. If she got away with this, it would cost me and not just financially. No team in the world would want me. She'd kill my racing career stone dead. I couldn't let her do this to me, not when I was on my way to making a name for myself in this sport.

'You'll probably go to prison for this,' she said. 'You won't like it there. No foreign travel. No TV interviews. No star of the future there.'

'Stop,' I said. 'Just stop.'

She'd closed the gap between us. There was real pleasure in her expression. She was enjoying her victory too much. I resisted the urge to shove her away. I couldn't give her any more ammunition to use against me.

'It hurts, don't it?'

'Look, it's time to end the game. You win. There's no one here listening. It's just you and me, so there's no need to keep pretending. We both know what happened that day and we both know you made it up. I can't prove it, but it doesn't matter. I just want this to end.'

'Is that right?'

Jenni's look of triumph looked unbreakable, but I knew it wasn't. It was time to disappoint her.

'Yeah, as I see it, you've beaten me. But I'm not so sure about the cops.'

A twitch pulled at the corner of her mouth.

'They've been by to investigate. They haven't found any evidence to back up what you've said. I still don't know where I supposedly ran you off the road, but I wonder if the skid marks back up your account? The analysis of skid marks is an accurate science. Did you know that? Worst of all, you don't have a witness.'

'So you say.' A tremor had entered her speech.

'I do say because if the case was iron clad, the police would have charged me by now.'

I was finally getting through to Jenni. The leer was gone and her confidence was waning.

'When the truth comes out, and it will, the cops are going to come for you and not me.'

Jenni was silent now.

I had her. As much as I enjoyed seeing the tables turned, it made her dangerous. She could lash out just as Steve feared and drop me in a bigger and darker hole. She wouldn't though, if I gave her a way out.

'It doesn't have to be that way,' I said. 'Y'know? We can work this out.'

'How?'

'What do you want? It's pretty obvious that you've gone to a lot of trouble, so you must want something. Are you really only interested in smearing me?'

The word 'yes' slipped between her lips, but fell short before completion.

'What do you want, Jenni? What do I have to do to make this mess go away?'

A light returned to her face. I'd given her hope, which I prayed would lead to greed. She didn't disappoint.

'I want money.'

'How much?'

Lap Twenty-Seven

'How much is she asking?' Dylan asked.

Steve, Dylan and I were in the situation room. We met most nights after Dylan had gotten back from Ragged to discuss what we had learned. Tonight, I had what I'd learned from Jenni Oglesby to share and Dylan had called me all excited to say he had some hot intel. Tonight was also going to be a little different because I'd invited Carrie Russell. I had a couple of questions for her.

'Fifteen grand,' I said.

'Shit,' Dylan said. 'How much do you have left from the sale of the Van Diemen?'

'About eight grand.'

'I can use Gates' upfront money to cover the rest,' Steve said.

'So you're going to pay her?' Dylan asked.

'Yes and no. I just need the money for show. I have to catch her in the act of taking it.'

'She's going to be sorry she crossed us,' Dylan said.

'And her partner,' I said.

'Partner?' Dylan said.

'She says she's Chloe's number one fan, but she doesn't know anything about her. That means someone is feeding her the lines. That also means this reckless-driving scam was set up by someone else.'

'Chloe?' Dylan asked.

'It feels like it. If she disgraces me, she's in line to take my *Pit Lane* title by default.'

'It's a hollow victory to win it by default,' Steve said.

I shrugged.

'So what's the plan?' Dylan asked.

'Make the payoff, document it, then hand it over to Sergeant Lucas and let him do the damage.'

'I hope it's that simple,' Steve said.

So did I.

Dylan stood up. 'OK, who wants to hear what I've found?'

'The floor is yours,' I said.

Dylan grabbed a marker and stepped up to the murder board. 'OK, a couple of interesting titbits. Kurt Haulk went through a difficult teen phrase. He grew up in a not-so-great area of Rotterdam. Don't ask me to pronounce it. He ran with a rough crowd. He's got form. Nothing heavy. He was caught up in a couple of assault charges that never went anywhere because of lack of evidence. Interestingly enough, one was an assault involving a knife. Make of that what you will.'

I could make quite a bit out of it.

'How'd you find all that out?' Steve asked.

'Some of it popped up on Google. I also joined a few Dutch motorsport forums and struck up a couple of conversations.'

'That's all fine and dandy,' Steve said, 'but what's his motive for killing Jason?'

I shrugged.

'We need more than a shrug,' Steve said. 'What else have you got, Dylan?'

'One for the timeline. I went back through Ragged's results over the last few years. The team was a pack runner until five years ago.'

'What changed?'

'Mike Whelan.'

Whelan was a big touring- and sports-car driver. He'd won touring-car championships in Britain, Germany and Japan.

'He won the ESCC title for Ragged that year and dominated the series, but instead of defending his title, he walked away from the team at the end of the season to drive a Corvette for some ropey team in the ALMS.'

'That's around the time Rags started taking money from Gates,' I said.

'Now that I'm one of the lads at Ragged, people are confiding in me,' Dylan said. 'The word is that Rags paid big to have Whelan for the team so the money would have had to come from somewhere.'

'But why leave a winning team?' Steve said.

'Why don't we ask him?' Dylan said. 'We've got the Norisring race this weekend and Whelan is going to be there for the Porsche Cup.'

The doorbell rang.

'That'll be Carrie,' I said.

I went to the back door and let her in. I took her into the situation room where Steve and Dylan introduced themselves. She went up to the murder board and timeline. She put a hand to her mouth while she read our conclusions. It was a long time before she turned to face us.

'You're serious about finding Jason's killer?'

'Yes,' I said.

'Andrew has threatened to take it out on Steve if we don't,' Dylan said.

I shot Dylan a look.

'Andrew is a shit bag,' she said.

No one disagreed with her, but he was a grieving shit bag.

'How can I help?' she asked.

'You told me that Jason broke things off with you three months ago to protect you. Can you think of anything that might explain that?'

Carrie shook her head.

'You also told Aidy that he'd been collecting evidence and hiding it in a picture,' Steve said. 'What started him on that road?'

'I don't know.'

'Did anything out of the ordinary happen? It could have been something seemingly small.'

'I've been racking my brain and the only thing I remember is Jason spotting Ragged Racing's cars once. We'd been shopping in Milton Keynes and as we were driving back, we passed this old service garage. The Ragged Racing truck was there with the cars.'

'Doing what?' I asked.

'I don't know, but Rags was there. Jason wanted to stop, but I didn't want to.'

'Do you know if he went back?'

She shook her head. 'I don't.'

'Do you know the address?'

'No, but I could show you the place.'

This could be Jason's ground zero. This was a lead too good to put on the back burner. 'Do you mind showing us now?'

The question surprised her. 'I suppose. It's on the way back home.'

'You're going to have to count me out,' Dylan said. 'I'm setting off with the team for the Norisring first thing in the morning.'

Carrie led the way while Steve and I followed her in my car. It took less than an hour to reach Milton Keynes where we pulled into the parking area of a disused accident-repair garage. I grabbed the torch from my glove box and we got out of my car.

I aimed the torch at the faded sign over the front of the building that said, Rudolph Repair.

Carrie stood next to us. 'The transporter was down the side and they were loading the cars into the back.'

'Was the place in business back then?' Steve asked.

'No. It was like this. I think that's what caught Jason's eye. Rags had that nice workshop in Banbury, so what was he doing bringing his cars here? I thought maybe he was downscaling and taking the place over. I hope this is of help because it's the only thing I remember.'

'It definitely helps,' I said. 'I'm going to dig around some more, so it's best you get off. I don't want to get you into trouble. It's a talent of mine.'

I smiled. She didn't.

'Are you sure? I don't mind staying.'

'I am.'

'OK. Just be careful. If I remember anything else, I'll call.'

Steve and I watched her go before we went around to the rear of the building, away from prying eyes. The windows were boarded and the doors padlocked. Steve got the crowbar from the boot of my car. I always kept a toolbox with me. It helped to be prepared. He popped the lock off the door and we let ourselves in.

I tried the light switches and the fluorescents blinked on, but I switched them off. We didn't need to let the world know we were poking about.

I searched for the bathroom and found it had running water. As Steve wandered around the garage, he picked up a compressed air-hose line and air came hissing out until the compressor kicked in.

Interesting. Why would a defunct business still have the power and water going?

The place had yet to be cleared out. It still had operational hydraulic lifts, a tyre-changing machine and most of the equipment a repair centre needed. I was surprised that this kit hadn't been sold off when Rudolph Repair went under. This gear was still worth a lot of cash second-hand.

I aimed the torch at the ground. There should have been a thick layer of dust on the floor, but it was pretty clean except for a couple of discarded newspapers. I picked them up and examined them.

'There's been a recent visitor,' I said. 'These papers are only two weeks' old.'

'This place is active,' Steve said. 'Time to go before they come back.'

We let ourselves out. As Steve was putting the crowbar back, I noticed I was being watched. A boy no more than fifteen was staring at me from his front garden across the street.

'Shit,' I murmured. 'We've got company.'

Steve followed my gaze across the street. 'What do you want to do?'

Decision time. Stand my ground or run away. I decided to stay.

'Wait here,' I said.

I raised a hand and jogged across the road. As I got close, the kid backed up a step.

He was weedy and just a couple of inches shorter than me.

I jerked a thumb over my shoulder. 'You know much about this place?'

'A bit.'

'You see this place every day. Is it in business?'

He took a step forward and cast a suspicious eye over me. 'Why do you want to know?'

'I'm in the car trade. I thought it might make for a good location.'

'Bollocks.'

Yeah, I wouldn't have believed that line either. It was the best I could come up with on the spot.

'You with that other bloke?'

I jerked a thumb at Steve. 'You mean the old guy?'

'No. This other guy. A bit older than you. He gives me fifty quid a week to watch this place and call him every time someone comes here. He hasn't called me back in over a week.'

So Jason was having this place watched. 'Yeah, I'm with that guy. He won't be around anymore. Jason, right?'

The kid nodded.

I regrouped by taking out my wallet. I had eighty-five quid, which was a lot for me to be riding around with under normal circumstances. I pulled the cash out and held it in my hand.

'I hear some fancy cars come in and out of there.'

The teen stared at the cash. 'Yeah, racing cars.'

'Yeah? What kind?'

The boy described Ragged's Honda Accords.

'Sweet.'

'Not sweet if they catch you over there. The wankers gave me a kicking for just looking. They won't like it if they find out you broke in there.'

'Hopefully they won't. There aren't any racing cars in there now.'

'No, they just use the place now and again. They bring the cars in, work on them for a few hours then leave.'

'They do this during the day?'

'No. Always at night.'

'How often are they here?'

'They usually come every few weeks or so.'

'Really, that often? When'd you see them last?'

'A couple of weeks ago. Look, you going to give me that cash or what?'

The second he snatched the money from me, he stormed back towards his house.

'I was never here, right?' I called after him.

'Never seen you before, mate. Just like the other bloke.'

I watched him disappear inside the house before I turned back to Rudolph's Repair. Carrie was right about one thing – why would Rags bring his cars to this dump when he had a modern workshop? The answer was he wouldn't, unless he had something to hide. Maybe Rags was cheating after all. I would have loved to have gotten some alone time with the cars, but they were leaving for Germany in the morning.

Lap Twenty-Eight

The ESCC was a support race at Germany's Norisring with the German Touring Car Masters as the feature. It was going to take the team two days to drive over there. I flew in to meet the team for the race on Friday. I was excited for this race since I'd never raced on a street circuit before. After the complexity of Spa, the Norisring is a relatively simple eight-turn lap around the streets of Nuremberg. For a street circuit, it's fast with plenty of overtaking opportunities. What makes the race notable in an odd way is that it takes place on what's left of the former Nazi party rally grounds.

Mike Whelan was here and I needed to speak to him, so I'd scoped out his team's location in the paddock. But as much as I needed to talk to him, I had my race to focus on, so I stuck close to my team during morning qualifying on Saturday. The team did well. I claimed fifth on the grid, while Haulk grabbed second place. A G-Tek BMW 3-Series claimed pole position, pipping Haulk by three one-hundredths of a second. The Townsend Motorsport Accords split Haulk and me. Naturally, Rags had wanted us to claim the front row and let us know about it in no uncertain terms. I wasn't sure what needled him more, the fact that the German BMW team had taken pole or that Russell Townsend's cars were matching our times. I wasn't particularly bothered. I always drove better in the race than I did in qualifying.

Rags' bear-with-a-sore-head routine gave me the excuse to put some distance between the team and me. Dylan caught me before I went in search of Whelan.

'Do you want me to come with you?" he asked.

'No, this'll go better as a one-on-one. Just keep your ears and eyes open. Call me if anything interesting happens.'

'You got it.'

I combed the paddock for Whelan's team. Since leaving Ragged Racing, he'd flitted between various sports-car championships. He'd done a couple of seasons in sports prototypes, but for the last season, he'd taken part in the Porsche Cup. The Porsche teams were corralled in the paddock next to a stadium. I caught Whelan as he was walking out of the team trailer.

'Mr Whelan, could I speak to you for a minute?'

He eyed me for a moment, but the racing overalls told him I wasn't an over-eager fan in need of an autograph. He put out a hand and I shook it.

'I'm Aidy Westlake.'

He tapped the name embroidered into my racesuit. 'I know who you are. I hear good things about you, and a few bad.'

He said this last part without malice. I wondered what paddock gossip had attached itself to my name.

'What can I do for you?'

'I'd like your advice. It has to do with Ragged Racing.'

Whelan pursed his lips and scratched under his chin. 'I was going to get something to eat. Why don't we have a bite together?'

'I think we should talk in private.'

'You're probably right. Let's take a walk.'

We circled around to the far side of the stadium away from the throng surrounding the pits. It was a dry, overcast day. Without transporters, lorries and awnings acting as a barrier, the wind cut across the paddock. I felt my body temperature drop a couple of degrees.

'What do you want to know?' Whelan asked.

'I wanted to ask you about your experiences with Ragged Racing.'

'Having problems?'

'You could say that.'

'Kurt Haulk is your teammate. I'm sure he can be of more help than I can.'

'It's kind of delicate and not something I can discuss with anyone at Ragged.'

'You've intrigued me now, so ask away.'

If I was wrong about the reasons why Whelan left Ragged, I couldn't afford to expose what I knew and risk tipping Rags off. I needed to ask a question that would touch a nerve in Whelan and I thought I had one.

'You gave Rags his first championship title, but instead of defending your title, you left. Why?'

I caught Whelan's flinch. It was a small reaction – just a hunching of his shoulders. It could be explained away by the biting wind, but only if you believed in fairytales.

'No mystery to that. I signed a one-year lucrative deal to drive for him. It was somewhat of a gamble for both of us at the time. Rags was small-time back then, but I saw something in what he was doing with the cars. He thought bringing in a name driver would attract sponsors and I saw that he was giving me the potential to win a title.'

That all sounded reasonable enough, but I didn't believe a word of it. 'You two proved you were a good combination. Why leave?'

'Better opportunities.'

More bullshit. 'So you call driving Corvettes in the American Le Mans series a better opportunity? Kilgore Motorsport was a three-wheel team at best, barely able to finish a lap let alone a race. I also find it interesting that you put an ocean between you and Rags.'

Whelan grabbed my arm, jerking me back. 'Watch your mouth. If you've got something to ask, I suggest you do it. If not, I'm hungry.'

'What you did doesn't make sense. Just tell me why you left the team.'

'I get the feeling you already know. So why don't you tell me why I left the team?'

'I'd say it had something to do with how Rags financed it.'

'Shit,' Whelan murmured, more to himself than to me. 'Is it happening again?'

'Is what happening again?'

'Aidy, don't piss me around. I'm trying to help you out.'

I held up my hands. 'OK, I'm sorry. Rags was paying for the team with money he borrowed from a loan shark, wasn't he?'

'Yeah. He was. I didn't know when I signed on. I wouldn't have joined the team if I had, regardless of how the good the cars were. I thought he was burning through his own money because he didn't have any sponsors. It became obvious about halfway through the season where it was coming from. By the end of the season, these heavy types were hanging around. One time, I walked in on these two blokes holding Rags down and slicing through his arm with a knife. After that, I wanted out, but those guys and Rags convinced me to stick around until the end of the season. It's the only time I've been truly scared in all the years I've been racing. Is Rags on the hook with those people again?'

'No, I don't think so, but I think he's into something else. Beyond the loan sharks, did you ever see anything else going on?'

'Like what?'

I didn't want to tip my hand here. I couldn't tell him about the drug running. 'I don't know. I'm wondering if he's moving stolen parts or something. I don't really know, but it's kind of spooking me.'

'I don't know about stolen goods or anything. I just saw the loan sharks, but once you dig yourself a hole like that, you'll do business with anyone who'll throw you a lifeline.'

Wasn't that the truth. 'Did anyone else know what was going on?'

'Not sure. I got the feeling that Rags kept the cupboard locked on that skeleton, but I'm guessing some of the crew twigged that something wasn't on the up and up. If you're looking for a friend within the team to talk to, I suggest you have a quiet word with Barry Nevin. He's close with Rags. If anyone knows what's going on, it's Barry. I hope that helps.'

'It does. Thanks.'

I shook Whelan's hand. He didn't release his grip.

'If I can give you a piece of advice: find another drive.'

At the best of times, changing drives was never an easy prospect. It was up there with tigers changing their stripes. Between my commitments to Gates, Barrington, Townsend and *Pit Lane* magazine, I was shackled to Rags.

'I'm only two races into the season.'

'I know there's a lot of politics tying you to this drive,' Whelan said, 'but junk it and find another.'

Whelan didn't know half the story. It was too late for that. 'I'm not sure I can do that.'

'Unless someone is holding a gun to your head, you have a choice.'

How about a knife? 'I appreciate the advice, but I can't.'

'Look, I'll make it easier for you. Let me tap up some contacts. If I can find you a drive elsewhere, will you take it? I'm serious, so I need a concrete commitment right now.'

Whelan intensified his grip on my hand to underline his point. I appreciated his offer more than he'd ever know. And if I proved Rags was mixed up in drug trafficking, there'd be no Ragged Racing to return to. Sometimes the lifeline people held out to you wasn't greased.

'You've got a deal.'

Whelan smiled. 'Good. Now get lost. I'll be in touch.'

I thought I should put an appearance in with the team and returned to the ESCC paddock next to the lake. I cut between the various team transporters and hadn't reached our area when I heard Rags saying my name. At first, I thought he was calling me, but I found him entrenched in conversation with Chloe Mercer. She had a guest ride in the Porsche Cup. I kept back. I wanted to hear this.

'You know he doesn't deserve the drive,' Chloe said.

'I won't say that. He's adapting well, but he does come with a little too much baggage.'

Don't kill yourself defending me, Rags.

'You mean he's a bloody liability.'

Chloe wasn't pulling her punches.

'Yes, he has the potential for that. That's why I called you. The question is, can you take over for him? You've bitched about him, but when I offered you his drive, you hesitated. I need a commitment. So what's it to be?'

Jesus Christ, I couldn't believe Rags had been plotting behind my back to replace me. I knew events had conspired against me, but I couldn't believe he was willing to cut me loose after just two rounds. Let's see if they'd say it to my face.

As I took a step forward, a hand grabbed my arm. It was Claudia. She shook her head and put her finger to her lips.

I tried to shrug her off, but she tightened her grip and pulled me away. She led me into the thick of the paddock away from the other ESCC teams.

'Rags is talking about replacing me.'

'I know. I 'eard a rumour. I was looking for you so I could warn you. You can't let that 'appen. We need you as part of the team.'

'Thanks for the support. How about you don't deserve to lose your drive, Aidy.'

'Sorry. You're right. This isn't fair, but I'm relying on

you. You 'ave to do something to save your drive and the operation.'

'I feel like slamming the car into the first crash barrier I see.'

'Aidy, please.'

'OK, OK, OK.' Claudia had done me a favour. I was over the shock. I was pissed off, but I wasn't cruising to torpedo my drive.

'So what are you going to do?'

'Make it impossible for Rags to ditch me.'

Three hours later, I was on the track on the third row of the grid for the race. Four cars sat ahead of me, but far more sat behind me. It was easier to lose my position than improve on it.

Rags' side deal still ate away at me, but I wasn't about to let it get to me. I turned to the only piece of racing advice my dad had ever given me. He made it to one of my races before he died. I was eight. It was a go-kart race in some junior league at an outdoor track in Kent. Dad had wanted me to follow in his tyre tracks and entered me in the league. I qualified twelfth out of sixteen and I was disappointed. On the grid for the race, Dad knelt alongside me with Steve. My head was down because I knew there was no way I could win from all the way down in twelfth. I didn't see much point in taking part. Dad had picked up on my disappointment. He leaned in and gave me the best piece of advice anyone had ever given me.

'Now that might look like a lot of helmets between you and first place, but you can't beat them all at once. You just have to take them down one at a time. Focus on the guy on front of you, overtake him then move on to the next. Before you know it, you'll be in front.'

I'd incorporated that approach into every race since. Today, just four helmets were between me and success.

'OK, Aidy, I'm looking for a good performance,' Nevin said. 'Talk to me. How are you feeling?'

I wasn't in the mood to communicate with my so-called team, so I tugged the jack from my headset. 'I'm feeling angry.'

The lights went from red to green and I used what my dad had taught me. I took down the helmets in front of me one at a time and won my first race.

'Fire me now, Rags,' I said to myself as I took the chequered flag.

Lap Twenty-Nine

Steve and I waited for Dylan's call in Steve's Capri parked a mile from Ragged Racing's workshop. He called just after nine p.m. to give us the all clear. Finally, we were going to prove Townsend's car tampering claims right or wrong. It was Wednesday night and my first crack at the team cars since the Norisring race at the weekend. The team hadn't got back from Germany until today.

The moment we turned on to the street, the workshop door rolled up. A cone of light pushed back the night, shining a light on tonight's risky activity. Steve drove the car straight into the workshop and Dylan brought the door down.

We had to work fast now. Steve and I climbed from the car. Dylan opened the boot and pulled out toolboxes and equipment. I grabbed the spec drawings I'd gotten from Townsend.

'You sure no one's coming back?' I asked Dylan.

'As sure as I can be. When these guys pack up for the day, they don't return. In the last week, only Nevin's come back. He just dropped by once to see how I was doing, but he hasn't been back since.'

That was about as risk free as tonight's adventure was going to get.

'Does anyone suspect you?'

Dylan grinned and flung his arms wide. 'You're joking, aren't you? I'm the flavour of the month. They love me here.'

The plan had worked. Dylan's role was to play the over-eager apprentice. In an effort to suck up knowledge, he'd asked to stay late so he could get the jump on the next day. Nevin had warmed to Dylan's enthusiasm and assigned him tasks to do after hours. Dylan had been working until nine on a regular basis for over a week now.

'They haven't seen anyone as dedicated as me since Jason,' Dylan said.

The significance of what Dylan had said hit us all hard and Dylan's grin withered.

'How do you want to do this, Steve?'

'A quick metallurgy test,' he said and produced a magnet.

I immediately got it and I smiled at my grandfather's simple brilliance, but Dylan looked confused.

Steve went up to Haulk's car and put the magnet next to the door panel, where it stuck tight. If Rags had wanted to lighten the cars, getting the bodywork reproduced in aluminium would be a great way of doing it. Once the paint was on, who'd know the difference?

'You wily old git,' Dylan said.

'Wily, yes. Old, no.'

Steve brought out a couple of other magnets and tossed them to Dylan and me. We ran them over every body panel on both cars. Everything that was supposed to be steel was steel. Round one went to Rags.

'OK, it's time to get out our measuring sticks,' Steve said. 'Aidy, put a car on the lift.'

I fired up my racecar and manoeuvred it on to a hydraulic lift and raised it up. It wouldn't be hard to manufacture wishbones that gave the car a couple of inches more width. It might not seem like much, but motor racing is a sport of degrees. A slight edge is all that's needed to get ahead and stay there. If Rags had made a couple of illegal tweaks that gained his cars half a second a lap, that would equate to fifteen seconds over a thirty lap sprint race. Depending on lap speeds, a fifteen-second lead could work out to be between a quarter to a half-mile lead. That's quite a cushion to have during a race. We measured the track, the wheelbase and the location of the suspension pickups. Everything conformed with the measurements on the design drawings. The story was the same with Haulk's car.

'Rags is playing it straight,' Dylan said.

'So far, he is,' Steve corrected. 'Now for the big test: let's check their power.'

You could make a car go faster a million different ways, but the number one method was to add more power. Things in the ESCC were very controlled. To keep the racing close, the engines were limited to three hundred brake horsepower and were sealed with a metal tab to prevent tampering. If someone removed the cylinder head, they'd have to break the seal. ESCC scruntineers inspected the seals before and after each race. It was as foolproof a system as humanly possible, but the human element was always the weakest link. If Rags had bribed or coerced the right people, he could get his hands on his own supply of ESCC seals and replace them at will. For what it was worth, I checked the ESCC seals and they showed no signs of tampering.

I brought Haulk's car around to the rolling road in the workshop. A rolling road is like a treadmill for cars. The driving wheels drop on to a set of rollers so the car can drive as fast as necessary and not travel an inch. In the meantime, a computer records everything from its speed and power output to its star sign. Steve and Dylan removed the plates covering the rollers and I dropped the car into place. I waited while Steve hooked the engine up to the computer and Dylan hooked an extraction hose to the exhaust. When Steve flashed me a thumbs-up, I pressed down on the accelerator. The car climbed up the rollers as its front wheels spun faster and faster. The whine of the engine was deafening in the enclosed workshop. Unfortunately, we weren't in a position to open the doors to let the sound out.

'More gas,' Steve said and I pressed down on the accelerator even harder.

It was disconcerting to see the digital readout in front of me state I was travelling at the equivalent of a hundred miles an hour while the car was stationary. If the car jumped out of the rollers, it would fly straight into the brick wall in front of me.

Steve waved his hand under his chin in a throat-cutting gesture. 'Kill it and bring me the other one.'

The result after two nerve-racking runs on the rolling road was that both cars produced the regulation three hundred break horsepower.

'It appears that Russell Townsend is talking a lot of bollocks,' Dylan said.

I was finding it hard to disagree. Townsend's belief that Rags was cheating was turning out to be nothing more than sour grapes. I'd already had my fill of that with Chloe Mercer bitching about my unworthiness.

Our discoveries pleased me, because Ragged wasn't cheating, but the downside of the cars being straight was that I didn't have a motive for Jason's murder.

'So far, we've just eliminated the obvious,' Steve said. 'Now it's time to see if Rags has indulged in some creative thinking.'

We spent the next hour examining the cars, checking everything against the design specifications and championship regulations. The cars checked out in every respect. They were straight.

'Er, I think we've got a problem,' Dylan said.

He had Haulk's car up on Steve's portable scales.

'This car is heavy.'

'How heavy?' Steve said.

'Close to forty kilos heavy.'

I was expecting an underweight car, not an overweight one. 'That can't be right.'

'Come double-check it.'

Steve and I helped Dylan reweigh the car. He was right. Haulk's car was forty-one kilos heavier than it should be. We weighed mine and found it to be thirty-eight kilos overweight.

'Are we living in Bizarro world where heavier cars go faster than light ones?' Dylan asked.

'Nope,' Steve said.

We combed the cars for a source of the additional weight and didn't find it. There was no way of hiding it inside the cars because the interior and seats had been removed. My thought was it was sealed up in the bulkheads but without cutting those open, there was no way of knowing. Dylan found the source when he removed a wheel from my car to check under a wheel arch. The wheel slipped from his grasp, but failed to bounce.

'Be careful,' Steve said, offering Dylan his hand.

'It's the wheel. It weighs a ton.'

'Someone needs to work out a little harder in the gym,' I said.

'OK, Mr Muscles, you pick it up.'

I chased after the wheel, which was still rolling drunkenly towards the workshop door like it was trying to escape. I stopped its progress with my foot and lifted it. It was heavier than I expected. I remembered the flat bounce when Dylan had dropped it, so I dropped it again. There was little bounce to the wheel.

I rolled it back to the car. I heard a rubbing sound as it rolled.

'There's definitely something up with this wheel,' I said.

Steve grabbed it and popped the tyre off one side of the rim. It should have been loose on the rim now, but something inside the wheel was keeping it in place.

'There's something inside this tyre,' Steve said.

Steve and Dylan were both big men with big hands. I was the

little guy who bought women's socks because they fit my size-six feet better. Steve and Dylan held back the edge of the tyre from the wheel rim and I slipped my hand inside. My stomach turned when I touched one of what had to be dozens of plastic bags from the feel of them. I grabbed one and pulled it out. It was a package of white powder. I had an uneasy sense of déjà vu taking me all the way back to a Belgian police station.

I pulled out my mobile and dialled Claudia's number. She answered on the third ring despite it being after midnight.

'Claudia, we have a problem.'

Lap Thirty

I met with Claudia and Barrington the following morning at the Holiday Inn next to Heathrow Airport. The room overlooked the airport road and the drone of passing cars penetrated the windows. There was coffee and a collection of notepads on a circular table, with an empty chair for me. The whole affair came over more like a sales-rep meeting than a clandestine meeting for HM Customs. It made me wonder how big an operation Barrington was running. It seemed pretty small-time, but it could be the iceberg approach, where I got to see the tip and nothing more.

Claudia brought out a digital recorder and placed it at the centre of the table. 'Tell us everything you discovered last night.'

I outlined every detail. Barrington hung on my every word. For once, he didn't mock me or exert his power. I guessed I was being useful to him.

'Now you're sure it was drugs inside those tyres?' Barrington asked after I was finished.

'As sure as I can be,' I said. 'The tyres were packed with bags of white powder.'

'Didn't you open one?'

'No way. I wasn't touching that stuff. And I wouldn't know cocaine from caster sugar.'

'It better not be caster sugar.'

'Who packs tyres with caster sugar?'

That silenced Barrington.

'Hiding the coke in the tyres is genius,' he said. 'I have to give the crafty bugger that. There's no chopping the car up or hidden panels and the drugs come gift wrapped in an easy to transport package. They're hidden in plain sight. There are dozens of wheels and tyres flying around, so everyone is going to ignore them.'

'I bet these loaded wheels get put on at the end of the race and taken off when the cars are back at the workshop,' I said.

'Have you seen anyone take the tyres?' Claudia asked.

'Probably, but I haven't been paying attention.'

'Who's responsible for changing them?' Barrington asked.

'No one special. All the guys are capable, from Rags on down, but Dylan's part of the furniture now and he hasn't seen anyone acting shady when it comes to the tyres. Which isn't surprising.'

'What makes you say that?' Claudia asked.

'If all the guys were involved, they'd either be cutting Dylan in or excluding him. Whoever's switching wheels must be doing this after hours when no one is watching.'

Barrington got up from his chair and paced up and down in front of the window. He flicked his thumbnail against his index finger as he paced. I thought I heard the gears turning.

'We could go in now,' Claudia suggested. 'We'd have enough to bury Rags. He'd give up his connections for a deal.'

Barrington turned his back on the mundane view. 'No, I don't want the mule, I want the network. I don't want to risk Rags not talking.'

'He'll talk,' Claudia said.

'I'm not so sure,' I said. 'Rags isn't a pushover.'

'I agree,' Barrington said. 'You say the wheels with the drugs in them are on the cars?'

'Yeah.'

'Where are the cars going?'

'We're testing at Zandvoort in Holland next Wednesday.'

'Why Zandvoort?' Claudia said. 'The ESCC has no scheduled race there.'

'I know.'

'Then why?'

'After catching a rival spying, Rags says he wants to test somewhere with a little privacy. Kurt Haulk has connections at the circuit and got us in.'

Claudia and Barrington looked at each other.

'So let me get this straight. Ragged Racing will be travelling to mainland Europe with almost a hundred kilos of cocaine to a secluded place where you have no business being,' Barrington said.

'Pretty much.'

'You want to catch them during the exchange?' Claudia asked.

Barrington grinned. 'Oh, yes.'

My emotions got stuck between floors. I'd be happy if Barrington wrapped up his investigation on Wednesday because it would mean our association was at an end, but so would my time with Ragged Racing. I'd told Russell Townsend I wouldn't torpedo my drive for him, but it looked as if I'd be doing that for Barrington.

I drove back to Archway to fill Steve in on the next phase. Instead of finding him hard at work, I came back to find half a dozen police cars and a police van filling the parking area. My stomach sank. This was it. Sergeant Lucas was finally here to arrest me. The heavy police presence seemed like overkill, but I supposed he was still pissed off over the van theft. I stopped the Honda behind a cop car, blocking it in.

I climbed out and a uniformed officer came rushing at me with hands out.

'You can't go in.'

'I think I'm the person Sergeant Lucas is expecting.'

The cop gave me a confused look. 'Wait here.'

He disappeared inside Archway and a moment later, Steve and DI Huston emerged. Her presence confused me.

Steve broke away from her and got to me first. 'It's going to be OK,' he whispered.

'What did he say?' Huston demanded.

'He told me it was going to be OK. What's going on?' I asked.

'We've been led to believe that you're in possession of the weapon used to kill Jason Gates, Mr Westlake.'

'What are you talking about? Is this is a joke?'

'No joke. Please come with me. I'd like you to explain this.'

I looked to Steve for answers. He just shook his head in bewilderment.

We followed her back into the workshop where half a dozen

officers were ransacking tool cabinets and emptying toolboxes. Others were pawing over the cars Steve was restoring for Gates. It was like watching wild dogs tearing apart a defenceless animal.

'I'm so sorry,' I said to Steve.

'I'd like your opinion on this,' Huston said and pointed at the situation room.

I groaned.

She stopped in the doorway where a couple of officers were removing the whiteboards, using Steve's tools. 'What are these?'

'What do they look like?'

'It looks like a suspect board. Have you been running your own investigation, Mr Westlake? It goes some way to explaining why I keep finding your paw prints all over my case. How about you explain the rest?'

'It's nothing. Just idle speculation. There's nothing wrong in that. Remember, I was a witness to Jason's murder.'

'Just a witness?'

'Just a witness.'

'Inspector,' an excited voice shouted. 'We've got it.'

I looked at Steve. I read the dread on his face.

A female officer burst from the toilets brandishing a cutthroat razor sealed in a plastic bag. Water dripped from the bag. 'It was in the toilet's cistern. There's blood on it.'

I closed my eyes. I knew what was coming next.

'Turn around, Mr Westlake. I'm arresting you.'

Lap Thirty-One

A uniformed officer drove Huston and me into London. Neither of them spoke to me during the drive. Not surprising. I'd lost my status as a free person. Others now decided when I spoke and who answered.

When we reached the station, Huston put me in the same interview room as before and left me there with the officer who'd driven us. It was familiar surroundings in an unfamiliar scenario. I'd seen the inside of a police interview room many times, but the charges levelled against me had always been minor. Until now.

The door opened. Huston walked in with two officers carrying the whiteboards from the situation room. As soon as they leaned them against the wall, they left along with the silent officer.

'You look nervous Mr Westlake. Actually, you look petrified.'

A murder charge did that to me. I couldn't see how Huston could make it stick, but you could make anything stick if you presented the information correctly. The room seemed smaller than it was. If they held me, my rooms from now on would be getting smaller and smaller.

Huston laid her file and the razor, now in an evidence bag, on the table between us. She loaded a cassette tape into the recorder and started it.

'Let's get down to business,' she said. 'Things don't look good for you, Aidy. I have the murder weapon and these odd jottings of yours. Do you want to talk about it?'

'I know this looks bad, but that knife was planted.'

The look of disbelief on Huston's face killed my will to continue with my defence. The truth sounded so weak. It always did when you had nothing but your word as backup.

'I have your statement that we took the night of Jason's murder. Is there anything you'd like to change?'

I foresaw myself stuck in this room for hours while Huston pounded me with accusation after accusation and picked away at my statement. I couldn't let that happen. It would be a waste of time and, worse, it gave the killer even more time to frame me. At least Steve knew I was here. I hoped he was getting me a solicitor. I needed to get out of here. I was on the verge of hooking Jason's killer. I couldn't do it from a jail cell.

'Look, I'm not going to change one word of my statement. What I told you is the truth. I want to talk about what you found.'

Huston held up her hands. 'Good. I'm all ears.'

'That razor. Assuming for one minute that it is the murder weapon, because at this point, you haven't matched the blood, you won't find my fingerprints anywhere on it.'

Huston smirked and nodded.

'But the important question is, if that is the murder weapon and I'm the murderer, why the hell would I keep it? If I had any brains, I'd have binned the weapon ages ago.'

'Is that a rhetorical question?'

'No, it's not. It's a bloody serious question.'

I knew I should be keeping calm but I couldn't help myself. Now that Huston had me she wasn't letting me go.

'You kept the knife because you're a collector.'

'Seriously? You'd think I'd come up with a better trophy case than my toilet tank.'

'You're not that imaginative. You wouldn't be the first.'

'You know what else makes a mockery of me still having the razor? The fact you didn't find it on me the night of the murder.'

Huston only needed a second to come up with an answer. 'You ditched it at the scene.'

'And my gloves, because there won't be any prints on it.'

'And gloves. Thank you.'

'So where did I ditch them? Because wherever I put them your people failed to find them at the scene. You see how none of this is making sense?'

Of course she didn't. She simply turned to her notes and flicked through them.

'I'm thinking you ditched the murder weapon in that drain with Jason's mobile. It explains why you returned to retrieve it. Why did you take the mobile in the first place – more mementos? God, I feel like an idiot for balling you out for touching it and destroying anybody else's prints. There were no other prints. Just yours. That was clever.'

Even dumb luck was conspiring against me. Unrelated and innocent events were fitting together to create a damning picture. My being covered in blood when the police found me just made that picture even worse.

'As it stands now,' Huston said, 'I have you at the scene, I have you with the murder weapon, but what I don't have is a reason. Care to shed some light on that?'

'There's no light to shed. I didn't kill Jason.'

Huston got up and went over to my whiteboards. They'd been sealed in plastic. She read our findings.

'Frankly, I find this disturbing. What the hell is this?'

I really didn't want her reading the board, but it might be my ticket out of here. 'What does it look like?'

'A murder board. You've got suspects, a timeline, motives and suppositions.'

'If I killed Jason, why would I have a murder board?'

'I see a couple of sets of handwriting. Have you been talking this over with your friends?'

'Yes.'

'So you and your pals have been playing detective while all the time you were the one who did it? Christ, that's cold.'

I was finished. It didn't matter what I said, Huston would have an answer. I just dropped my head into my hands and a despair-filled laugh leaked out of me. If the situation weren't so crazy, it would have been funny.

'Something funny, Aidy?'

'You're making me out to be the greatest criminal mastermind since Jack the Ripper. Listen to yourself. Is any of this likely, let alone possible?'

'You tell me.'

A knock at the door stopped me from answering. Huston suspended the interview and stopped the tape. O'Neal let himself in. I hadn't seen him since the night of Jason's murder.

'Got a minute?' he said to Huston.

She picked up the razor and her file and stepped out of the room. A uniformed officer replaced her. He stood by the door and dropped the weight of his gaze on me.

I offered a friendly smile. My babysitter didn't return it.

After a couple of minutes' silence, Huston's angry voice penetrated the interview room's walls. Both the uniformed officer and I whipped our heads around in the direction of the door.

'You've got to be fucking joking!' she shouted. 'Shit.'

A second later, the door flew open. 'You're free to go.'

'What?' I said.

'All charges have been dropped. Sorry for the inconvenience.' The apology came out with frost clinging to each word.

I stood up. 'I don't get it.'

'Seems like you have some very powerful friends. So powerful that they don't even have to leave their name. Just one word from them and you are magically free to go about your business.'

The sudden rush of relief left me breathless.

'Once we sign you out, you can leave and all your possessions will be returned to you.' She nodded in the direction of the whiteboards.

'You can keep the razor since it's not mine. Hopefully, it'll help you. By the way, what made you think I even had the murder weapon?' I asked.

Huston said nothing.

'An anonymous tip?'

'Your freedom awaits, Mr Westlake.'

'You might want to check out who tipped you off,' I said, but Huston was already walking away.

'This way, Mr Westlake,' O'Neal said.

O'Neal saw me out. Steve was waiting for me in the reception area and I hugged him.

'I'll just get your possessions,' O'Neal said.

'Thanks for coming,' I said to Steve. 'Barrington?'

'Yeah. I called him. He flexed his muscles and hey presto,' Steve said.

'At least he's good for something.'

'He says he hopes the same about you. He also said to remind you that you've got a job to do and you need to finish it.'

Lap Thirty-Two

The Zandvoort circuit sits on the coast just twenty miles from the heart of Amsterdam. Sand dunes hide the North Sea lurking behind. Steve had warned me to watch out for the sand. It's not uncommon for it to blow in from the dunes to dust the main straight. It's one of those little things that makes getting to know a track that little bit trickier. In its heyday, Zandvoort was a regular stop on the grand prix calendar, but the last Dutch Grand Prix was in 1985. Despite losing its Formula One lustre, it's still a busy circuit for Dutch national titles and European championships. Regardless of our nefarious reasons for being in Holland, I was looking forward to driving here. The world was teeming with historic tracks that had hosted some fantastic races and I wanted to leave my tyre tracks on as many of them as I could.

The team set off on Tuesday with Dylan. The convoy of two transporters drove from England to Holland via the Channel Tunnel. Dylan acted as my eyes. He called me with updates every few hours. There'd been no detours, stop-offs or meetings. They simply drove to the circuit, parked the transporters and went to their hotel for the night. I reported this back to Barrington.

'Someone will come for the drugs while you're on the track.'

Claudia was out of the picture for this part. According to Barrington, she had to protect her cover. That was reasonable, but I got the feeling that he just wanted to be there at the kill.

Instead of driving, I flew into Amsterdam's Schiphol Airport first thing Wednesday morning with Haulk. The forty-minute flight trumped the eight-hour drive.

Rags met us at the airport. Haulk rode shotgun with Rags while I took the back seat.

'How's the setup?' Haulk asked.

'Good. Your name opens more doors than American Express. We've got the circuit to ourselves and we'll be ready to hit the track by the time we get there. The best thing is that there won't be any of Townsend's spies on deck.'

Rags went on to outline the day's game plan and I tuned him out. All I could think about were those packets of cocaine hidden inside the wheels of my car. Was Rags a mule? It sure looked that way. I tried to marry that up with the man talking ten to the dozen about lap times, tyre performance, and engine power and failed to get a match. If it was true, was Rags working alone? How many of the crew members were involved? I couldn't see how this was going to end well.

We arrived at Zandvoort to find the cars in the pit garages with their engines running. Dylan brought over my kit bag. He'd stored it on the transporter so I didn't have to take it through the airport.

I took the bag from him. 'Anything interesting happen?'

'Nope.'

I eyed the wheels on my car. 'Are they the loaded tyres?'

'As far as I can tell. Those are the wheels that we took off the other night.'

Surely we weren't going to drive with ten kilos of coke in each wheel. The cars would handle like a bus and the drugs wouldn't survive the beating. 'Don't take your eyes off those wheels after we do a tyre change.'

He nodded. 'Barrington?'

I glanced out over the dunes. 'He says our every move is being watched.'

Nevin called my name. 'Aidy, we're good to go. We just need the human component.'

'Human component ready to go.'

Nevin handed me the checklist and as I changed, I called out the tasks. I kissed my mum's St Christopher and got behind the wheel.

Zandvoort is similar to Snetterton in that it's relatively flat with one corner after another with little respite. I knew it was going to be a challenging circuit and I struggled. I picked the wrong lines through the bends and each turn was a dance with the gravel traps. I knew I was slow. I could hear it in the engine noise. I just wasn't pushing the power band. To compensate, I cut my braking distances and ended up slewing past my turn-in points.

'C'mon, Aidy, pull it together,' Nevin said through my headset. 'Don't let this place rattle you. You're better than this.'

Zandvoort wasn't getting to me, Ragged Racing was. Instead of watching for braking points, apexes and exit points, I saw tyres packed with cocaine. I saw people I admired, liked and trusted with my personal safety as possible drug mules. And worst of all, I was now picturing one of them as Jason Gates' murderer. All of it ate away at me. Driving flat out at ten-tenths took single focus and I was nowhere near. I'd be better off driving blindfolded.

Rags' voice came in over my headset. 'You going to wreck my car?'

If Rags was breaking ranks to talk to me instead of Nevin, my driving had pissed him off.

'No, sir.'

'You'd better not, Aidy. You know what makes a good driver? Consistency. The ability to make lightning strike in the same place again and again. You, son, are too hot and cold. That's no good to me. I'd rather have lukewarm. Pull it together or get off the track. Your decision. What's it going to be?'

'I'm staying out.'

'Good. Back off. Wait for Haulk. Latch on to his tail and see how a real driver does it.'

I backed off and when Haulk ripped past me on the approach to the Audi S curve, I floored the accelerator. With momentum on Haulk's side, he continued to pull away from me, but it wouldn't be for long.

Nevin had asked for the human component. That was what I needed to be. I squeezed all thoughts of drug trafficking from my mind and put everything I had into keeping up with Haulk's car. I mimicked his lines around the track. I put down mental markers where he braked, where he turned, where he clipped the apexes. I needed this information not only to learn the circuit, but to overtake him.

After five laps, I was keeping up with him, even when he pushed that little bit harder, then I reeled him in a tenth of a second at a time. In showing me his line around the track, he'd exposed his driving style. Just like a card player revealing his tells, I knew what Haulk was going to do. I watched for the telltale puff of exhaust smoke every time he changed gears and held the gear just that second longer before shifting to wring every last rev out of my engine. Every time the rear of his car rose up when he braked for a corner, I stayed on the power for a fraction longer. And I reeled Haulk in.

I could smell it as well as see it. The acrid stink of burnt exhaust fumes filtered through the vents in my car. Instead of repelling me, the scent spurred me on. I was on the hunt and I had my prey.

On the tenth lap, I crawled all over Haulk's rear bumper as we went into the sweeping right-hander before the start-finish straight and, on the exit, I jerked out from behind him and drew alongside him. He saluted me as I breezed past.

'Very impressive,' Rags said through my headset. 'Now bring it in before you go and ruin it.'

Both Haulk and I slowed for a cool-down lap and I rolled to a halt in front of my pit garage.

Dylan opened my door and helped me out of the car. 'Mate, that was quick.'

'Really?'

'Telemetry doesn't lie,' Nevin said, holding his laptop. 'Nicely done.'

'Aidy, Nevin, over here,' Rags called out.

'Time for us to listen to our master's voice,' Nevin said, before addressing the crew. 'I want fresh rubber all round and a full tank when I get back.'

I exchanged a look with Dylan. He knew what he was supposed to do.

We met Rags at the pit wall. 'We need to talk,' he said.

My heart fluttered.

'I like how you responded out there, but I don't want to have to give you a bollocking to get you to perform.'

'I know. I'm sorry.'

'Don't be sorry. Get your act together. You just took the ESCC champion apart in ten laps. I want that every time without shouting for it. I meant what I said about you blowing hot and cold. I can't have that. I want fast and predictable. Does that make sense?'

'It does.'

'So, is there a problem?'

Yeah, close to a hundred kilos of coke, I thought. 'It's an adjustment thing.'

'There isn't time for adjusting. You have to be on from the start.'

'In the lad's defence, we didn't think he'd have a win under his belt at this point,' Nevin said. 'He's doing better than we thought and our expectations are higher.'

'Maybe so, but he's shown he can mix it up with the best, so he has to do that race after race.' Rags turned to me. 'Can you do it?'

'I can do my best.'

'Not good enough. Can you do it?'

'He can,' Nevin said.

'Then I'm making it your job to get the best out of him.'

'Consider it done.'

Rags fixed me with his stare. 'Are you going to break my heart?'

Quite possibly, I thought.

Rags briefed Haulk and me on a plan of action, which included a day of driving on full tanks, quarter tanks and tyre testing. Tyre testing meant we'd be burning through a lot of tyres. It would be easy to lose the cocaine-loaded tyres in the mix.

After the briefing, I pulled Dylan to one side. 'Where are the wheels?'

'Over there. When we pulled them off, I stacked them and marked them with a blue dot.'

He nodded to the corner of the pit garage where the eight wheels were stacked.

'And the others?'

'In similar spots.'

'Keep an eye out for anyone coming by to take them.'

'Will do.'

'Aidy, ready to cause some more havoc?' Nevin called across the pit garage.

'Yeah, just give me a minute.'

'This is a game of seconds. No time for minutes.'

I smiled at Nevin and said to Dylan, 'Call Barrington. Tell him to expect a tyre delivery.'

The sound of my car firing up told me it was time for me to get back out there. I returned to the pit garage.

'Get in the car and earn your pay,' Nevin said.

'What pay?'

He smiled and handed me my helmet. 'Just get in the car.'

I wore a groove in Zandvoort, piling on lap after lap. Rags didn't give Haulk or me any downtime. Today was costing the team a pretty penny and Rags seemed to be on a mission to get the most out of that penny. We logged over a hundred laps before we called it a day. The two cars had guzzled tanks of fuel and shredded dozens of tyres. The crew would be working hard to overhaul the cars as soon as they got back to the workshop. A hundred miles of track punishment was the equivalent of ten thousand road miles. The oil would be soup, the brakes would be bare and the wheel bearings would be shot. The cars would be old men after a season of this punishment.

I climbed from the car, not realizing how sore my back and arse were. I'd feel it in the morning. Nevin handed me an energy drink and I tottered into the pit garage. I peeled off the top half of my racesuit and tied the sleeves around my waist.

I sucked down half the sports drink, but my throat closed up when I spotted the eight wheels still sitting where they'd been all day.

Dylan sidled up to me. 'No one's been by for them.'

It didn't make sense. I grabbed my kit bag and went into the men's toilet to change. While I was in there, I called Barrington. He didn't answer and my call went to voicemail. I left a message telling him to call me.

After I cleaned up, cheering greeted me in the pit garages.

'What's going on?' I asked Nevin.

'Dinner's on Rags.'

'Nice.'

I helped my crew pack up the car and equipment. The move bought me plenty of goodwill with the team. It also forced Haulk to help out. What was he going to do otherwise – just stand there?

Rags disappeared to his car and made call after call.

Who was he calling? His connection in Holland? Or Honda to tell them how testing had gone?

I made a move to grab the wheels carrying the drugs. I thought someone might stop me, but no one did. As I went to load them on to the tyre rack, my crew shooed me away. 'No stealing our jobs,' Roy Carroll said.

When everything was packed up, Rags led the convoy. As we had in the morning, Haulk and I rode with Rags. Dylan rode with the crew. We drove through the town of Zandvoort and picked up the road that took us east towards the airport.

The chatter in the car was upbeat. Rags rained compliments on us for our performances. I struggled to keep up with the conversation. All I could think about were those cocaine-loaded wheels. Why hadn't anyone come for them?

We left the town of Zandvoort in the distance and travelled on a quiet stretch of road. Just as the road signs announced Bentveld was the next town, Dutch police cars poured out from a side road, lights and sirens blaring. Two cop cars raced in front of Rags' car and slowed, blocking the road ahead. A string of police cars came up on our left side to pin us in. There was no going around them and Rags stamped on the brakes to avoid slamming into the back of them.

'What the fuck is going on?' Rags bellowed.

Barrington, I thought.

Rags pulled up short, causing the transporter behind to lock up its brakes and rear-end us. The impact felt like a punch in the back and sent Rags' car forward a couple of feet.

'These fuckers are going to pay,' Rags snarled and flung the door open.

'Stay in the car,' Haulk said.

Rags ignored the good advice and jumped from the car.

'Shit,' Haulk said and jumped out.

'If you can't beat 'em, join 'em,' I said and opened my door.

Three cops, talking in a mix of both Dutch and English, were telling Rags to calm down and get back into his car. Rags just shouted at them, demanding to know what the hell was going on and who was going to pay for the damage to his vehicles.

Two more cops appeared in front of Haulk and me. Haulk immediately fired off something in Dutch that disarmed them. We jogged over to Rags and a plain-clothes cop who had a sheaf of papers in his hand. Haulk cooled the situation down by talking to the cops in Dutch. Rags crossed his arms and just smouldered while Haulk spoke to the detective in charge.

I looked back down the line of vehicles. The whole crew was at the side of the road looking bewildered and confused, Dylan amongst them. He looked worried. I understood his fears. This wasn't on the script.

With half the road blocked, a handful of cops took over traffic duties. Cars drifted by the scene, staring at the transporters and us.

I looked for Barrington. He was the ringmaster of this circus, but I didn't see him at first. He swept past me at the wheel of a car, moving with the traffic and fixed me with a disapproving stare.

'What kind of bullshit is this?' Rags bellowed.

'The warrant says they're looking for narcotics,' Haulk said.

I inched closer to Haulk and Rags.

'Seriously, they think we're moving drugs?' Rags said to Haulk, then turned his disgust to the cop in charge. 'I have just dropped a small fortune in your country today and this is how I get treated?'

I wondered how much involvement Haulk had in the smuggling. It had been his idea and connections that brought us to Zandvoort today. Had his problems with the law ended in his teens or had he matured into something more insidious?

'Sir,' the lead detective said, 'I just want to search your vehicles. If we find nothing then you'll be free to go. The quicker you stop protesting the quicker you'll be on your way.'

Rags was silent for a minute. This was one race he couldn't win. He threw up his hands. 'OK, do it. Waste your fucking time.'

The detective signalled to his men and they descended on the transporters and Rags' car. Rags told the crew to open the transporters up. Once the doors were open, the police ordered everyone back and they descended on the vehicles.

Barrington played it smart. The cops didn't go straight for the wheels. They rifled through toolboxes, storage cabinets in the transporters and the cars. The drugs had to be discovered organically. First, search the obvious, then get inventive.

'This is bullshit,' Rags said for the umpteenth time.

He didn't get any arguments, not that anyone was saying anything. Everyone stood in silence while the police worked.

I didn't know what to make of Rags. He reacted how I would expect someone to react if they were innocent. These weren't the protests of a guilty man. I looked at the crew for anyone who was sweating. The only person who looked even close to guilty was Dylan.

The lead detective clambered up into the transporter and grabbed a wheel off the tyre rack. 'I want the tyres removed,' he said to Rags.

'What do you want?' Rags said.

'I want the tyres off these wheels, so I can see inside.'

Rags coughed out a laugh so loud with derision that it left a trail. 'You've found nothing, so you want to be as awkward as possible. Is that it?'

'I'm not debating the subject, sir. Just do it.'

'Nevin,' Rags called.

Nevin tapped Dylan on the shoulder and they jumped into the transporter to pop the tyres from the rims.

My breath caught when Nevin picked up the first of the wheels with the drugs inside. He and Dylan popped the rim. Nothing. No coke. Just air. I fought the urge to ask what was going on. These were the marked wheels, yet they were empty. Dylan and Nevin popped the next marked wheel. Again, nothing. Every wheel revealed the same – nothing.

Dylan jumped down from the transporter and stood next to me. 'What just happened?'

'I have no idea.'

All I knew was that Barrington wasn't going to be happy.

Lap Thirty-Three

The Dutch police disappeared into the sunset. In typical fashion, they left the carnage of their fruitless search behind them. Cars, parts, tools and tyres littered the side of the road with no apology or offer to help put everything back.

No one spoke or moved, because Rags hadn't spoken or moved. He just stood stock still, glaring at the cop cars' taillights.

'Get this shit packed up,' he said when the last of the cop cars was long gone.

I grabbed a couple of wheels.

'What the fuck are you doing?' he barked at me.

'Helping.'

'You're not here to help. You're here to drive. And you're not driving right now. I want you and you –' Rags pointed at Haulk and me – 'out of here. You've got a plane to catch. Now, get in the damn car. The rest of you, I expect everything on the roadside back on the transporter.'

Barrington had overplayed his hand with the road stop, but not all was lost. He'd beaten the bushes, so it was likely that something would come flying out. I was interested to see what Rags did next.

'See ya back home,' I said to Dylan.

'I'll tell you if anything interesting happens.'

Haulk patted me on the back as he crossed behind me. We followed Rags to his car. He left a thick pair of rubber streaks as he pulled away.

'What do you think that was about?' Haulk asked. He was a brave man to ask considering Rags' mood.

'What the fuck do you think? Someone is fucking with my team. First, they stitch Aidy up on reckless-driving charges. Now they've called in a bullshit trafficking claim that casts a dirty light on our team.'

It was the first time Rags had showed any sign that he believed in my innocence. That threw me. Did he really believe what he'd just said? Was he unaware of the fact his team was being used as a drug-smuggling operation or was it just smoke for our benefit? Barrington saw the whole team as dirty, but that might not be true.

'Who's they?' Haulk asked.

'Another team. They can't beat us on the track, so they want to ruin us off the track.'

'Which one?'

'Take your pick. Any one of these fuckers would like to take us down.'

The conversation was quelling Rags' anger, but it wasn't lightening his foot on the accelerator. We were hitting motorway speeds on the two-lane road.

'What about Jason Gates?' I asked. 'Do you think his murder is part of this too?'

The vibe inside the car shifted awkwardly.

Rags eyed me in his rear-view mirror.

'I find it hard to believe that someone would kill Jason just to fuck with the team,' I said. I looked to Haulk and Rags to either agree or shoot me down and got nothing.

'I don't want to talk about that,' Rags said.

And we didn't talk about anything else until we reached the airport. Haulk and I grabbed our bags from the boot before Rags slammed the boot lid shut.

'If anyone approaches you two for comment, play dumb and refer them to me. OK?'

We nodded.

Rags burnt more rubber rejoining the airport traffic and I wished I was going with him. I didn't want him out of my sight.

'Aidy, I hear the siren song of the airport bar calling our names,' Haulk said. 'We deserve a drink.'

There was no arguing with that point.

We passed through airport security and Haulk bought me a drink while we waited for our flight to be called.

'If Rags wasn't such a magician when it came to the cars, I'd be off this team,' Haulk said. 'I like my excitement on the track, not off it.'

'Preaching to the choir,' I said.

'You're the lucky one here. You're on a one-year deal. This kind of crap won't stick to you, but I still have another year on my contract.'

How little he knew. I'd count myself bloody lucky to come out of this one unscathed.

I spent the next hour listening to Haulk's war stories from his racing career. It was an education for me. He'd done it all and I hoped I would too, if I could keep Andrew Gates, HM Customs and the police at bay. One of those might be doable. All three seemed impossible. Haulk's stories continued during the flight, but ended when we reached Heathrow, where we went our separate ways.

Steve was waiting for me at the airport. He took my bag from me.

'How'd it all go?' he asked.

'Good and awful. Barrington pulled the team over and found nothing. Everything's in shambles.'

'Where's that leave us?'

'I don't know.'

Steve had just weaved his way through the airport road system when my mobile rang. Dylan's name appeared on the screen.

'Where are you?' he asked. Excitement boiled over in his voice.

'Just leaving the airport.'

'Don't go home.'

'Why? What's going on?'

'I'm in Rags' car. I'm driving it back. He's on the next flight to Stansted.'

'Why's he flying?'

'It has something to do with a phone call he got. He got back to us just as we'd pretty much loaded everything back on to the transporter; then his phone rang. He took the call in his car, but from his body language, it didn't go well. Afterwards he tossed me his keys and said to drive him to the airport. He's on an EasyJet flight that's scheduled to land around nine thirty.'

'He's flying back to meet with someone.'

'No shit. That's why you need to follow him.'

That gave us a little over two hours to get from Heathrow to Stansted. The sixty-mile trip should only take an hour, but with the evening traffic, we could be unlucky.

'You might have just saved us.'

'I know, so don't screw it up. Keep in touch.'

'Will do. Thanks, mate.' I hung up on Dylan and told Steve
to drive to Stansted. 'We have to get there before nine thirty.'
'We'll do it.'
Traffic was thick but flowing. Steve kept his foot down, cutting
in and out of traffic. Every mile seemed to take an age to cover as
the minute hand on the dashboard clock swept across its face. Despite
my fears, we arrived at the airport with forty minutes to spare.
Steve parked in the short-stay car park. I told him to be ready
to move when Rags touched down.
'At nearly five pounds an hour, you bet your arse I'll be ready
to move.'
I smiled. Steve smiled back.
'Just don't let him see you,' Steve said.
'I won't.'
I paced in the arrivals lounge, counting down the minutes until
Rags' flight arrived. I didn't think we'd get another shot at this.
Not after the road stop. Everyone was going to be cagey from
now on.
I called Barrington's number. He didn't answer. I tried twice
more over the next twenty minutes and still got no answer. I
didn't know what his game was, but it was pissing me off.
I called Claudia and she answered on the first ring. 'Aidy.'
'Claudia, can you get me Barrington? He's not answering his
phone.'
'Aidy, what 'appened? John went ballistic. 'E said there were
no drugs.'
'I'm not sure, but I'm at Stansted waiting for Rags. He's
ditched his car and he's flying back to meet with someone. This
may be our chance to find out who he's working with.'
'John is still in 'olland. 'Is 'ole team is. Today was supposed
to be the big bust.'
Yeah, don't rub it in. 'Shit. Rags will be on the ground in
twenty minutes. Where are you?'
'I'm in Norfolk with the ESCC.'
She was too far away to meet us in time.
'I'm going to follow Rags to his meeting. Tell Barrington what
I'm doing and to call me if he wants me to do anything.'
'OK. Be careful, Aidy.'
She sounded like she cared.
'I will. Thanks.'

I hung up and counted down the minutes as I watched the Arrivals screen for updates. I almost cheered when Rags' flight went from 'On time' to 'Arrived'.

I called Steve. 'Rags' plane is on the ground. Come around to Arrivals to pick me up.'

'Keep an eye out for whoever is picking him up.'

I hadn't thought of that. 'Will do.'

I hung up and disappeared into the crowd in the lounge. I didn't want Rags spotting me the second he appeared. I scanned the faces of the people waiting patiently. It was the usual mix of friends, family, business acquaintances and drivers with hand-written signs. No one stood out as a drug kingpin.

My heart hit the red zone when Rags poured into the lounge with a glut of passengers. I remained still, waiting for him to reach out to his connection. Instead, he slalomed between groups of people, acknowledging no one.

I gave him a twenty-yard head start before following him. I pulled out my phone and called Steve. 'He's here and he's not got anyone waiting.'

'What's he doing?'

'He's on his way to hire a car.'

'I'll keep circling until you need me.'

I hung up.

I watched Rags pay for the car and cross the terminal for a courtesy bus to take him to the vehicle. Steve picked me up and we followed his bus to the car depot. Still on the Terminal Road, we couldn't pull over, so Steve overtook the bus, pulled off at the roundabout and parked on the grass. I jumped out of the car, backtracked up the road and watched for Rags.

I ran back to Steve and jumped into the passenger seat. 'Red Ford Mondeo.'

Steve let Rags pass us by before rejoining traffic. Steve's old Capri stuck out amongst the modern cars on the road, but considering Rags' driving, he seemed to be a man on a mission who was paying little attention to his surroundings. I think I could have stood next to him in the terminal and he wouldn't have noticed me. He certainly had plenty on his mind.

Rags picked up the M11 going south towards London. From there, he took the M25 anticlockwise. We were catching the M25 late, so traffic was light.

'He looks like he's going home,' Steve said.

Steve's words jinxed us. Rags joined the A1(M) and headed north.

'He's not going home,' I said.

Rags went as far as Hatfield. He cut through the town, drove on to an industrial estate and stopped at a derelict factory. He climbed from his hire car armed only with his mobile phone and slipped through an open doorway.

Steve pulled up at the side of the road. 'Looks like he's first to arrive.'

I wasn't so sure. Time would have been on the side of the person who'd demanded Rags fly back from Holland. 'Make a loop.'

Steve followed the roads encompassing the warehouse. It was after eight p.m. and everyone at the neighbouring industrial units had finished their working day. There were no other cars parked. It looked as if Steve was right about Rags being alone.

Steve completed his loop and stopped. 'You going in?'

'Yeah. The place is big enough that I can hide and no one will see me.'

'You want me to come?'

'No. It's just me and Rags at this point. You stay alert in case this party gets gatecrashers.'

Steve nodded. 'Just be careful.'

'Aren't I always?'

'No.'

I slipped from the car and jogged across the weed-ravaged car park. I circled around the building and entered on the far side from Rags. No fancy lock-picking skills were required. The door had long since been kicked in. From the look of this place, whatever this factory had once been, it was now the local punching bag for graffiti artists and vandals.

I used the backlight on my mobile to illuminate my way and found myself in the offices.

I could hear Rags talking to himself and cursing whoever had the audacity to keep him waiting. His voice helped guide me even better than my mobile. I reached a stairwell and climbed to the top. It opened out into a suite of offices overlooking the factory floor. The windows insulating the office workers from the factory noise were gone, so I kept quiet. I dropped to my knees and peered through a window frame.

Rags stood a hundred feet away, lit by his car's headlights. He paced back and forth within the boundaries of the light, staring at his mobile, seemingly willing it to ring.

He kept up this performance for twenty minutes before dialling a number. His pace quickened as his call went unanswered.

'I'm here. Just as you asked. Now where the fuck are you? The cops are on to us. The Dutch police had a warrant. How long before the cops here have a warrant to do the same? You can't hide from me. Call me now.'

A call didn't come. Rags called back two more times over the next hour before snatching up a length of pipe he found and hurling it across the warehouse. The sound of it clanging on the floor echoed off the walls.

'I'd say you've been stood up, Rags,' I whispered. 'Worse luck.'

Rags stormed out of the factory.

I stood and winced at the sound of the Mondeo's engine screaming in pain as Rags slammed the car into reverse and roared away. Just as he did, his headlights swept through the building and splashed across something familiar – a tubular steel chair with a broken wooden back. The sight of that chair brought back ugly memories.

My mobile rang. It was Steve.

'Everything OK?'

'Yeah. Rags got stood up.'

'It happens to the best of us.'

'Bring your car over. I need your lights. There should be a loading door close to where Rags parked.'

'I see it.'

'OK, I'll meet you there.'

I raced down the stairs two at a time and across the factory floor. I found the loading door and raised it. Steve poked the nose of the Capri through the door and lit the place up with his high beams. His spotlights struck the chair I recognized. I picked it up and examined it. The last time I'd seen this chair, I'd been pinned to it.

I tossed the broken chair aside and dropped to my knees. I ran my hands over the concrete and found the gouges that a five-pound mallet had made.

Steve emerged from his car and crossed over to me. 'What's going on?'

'I've been here. Crichlow brought me here the night Jason was killed. This place belongs to Andrew Gates.'

Lap Thirty-Four

S teve and I were at work on Gates' Jensen Interceptor when we heard the sound of a car sliding to a halt behind Archway. I checked my watch. It was just after ten. I'd called Claudia with an update after I'd left Gates' factory last night. Barrington still wasn't taking my calls. An hour later, she'd called back telling me Barrington wanted to meet the next morning.

'It's him,' I said to Steve. 'Brace yourself.'

He frowned.

A moment later, Barrington burst through the door with Claudia in tow.

'What the hell happened yesterday?' he shouted across the workshop. 'I didn't get you out of jail just so that you could fuck me. If you did, God help you, son, I'll make sure you won't get a job driving shopping trolleys at Tesco's.'

I expected this display after the botched search yesterday. It was time for him to throw his weight around to frighten the natives.

Steve pulled on the Interceptor's throttle cable. The engine note increased until it drowned out Barrington's words.

Barrington glared at Steve. Steve released the throttle cable and the noise dropped to a soft idle.

'Please close the door,' Steve said, keeping his tone low and calm.

Disgust darkened Barrington's expression. 'Do you know who I am?'

'I don't give a shit who you are. This is my place of business, so you'll show some respect. You can start by closing the door.'

Claudia took a step backward. 'It's OK, I'll do it.'

'No, not you, love. Let him do it.'

'I can have this place shut down in a second. I just have to say the word.'

'No, you can't. No crimes have been committed and you don't have a warrant. You can't do shit.'

'Just try me. I got your grandson out of jail, but I can put him right back there and he'll never be heard from again. I'll bury him.'

'Keep up with the mouth and you won't leave this building upright.'

Barrington laughed dismissively. 'Are you threatening me?'

'Just fair warning and I warn only once.' Steve picked up a two-foot-long adjustable spanner. 'No one threatens my grandson. Not you. Not anyone.'

Steve was the best. He was my bulletproof vest.

'I understand that the situation you're in has gotten away from you, so you need to keep a grip on what you have left. You conscripted this lad to help crack your case. If you still want his help, you'll keep it civil. You can start by closing my door.'

Barrington held his ground for a moment before returning to the workshop door and closing it.

I looked at Claudia. The set-to had failed to ruffle her feathers. I was in the presence of the Unflappables.

'OK, let's get down to business,' Steve said and led the way to our situation room. He sat on the table and Claudia sat next to him, while Barrington and I remained standing.

Barrington looked at our freshly re-mounted murder board with names, facts and connections linking the various players to each other. He read the wanker comment under his name and smiled. 'Christ, what is this place – the clubhouse for the Nancy Drew Appreciation Society?'

'What did I say about keeping it civil?' Steve said.

Barrington raised his hands. 'OK, OK, I'm on my best behaviour now.'

Claudia went up to the wall and studied our findings. She looked at me and smiled. 'Nicely thought out, gentlemen.'

Barrington turned his disappointment on me. 'Want to explain yesterday's fiasco?'

'Correct me if I'm wrong, but weren't you running the show yesterday?' Steve asked Barrington.

'OK. Fair point. Tell me what happened.'

I outlined the day's events, including how Dylan had marked the wheels with a dot of blue paint.

'I can't explain how they got the drugs out from under us,' I said.

'I can,' Claudia said. 'You didn't discover a shipment going to 'olland. You discovered one that had just come into the UK and was unloaded before you left for 'olland.'

That put a different spin on things. 'That means Rags picked up the shipment at some point during the Norisring race.'

'Correct,' Claudia said. 'I think we 'ave a couple of options.'

'We don't have any options,' Barrington said. 'None of this matters now.'

Claudia blushed at being chopped off at the knees.

'I think it does,' I said.

'Well, it doesn't,' Barrington said. 'I'm here to tell you that you're off the hook.'

'What?' I said.

'We've shown our hand,' Barrington said. 'The traffickers know we're on to Ragged Racing. They'll find a new mule. This case is dead in the water.'

'You're walking away?' I said. 'You're joking.'

'No joke. I took a big risk and it didn't work.' He looked deferentially to Steve. 'All I can do is regroup and try again.'

Claudia couldn't look me in the eye and her gaze fell to the floor.

'No,' I said. 'Look at what you've got.'

'Enlighten me. What have I got?'

'The drugs in the tyres. You can bust Rags and turn him in.'

'What drugs? They're gone. All I have is your word that they were ever there.'

'I bet if you swept Ragged Racing's workshop you'd find traces of cocaine.'

'You're probably right, but it wouldn't give us any concrete evidence as to how much had passed through there or who was involved. A good lawyer would claim the residue was from personal consumption.'

'Look, last night, Rags went to a factory owned by Andrew Gates in a panic. Now you've got an iron-clad connection between Andrew Gates, Rags and this drug operation.'

And possibly the reason for Jason's murder. There was no way drug traffickers would let him live after he'd stumbled on to their operation. I wondered if Jason had suspected Ragged Racing was involved in the drug trade or if his need to dig into their affairs was triggered by something else and finding the drug trafficking was an unfortunate accident.

'Did Gates show?' Barrington asked.

I sighed. 'No.'

'That tells me everything. Gates is done with Rags. The Ragged Racing pipeline is capped. His no-show was a message telling Rags his services are no longer required.'

After all we'd done, this wasn't right. As much as I wanted to be out from under Barrington's operation, I didn't want to walk away from the job now. We were so close to trapping these people and finding Jason's killer. I couldn't believe he was binning the operation.

'Look, I understand your frustration because I'm feeling it too.' Barrington's tone had switched from antagonistic to consolatory. 'I could have played it safe and wrapped up Rags a long time ago, but mules are a cheap win. You shut down one distribution line and another three replace it. I need the whole thing, from cartel to distributor, to really make a difference.'

I wondered how much heat Barrington was taking for this failure. It had to be a lot. He'd gone all in and gotten blown away by a better hand.

'At least we now know Andrew Gates is part of this,' Barrington said. 'He was a piece of the puzzle we didn't even know we were missing. We can regroup with Gates as the focus.'

Gates had everyone fooled on that score. Eddie Stores never knew Gates to deal in drugs and Gates had almost torn my head off for alluding to drug dealing within his organization. No wonder Jason didn't trust his brother. 'So that's it?'

'The battle was lost, but the war is still winnable. I'd just like to say thanks for your assistance and apologies to you and your friends for squeezing you so hard.'

'What about Jason Gates' murder?' I asked.

'What about it? It's a police issue, not a Customs one. It's down to them to solve, not me.' Barrington looked to Claudia. 'Let's go.'

She remained seated next to Steve. 'I need to go over a couple of things with Aidy. I'll catch the train back into town,' she said.

Barrington nodded and walked out. No one said a word until we heard the roar of a car engine.

Steve wiped the eraser across Gates' name.

'Put his name back,' I said. 'This isn't over.'

Claudia hopped off the table and rested a hand on my shoulder. 'I know you've been through a lot, Aidy, but it's finished.'

'For you, Barrington and Customs maybe, but nothing's changed for me. Andrew Gates still wants to know who killed his brother and he expects me to find out.'

This was the perplexing part of all this. Andrew Gates was connected to the drug trafficking and Jason had stumbled upon it. So did Andrew have his brother killed? It was possible but not when you factored in my involvement. Gates wanted me to find Jason's killer. If he was behind the murder, he had no reason to bring me in. That meant someone had killed Jason without his permission and he was using me to find out who'd crossed the line.

Steve nodded and rewrote Gates' name on the board.

'Aidy, what are you playing at?' Claudia asked. 'You don't 'ave Customs' protection now.'

I wasn't sure I ever had it in the first place. 'This case may be dead as far as Barrington's concerned, but I say it isn't. We still have plenty to work with. The question is, do you want to be a part of it?'

'Aidy, I can't go against orders.'

'But you want to. You're a good undercover agent, but you wear your emotions on your sleeve. I can see that you disagree with Barrington. You know there's more mileage in this one.'

'Regardless of 'ow I feel, I'm not going to blow my career for you.'

'You don't work for Customs. You're only on loan to them. Are you telling me that you blowing off the British wouldn't go down well with your bosses in France?'

Claudia grinned.

'You know you want in,' Steve said, providing an additional piece of arm twisting.

'Tell me what you 'ave planned, then I'll decide whether I'm in or not.'

Lap Thirty-Five

I was having breakfast at home the following morning when Dylan called.

'You're not going to believe this.' He was boiling with excitement.

'What?'

'Rags just sent the whole team home until further notice.'

'Did he say why?'

'He just said he needed time to follow up on things after the Dutch cops stopped us.'

The wheels were coming off Rags' world and he was heading for a crash. I wanted to be there when it happened. The best time to hit him was at his weakest.

'Where is he?'

'He's still at the workshop.'

'OK. I'm coming up.'

'Wait. I've got more. I know who doesn't have their keys. It's Nevin.'

Haulk had said that Nevin had taken Jason under his wing. Naturally, Jason would go to him. I wondered how Nevin featured in all this now.

'Where is he?'

'I'm following him.'

'Get him alone. I want to speak to him.'

'I'll call you.'

I grabbed my car keys and blew out the door. I got as far as the Honda when Sergeant Lucas pulled up.

'Is your grandfather around?'

'No, he's at work.'

'OK. Could you let him know we found his van?'

'Sure. Where'd you find it?'

'Over by Thorpe Park. Someone stripped it and torched it. It's a real mess.'

I didn't like the casual tone Lucas was using. He hadn't liked that his key piece of evidence had been stolen and to find it obliterated wasn't going to leave him in a jovial mood. He was gearing up for something.

'Could I have a word, Aidy?'

'I have an appointment and I can't miss it.'

He parked himself at the end of the driveway. The only way out was through him. 'I wasn't really asking.'

I circled the car and leaned against the boot. 'I suppose I have a few minutes.'

Lucas didn't reach for his handcuffs, so I guessed I was safe for the moment.

'Thank you, Aidy. I appreciate that.'

I hated police smugness.

'I'm troubled by this case. I feel that I'm the only one who doesn't understand what's going on.'

I really didn't have time for this. I could see Nevin slipping away. But at least Lucas was finally seeing the cracks in the case.

'You're not alone. I'm just as lost.'

Lucas' mistrustful look said otherwise. 'I'll tell you what doesn't make sense to me. I have a crash site that doesn't support the statement. I have a piece of critical evidence in the form of your grandfather's van that goes missing before I can examine it. Care to explain?'

I could, but I had the feeling Lucas didn't need my help. He seemed to be on the right track.

My mobile burst into life. It was Dylan. I bet he had Nevin. 'I can't explain what I don't know myself. Really, I do have to go.'

I went to leave, but Lucas stepped in front of me to block my path.

'There's something going on,' he said, 'and I suggest you tell me before I find out.'

My phone rang again. I couldn't lose Nevin. Not now.

'Sergeant, I suggest you ask the victim why she was in Egham when she lived all the way over in Harrow.'

Shock spread across Lucas' face. 'How do you know that? Have you been in contact with her?'

Oh, crap. I'd screwed up. I could kick myself for my stupidity.

'What's going on?'

'Nothing. Now, you will have to excuse me.'

I pushed by Lucas and got into the car. He kept barking

questions at me, but I reversed out before the questions changed into an arrest.

As soon as I was on the road, I called Dylan. He'd caught up with Nevin at an ASDA. Somehow, he was now riding in Dylan's car. I didn't ask Dylan how he'd convinced Nevin to ride with him, but Dylan was a foot taller than Nevin and twice as strong. I was nervous now. My friends and I were really sailing close to the wind. I hoped we didn't end up shipwrecked.

I caught up with them in a field outside of Banbury. I stopped my car behind Dylan's Subaru. Nevin burst from the car the second I appeared. Dylan climbed out, looking tired. I could only imagine the conversations they'd had.

'What the hell is wrong with you?' Nevin demanded. 'Why did you have this idiot drag me over here?'

'You didn't do anything stupid, did you?' I said to Dylan.

Dylan held up his hands. 'Do you see any bruises?'

'Hey, I'm talking to you!' Nevin barked at me.

'I'm sorry for all this. I just wanted to give you these.'

I fished out Nevin's keys and tossed them at him. He caught them and the colour drained from his face as his indignation turned to fear. He failed to take ownership of his keys. He didn't pocket them or clutch them in his fist. He just cradled them in both hands.

'They are yours, aren't they?'

'I don't know what you're playing at, Aidy, but I don't like it. How did you get these?' Nevin's voice had dropped to a whisper.

'From Jason. He had them on him when he died.'

The keys fell through Nevin's hands into the mud at his feet. He stared down at them but made no attempt to retrieve them.

I liked Nevin and I hated squeezing him like this, but I didn't have a choice. I needed the truth from him. 'I still need an answer, Barry. Are they your keys?'

'Answer him, Barry,' Dylan said. He stood a respectful distance from Nevin, but if he bolted, the two of us had the angles covered.

'Yes, they are.'

'Why did Jason have them?'

'I don't know.'

'I don't have time for this, Barry. Seriously, I don't,' I said. 'Know when you're caught. I have the detective in charge of

Jason's murder crawling all over me. If I tell her who those keys belong to, she'll leave me alone and come after you. Do you want that?'

Nevin said nothing. I reached for the keys and he stamped a foot over them.

'Don't.'

I straightened. 'Give me one reason why I shouldn't.'

'I can't.'

'You can and you will, because I'm not leaving without an explanation. As I see it, you're a guilty man. Was that guilt the reason you attended Jason's funeral when no one else from Ragged did?'

'Call her, Aidy,' Dylan said. 'Throw him to the wolves.'

'No, don't. Please. Let me explain.'

Nevin ran his hands through his hair. He removed his foot from the keys, picked them up and slipped them into his pocket without wiping the mud off.

'OK. I stayed in touch with Jason after he left. I liked him. We'd go for a pint from time to time. The last few times he kept asking about the team and the operation. I thought Russell Townsend had put him up to it, but at Earls Court he asked me to help him. He said Rags was up to his neck in something shady and he wanted to check out the car and transporter. I told him I didn't want any part of his bullshit. There's no way Rags would cross that line.'

'But you had second thoughts?'

Nevin nodded.

'Because Rags has coloured outside of the lines from time to time, like when he played with loan sharks?'

'You know about that?'

'Nothing stays a secret forever.'

'Yeah, well. In those dark days, when Rags got behind with his payments, the heavies weren't shy about dropping by. That got me wondering if he was in trouble again, but I believe in Rags and I wouldn't go behind his back. I told Jason I wouldn't help him directly, but he could check things out himself, so I slipped him my keys at the end of the day. I said if he found anything, he was to come to me first.'

'And did he?'

'I don't know. Someone killed him before he got back to me.'

I opened my mouth to ask another question when I picked up
on something Nevin had said. He said that he believed in Rags
and wouldn't go behind his back. A frightening conclusion
presented itself that left me nauseous.

'Barry, don't tell me you told Rags.'

Nevin swallowed.

'Barry?'

'I had to. I couldn't go behind the man's back. He's my friend.
I told him what I'd done. He told me not to worry about it and
that he'd take care of it. Christ, do you think he killed Jason?'

I couldn't believe Nevin's naivety. I retreated back to my car.

'Where are you going?' Nevin asked.

'Don't let him go and don't let him call anyone,' I told Dylan.

'No worries. Where you going?'

'To talk to Rags, of course.'

Lap Thirty-Six

I reached the Ragged Racing workshop around lunchtime. Rags'
Mercedes was the only car parked out front. I pulled up
alongside it and went inside. I found Rags in his office staring
at the ceiling. Had he been sitting there since he'd sent everyone
home?

I took that as a good sign. He was a desperate man. Desperate
men made decisions from a place of weakness.

What wasn't a good sign was that I was possibly meeting with
Jason's killer alone. He had every reason and now the opportunity
to have killed Jason that night. I was keeping that titbit to myself
for the moment. I had to hook Rags with a separate line first.

I leaned in through his door. 'Got a minute?'

'Can't it wait, Aidy?'

'No.'

He sat up in his seat. 'OK. What do you want?'

'Assurances.'

'What assurances?'

I took that as an invite to enter his office. Instead of taking
a seat, I stretched out on the sofa against the opposite wall. I

was being disrespectful on purpose. I had a part to play. 'I
know you've been talking to Chloe Mercer about replacing
me. I'm here to tell you that's not going to happen. What also
isn't going to happen is you dumping me at the end of the
season.'

'You've got some nerve.'

For the first time, I saw the spark back in Rags' eyes. Not
surprising. He thought he was talking to someone he could
dominate. I just grinned, reached into my pocket and tossed him
a packet containing a few ounces of cocaine. It landed on his
desk. Claudia had gotten me the cocaine from Custom's supply
once she'd gotten on board with our plan.

Rags eyed the packet but made no attempt to touch it. 'What's
that?'

'You should know. I found that in the wheel of my car. Actually,
it was a lot more than that, but I just needed a sample.'

Rags picked up the resealable bag and opened it. He wetted
his little finger, dabbed it in the powder and tasted it. The colour
drained from his face.

'I know what you're doing and I want in.'

Rags spat the cocaine out. He resealed the bag and tossed it
back on his desk. 'And what's that?'

'Do I really have to say it?'

'Yes.' Rags' voice cracked.

'You're transporting drugs in your cars. You're hiding them in
the tyres of the cars and when we reach the tracks, someone
comes and takes the wheels. Genius, really. No one gives these
transporters a second look at the border crossing. The Customs
people are all dazzled by the big, shiny racecars, so it never
occurs to them that it would be a Trojan horse.'

'Except for you.'

'Not really. I wouldn't have guessed in a thousand years if I
hadn't noticed it leaking from one of my tyres,' I lied. 'I thought
it was chalk dust. Dylan tried to pop the tyre and guess what
came tumbling out?'

Rags said nothing.

'It was so obvious you were up to something. You were
spending money on exclusive testing and R&D like it was water,
but you didn't have the sponsorship to back it up. I'd bet you're
two hundred grand shy of balancing the books every season.

Everyone thinks you're up to something, but no one would have guessed you were a drug trafficker.'

I could have kept going, bringing Andrew Gates into the mix, but I'd be overplaying my hand. I was playing the part of the greedy driver in over his head. I wanted Rags to bring me into the fold and take me to Gates.

'You think you're pretty clever, don't you?'

'Not really. I'm lucky more than anything, but I'm clever enough to know an opportunity when I see it.'

'And you see one here?'

'Yeah.'

Rags shook his head in disappointment. 'I didn't think you were the type for this sort of thing.'

'I could say the same about you.'

My answer forced a slight smile from Rags. 'So you want a longer contract in return for your silence, is that it? What, three years?'

'To start with.'

'To start with? What more do you want? A lifetime contract?'

I shook my head. 'No, a three-year deal will do me very nicely. We can always renegotiate at the end or I can move on. But no, I want a piece of this. I need a pension plan and what you're doing is it. I want five grand a month. That'll guarantee my silence.'

Rags threw back his head and laughed. 'Christ, you must be a racing driver, because you've got the worst fucking timing off the track. Remember that little roadside incident at Zandvoort? That was the nail in the operation's coffin. It's over.'

Rags picked up the little baggie of coke and tossed it to me. It landed at my feet.

'You should have taken more because your pension plan is worth precisely as much as you can sell that for. I'll give you your three-year contract. Fuck it, I'll give you ten, but Ragged Racing will be done before the end of the season. You were right. I don't have the money to keep this team afloat. I could have gotten loans, but the problem with them is that you have to pay them back and without a sponsor, loans only delay the inevitable. I needed money without ties and the money I get from trafficking keeps this team afloat. Without it, it sinks fast. You raided the piggy bank after it was emptied.'

Rags laughed again and pushed past me on the way to his office. 'Now, let's write up that contract.'

I was prepared for this eventuality. I let him reach the door to the offices before I called to him. 'I still want my five grand a month. I don't care how you come up with it. Just make it happen or I'm going to the cops and you can explain yourself to them.'

'Tell them. See how far that gets you. They won't find anything and if you do, I'll tell them you're a mean-spirited little prick trying to screw me over because you can't hack it in the big time. Trust me, I can sell that and the cops will buy it. Goodnight, Aidy. See you next week.'

'Call your boss. I want to speak to him.'

'No. You're getting out of your league now. These people won't buckle to your threats.'

'I'm not threatening him. I have an offer for him.'

'What have you got to offer?'

'A new pipeline.'

'What are you talking about?'

'The cops are on to you, but they're not on to me. Steve is receiving and shipping cars from all over the world. Why can't there be something inside of those cars?'

'You want to drag your grandfather into this?'

'He doesn't have to know. I can make it part of his personalized service. Who wouldn't want their restored car delivered to them by up-and-coming racing driver, Aidy Westlake?'

Rags was silent for a moment. I hoped my bait was enticing. 'I'll cut you in. You'll keep Ragged Racing on the track.'

How could Rags turn down an offer like that? The chance to recover a hopeless situation had to be irresistible.

'Do you really want to follow through on this?'

'Yeah.'

Rags was silent. He was thinking about it. It was there on his face. He was looking into the future and he saw himself there.

'Come into the office.'

I followed him in. He punched a number into his mobile, but no one picked up. I didn't think anyone would. He didn't have anything to offer, until now. His call went to voicemail.

'Hey, it's me. Aidy Westlake knows everything, but he wants to make us an offer. He has an alternative to what we're doing. I think you should listen to him.'

Rags hung up and tossed the phone on his desk. We didn't say anything to each other. There was nothing to say.

It was an hour before his mobile burst into song.

Rags answered. He was cool, calm and collected with his explanation. He wasn't the same Rags I'd witnessed at the factory, coming apart one piece at a time when his calls went unanswered. He was back in the game.

He listened to his boss for several minutes before hanging up.

'Be back here at ten tomorrow night. Make sure you have all your facts straight. You won't get a second shot at this.'

Lap Thirty-Seven

Since my meeting with Rags wasn't until tonight, I had the day to kill, so it was time to kill Jenni Oglesby's black-mailing scheme stone dead. I had Rags to deal with. I didn't need Jenni's scam distracting me. I called her over a late breakfast.

'You got the money?' Jenni Oglesby asked.

It was just a phone call, but my heart was banging away in my chest. I glanced at Steve and Dylan sitting across my desk at Archway for some comfort. They looked just as wound up as I did. So much for a problem shared is a problem halved.

I tapped the envelope with the fifteen grand in it. 'Yeah, it's here in front of me.'

'Good. Meet me at the Englefield Green Town football ground. Do you know where that is?'

'No.'

I wrote down the directions she gave me.

'I'll be waiting,' she said and hung up.

'You ready for this?' Steve asked me.

'As ready as I'll ever be.'

'He's got nothing to worry about. He'll have me there backing him up,' Dylan said. 'Jenni's had the upper hand until now. Her taking a payoff changes everything. The second she takes the money, it's over. She's a blackmailer and Aidy is the victim. Done and dusted.'

Steve took the pad with the directions written on it from me. 'She wants to meet at a football field?'

I nodded. 'On the centre spot.'

'A big, open space. That makes it hard for you to get close,' he said to Dylan.

'Don't worry. I'll get it all recorded,' he said.

'Let's go then. She wants to meet now.'

Dylan rode with me. I didn't see the need for two cars. It was going to be a straightforward exchange.

As I drove, Dylan downloaded an app called Dictaphone to my mobile. It effectively turned my phone into a digital recorder. He checked and double-checked the function. With the phone in my jacket pocket, the recording app captured my voice with little loss of quality. The beauty of turning my phone into a recording device was that no one would think twice about me having my phone with me.

Englefield Green was a short drive from Windsor. The football pitch's stand came into view, sticking up over the neighbouring houses. I pulled over at the side of the road.

'Do you think she's got anyone watching?' I asked.

'Out here? If someone's put her up to this, I'd expect her to have friends with her.'

Outnumbered and outgunned, I thought.

'OK, game time,' Dylan said. 'Give me a couple of minutes to get into position then do your thing.'

I nodded.

He jumped out of the car and jogged ahead.

A few minutes later, Dylan called me. 'OK, I've got a good spot with a clear view of the pitch. Jenni's waiting for you. And she's alone. I like how this is shaping up. Go get her.'

I hung up on Dylan, turned on the Dictaphone app and pocketed the phone. At the stadium, I stopped next to Jenni's Ford Fiesta. It was the only other car in the car park. To call the Englefield Green Town's ground a stadium was an exaggeration. It was home to a non-league club several tiers down from anything close to a professional club. There was only one covered stand, running the length of the field. The other three sides were exposed to the elements and had no seating. I got out of my car and walked through the main gate on to the pitch.

Standing on the centre spot, Jenni Oglesby turned to face me.

She was smart. She'd brought me out to a place I didn't know. Insisting that I meet her here gave her the upper hand. The Achilles heel in all this was the money exchange. She could take as many precautions as she liked, but taking the money left her exposed. It made her a blackmailer.

'Got the money?'

I pulled the envelope part way from my jacket pocket. A smug smile spread across her face at the sight of it. She held out her hand for it.

'Not quite yet.'

Her smile changed to a frown. 'I'm not here for games.'

'I need assurances.'

'What assurances?'

'That you'll drop the claim against me. I've got the Surrey Police breathing down my neck.'

'I'll make sure they leave you alone.'

'How? If I give you this money like you asked, what assurances do I have that you'll do it?'

The smug smile returned. 'You don't. Money, please?'

I removed the envelope and held it out to her. She took it, but I maintained my grip.

'Don't piss about,' she said. 'Let me have it.'

'Not yet. I need to know why you did this. Why me?'

'Why not? Now give me the money.'

'You know I didn't crash into your car.'

'That's what you say.'

Her playing coy wasn't getting me anywhere. I imagined Dylan listening in on the conversation, willing Jenni to incriminate herself.

'You orchestrated this. You wanted to crash, but I stopped in time. You rolled the car instead, but you knew the charge wouldn't stand up.'

'Give me the money.' She yanked on the envelope, but I held on.

'You stole my grandfather's van, didn't you? With no damage on the van, you had to take it, before the police saw it wasn't involved in a crash.'

She loosened her grip on the envelope and smiled.

'Yes. Tell your grandfather that he should watch his mirrors. Then he might know when he's being followed.'

I had an admission of guilt at last. It wasn't perfect, it wasn't everything, but it was a start and enough to get Sergeant David Lucas off my back and on to Jenni's. But I wanted more.

'I wasn't some random victim, was I? You singled me out. Who put you up to this?'

Before I could get an answer, Jenni snatched the envelope from me and bolted for the car park. I chased after her across the pitch. My feet slid on the sodden ground, but I ate into her lead.

Just as I caught up to her, she held up the envelope and screamed, 'I got it!'

My breath caught in my throat. Jenni had set me up. I expected cops to appear from every corner, but none did. I caught a flash of someone bursting from the coach's dugout and racing towards the car park. I kept running.

'Don't let her get away!' Dylan yelled.

He was racing across the pitch from the far side, but was too far away to provide any help.

I followed Jenni into the car park, closing on her with every stride. She'd never get to her car in time, but someone already had. It shot back, spitting dirt and stones as it spun ninety degrees. The passenger door flew open and Jenni dived in.

I jumped in front of the car's path and spread my hands. I stared at the driver and I couldn't speak. It was Tim Reid.

As surely as shock was on my face, embarrassment was on his. He revved the Fiesta's engine.

For a second, the pieces failed to fall into place. Then they did.

'Get out of the car, Tim.'

He lifted the clutch and the car surged forward, stopping at my feet.

'Go!' Jenni screamed.

Reid just stared at me, his foot still on the accelerator, the engine screaming.

'Get out of the car,' I said again, this time with disappointment in my voice.

Dylan slammed into the side of the Fiesta and yanked open Jenni's door.

What happened next was a reflex action. I knew what was going to happen before it did, but I was too close to change it. Reid's foot came off the clutch and the car leapt forward. There was no getting out of the way. The car scooped me up. I rolled up the bonnet and bounced off the windscreen. The world spun for a brief, disorientating moment before I struck the ground on my hip.

Dylan was at my side before I knew which way was up. 'Christ, you OK?'

'Yeah.'

Reid hadn't hit me with any great speed and that had saved me from serious injury.

We both whipped our heads around at the sound of the car's brakes locking up on the dirt. Two police cars blocked Reid and Jenni's escape. Sergeant David Lucas emerged from one.

'Turn off the bloody engine!' he shouted. 'You lot have some explaining to do.'

Lucas separated us when we reached the station. I sat alone in an interview room with a cup of now cold coffee. I'd been there for over ninety minutes. I took my long-term neglect as a sign that Lucas wanted everyone else's account before he got mine. I found that unnerving, but took comfort from the fact that I hadn't been charged with anything. For the moment, anyway.

Lucas opened the interview-room door just after the two-hour mark. He came in carrying my envelope that contained the blackmail money, my mobile and a video camera. He laid them out on the table between us.

'Well, you've had an interesting morning.' He picked up the mobile phone. 'I'm especially impressed by your cut-price James Bond gadgetry.'

I said nothing. No answer was the right one at this point.

'What I'm not impressed by is your attempts to interfere with an ongoing police investigation and pervert the course of justice.'

I could have said, 'They started it,' but I didn't think Lucas was in the mood to hear that defence.

'You want to tell me what's going on?'

'I didn't crash into Jenni Oglesby's car, but I couldn't prove it. After your investigation got leaked to the media, I knew someone was acting out of spite, so I tracked Jenni down.'

'I'd really like to know how you did that.'

I ducked the request and kept on talking. 'I asked what it would take to make her drop the charges. She said fifteen grand. My friend and I recorded the exchange because I knew if I could get her to admit anything, I had her.'

Lucas picked up the video recorder. 'She had a similar idea. Her video showed you paying her off. Without the sound, she could have inserted any story she liked. Luckily, you were a little smarter. You got audio.'

My arse was saved? I wondered why Lucas was suddenly being so forthcoming after he'd been so closed off. 'Are you dropping the charges against me?'

'Yes, but I'm considering bringing others.'

That sounded like a hollow threat to remind me of how lucky I was.

'It seems these two in our custody were out to discredit you.'

'Why?'

'Professional jealousy, by all accounts.'

Professional jealously? Tim Reid being jealous of me made even less sense than Chloe Mercer, who I'd thought was at the root of all this.

'So this is all over?'

'For you, yes. For the other two, it's just beginning.'

'How did you know about today? Did you follow me?'

Lucas leaned back in his seat, crossed his arms and frowned. 'Yes, Mr Westlake, we've had you under surveillance over a traffic offence because we have that kind of manpower. No, police work led us to today's conclusion. Your intervention wasn't necessary. My investigation was centred on Miss Oglesby. Cracks were appearing in her story. I found her claims suspicious.'

'And today brought it to a head.'

'Yes, but we would have gotten to the truth in our own time.'

Not before it had well and truly dragged my name through the mud. I didn't care what Lucas thought. It was over and now I could repair the damage.

'Who is Jenni Oglesby and how's she connected to Reid?'

'She's his niece. Now, I'll need a full and frank statement from you.'

I nodded. 'Could I speak to Tim?'

'I don't think so.'

'I just need a minute. I'm not interested in gloating. I just want to understand.'

Lucas mulled my plea over. 'I'll ask. You can speak to him if he agrees.'

'Thanks.'

Lucas left the interview room and returned a minute later. He leaned through the doorway and beckoned to me with a finger. I followed him to another interview room two doors down.

Reid smiled sheepishly at me when Lucas swung the door open.

'You two have got two minutes and I'm leaving this officer with you.' He nodded at the officer in the room. 'Those are my terms. Take 'em or leave 'em.'

I answered by taking a seat opposite Reid. Lucas closed the door.

'You want to know why,' he said.

'Yeah, because I don't get it, Tim. Why'd you do this? I never did anything to you.'

He leaned back in his seat. 'You did. You won the shootout. You took my job.'

'What?'

'*Pit Lane* was sounding out teams to partner up with on this Young Driver thing. Rags liked the publicity it would bring and struck a deal. I thought we'd be running a three-car team. I found out after the shootout that my contract wasn't being renewed. Rags dumped me over a gimmick. Dumped me for you.'

There was acid behind that last remark. It made my skin prickle. It saddened me to see someone I hardly knew have such vehement feelings.

'Who cares if Rags dumped you? You're Tim Reid. You have your pick when it comes to drives.'

Reid shook his head. 'You don't get how things work. Ten years ago, I might have had the pick of the bunch. I'm forty-eight now. This is a young man's sport, and it's getting younger. Look at how many drivers in the ESCC are under thirty. If you haven't made it by the time you're twenty-five, you never will.'

He dropped his head in his hands. 'I just wanted my drive back.'

He wanted his drive back. That was it. I wanted a bigger reason than that to justify putting me through all that he had over something so petty. 'Jesus Christ, you were trying to kill my career so that you could have your old drive back?'

'Keep it civil,' the police officer in attendance said.

I let my anger bleed off for a minute. 'And you used Chloe Mercer to do it. Why bring her into this? What were you hoping, that I'd deck her or something?'

Reid looked up. 'Sure, if you'd done that it would have been a bonus. I just needed someone to play the bad girl for me and she fit the bill. Look, if it makes you feel any better, it wasn't personal. I went after you because you won the shootout. If the results had been different, I would have gone after someone else.'

'So the idea was to discredit me so Rags would welcome you back.'

'Pretty much.'

'That was never going to happen. Rags was talking to Chloe about replacing me.'

Reid rolled his eyes. 'I suppose that's what I deserve.'

I wanted to feel sorry for Reid, but I couldn't. I was too close to it. He'd tried to throw me under the bus to save his career. It was hard to be generous under those circumstances.

The door opened and Lucas appeared. 'Time's up.'

I stood up. I had nothing more to say.

'I'm sorry, Aidy. Truly, I am.'

'It's a little late for that.'

Lap Thirty-Eight

It was seven p.m. before Dylan and I got out of the police station. After we gave our statements, Sergeant Lucas kept us while his higher-ups decided whether we should be charged for our interference. Eventually, Lucas appeared to tell us we were more trouble than we were worth and to get out of his sight.

We arrived back at Archway to find Steve and Claudia waiting for us. Claudia tapped her watch when she saw me. I didn't need reminding. Three hours' notice wasn't a lot of time to prepare anything. We entrenched ourselves in the situation room. Everyone's gaze was on me.

'Are you sure you want to do this?' Claudia asked me.

I glanced over at Steve. His expressionless stare gave me no encouragement. I didn't think he wanted me to go through with this, but he'd back me.

'I'm sure.'

'Because if you don't, we'll catch these guys eventually. They will screw up. They always do.'

But they'll only go down for the drugs, I thought. Barrington's interests didn't lie with finding Jason's killer.

'I like the idea of catching these people sooner.'

Claudia flashed a brittle smile. 'OK. The thing to remember is to be patient. This is the first stage. You are just baiting the line. Sell them on the idea that Archway can be their new drug pipeline. We need these people to fall in love with your proposal. There won't be any drugs at tonight's meeting. It'll be all talk. Tonight is about seduction.'

'No shagging on the first date,' Dylan said.

Steve and I laughed.

'Please take this seriously,' Claudia said. 'This is very dangerous. We 'ave no protection or support.'

'We are taking this seriously,' I said. 'We're just a little anxious.'

'The best cure for anxiety is to do what you're anxious about.' Steve stood. 'So let's do this.'

Steve led a two-car convoy up to Ragged Racing's workshop. Dylan rode with Steve and Claudia rode with me. On the drive up, she talked me through tactics and strategy. All too soon we arrived at the industrial park.

Steve and Dylan climbed from the Capri and into the back of the Honda.

'This is it, I suppose,' Dylan said. 'You want me to come with you?'

'No, I want to go in alone. It's better to give them the impression they have the upper hand.'

'They do,' Steve said. 'Remember that.'

That was a confidence shaker.

Claudia pulled out her mobile. 'If you need 'elp, call. We'll come running.'

That was if I got the chance to make a call. 'I know. Now get out.'

They climbed from my Honda. Steve opened my door and took my hand. 'Be careful, son.'

'I will.'

Steve closed my door and I pulled away. I rounded the corner and light spilled from the entrance to Ragged Racing. I was expected. I wondered how many were waiting for me inside. Five? Ten? Well, there was only one way to find out. I parked next to Rags' Mercedes and let myself in.

I found Rags in the workshop, alone. He stood in front of my car running his hand over its contours. He was a man admiring his own handiwork. It was worth admiring. He'd built quite an empire for himself, but at what cost?

I felt like an intruder with my presence, so I let the sound of my footsteps on the concrete floor announce my arrival.

'I was thinking about Jason today,' Rags said without turning around.

He wants to talk, I thought, so let him talk. 'In what way?'

He turned around and leaned against my racecar. He tried smiling at me but it failed to take shape. The Rags the ESCC had come to know and fear was gone. His mistakes had caught up with him.

'I was thinking what a great guy Jason was. He was hard-working, smart, attentive and honest.'

'And he didn't deserve to die.'

'No. He had integrity. The kind this sport needs. The kind I used to have.'

Rags was going to confess. He just had to be pressed and pushed in the right places. He knew it was over.

'Was his death connected to what we're doing tonight?' I asked.

Rags nodded.

Only one question came next. My mouth went dry at the prospect of asking it. 'I know that you knew that Jason was going to search the transporter the night he was killed. Did you kill him?'

'I might not have done the deed, but I phoned it in. I took my hands off the wheel and let someone else steer. If I had half the guts Jason had, I would have faced him myself. I don't think I could have dissuaded him, but at least he would be alive and we wouldn't be here tonight.'

I said nothing. Rags was struggling with the guilt, but he deserved to struggle. He'd let a man die. And if he'd let one die, he'd be likely to do it again.

'You disappoint me. I thought more of you.'

The remark surprised me. 'How so?'

'You seemed honest. Your grandfather has a reputation for playing by the rules. I didn't think you'd want anything to do with this.'

It was time to get into character. 'Yeah, well, being honest doesn't put money in the bank.'

Rags shook his head. 'There's more to life than money.'

'That's easy to say when you have it. My dad made it to the top of this sport and didn't have a penny to show for it. Worse, he died owing money. It almost cost my grandfather his livelihood. That wouldn't happen in any other industry. I may be my father's son, but I won't starve because of some ideal. I want to succeed in this sport and I don't care how I do it.'

A tremor that I hadn't intended invaded the tail end of my speech. I was breathing hard when I'd finished. Maybe I wasn't entirely playacting.

'I thought like you and look where it's gotten me,' Rags said.

'To the top of your game.'

Rags shook his head. 'You're too young to get it. That's your problem. But you'll work it out. Hopefully before your mistakes swallow you up.'

'Can we get on with this?'

'Why don't you just go? Forget about this shit. I'll tell my people that you had second thoughts and I paid you off.'

'But you haven't.'

'I will. I've got ten grand waiting for you in my office. You can have it and I'll make sure you get more.'

Something was wrong. Rags was trying to sideline me and it unnerved me, but I had to follow through with the plan. 'You're not squeezing me out. I want what I came here for and that's a piece of the action.'

The sound of a car pulling up outside drew our attention.

Rags looked back at me and raised his hands. 'Have it your way, Aidy. I did my best for you. Don't you forget that.'

My heart thundered in my chest. This was it. I was going to come face-to-face with Jason's killer.

As Rags went to the door to let our visitor in, my mobile vibrated in my pocket. It was Dylan. I answered it.

'Be quick.'

'Mate, we're busted.' Dylan was out of breath. His voice was uneven like he was running. 'It's Barrington. Him and two of his boys just swooped in. They've got Claudia and Steve. I'm trying to give these fuckers the slip so I can back you up.'

A voice in the background barked something I couldn't quite

make out. Then a second voice, much closer to Dylan's phone, told him to stop. I recognized Barrington's voice.

'Shit,' Dylan said.

The panic I heard in Dylan's voice spread to me.

Barrington had to be right next to Dylan as I heard his voice clearly. 'Use my personnel for your own private investigation? I don't bloody think so. Your fun and games are over.'

'Aidy, get out,' Dylan said. 'You're on your own.'

But it was too late. Rags was returning with our drug connection – Crichlow. And I was totally alone now.

Lap Thirty-Nine

Barrington had inadvertently screwed me by taking my only backup. I tried not to let that thought scare me and bottled my panic. I clung to Claudia's belief that tonight was just a first date. Nothing would happen.

Crichlow looked at me bemusedly as he walked up to me. I was sure he thought his grand entrance would be a big surprise to me. My only surprise was that Gates wasn't there with him.

'Who were you on the phone with?' Crichlow asked.

'Just my grandfather. He gets worried when I'm late.'

'Let's have the phone. I don't want anything interrupting our business.'

My mobile was no longer a lifeline, so I handed it over. Crichlow pocketed it.

'I bet you're wondering what the hell is happening, Aidy,' Crichlow said.

Rags looked from Crichlow to me. 'Do you two know each other?'

'Isn't Andrew joining us?' I said. 'Or doesn't he like to get his hands dirty now that he's an upstanding businessman?'

'Andrew? What's he talking about?' Rags said. 'Is he talking about your boss?'

'He isn't my boss.'

Not in all things, I thought. Did that mean he was here without Gates' permission? I remembered something Eddie Stores had said about Gates. It was all starting to fall into place and it was creating a dangerous picture. 'You're the one Andrew caught dealing drugs.'

'How'd you find out about that?' Crichlow barked. His angry words bounced off the metal walls.

'You never stopped dealing though, did you?'

'Watch your mouth.'

'I heard that Andrew left his mark on you. Can I see?'

Crichlow lunged, grabbed me by my shirt and thrust me back. I struck the ground on my back. Rags caught his arm, snagging his sleeve. A crisscross of scars made a patchwork of his arm over the four-inch length of exposed skin. They weren't just stripes like on Rag's arm.

Gates wasn't part of this. It was Crichlow. He was responsible for everything and he knew I knew. I bottled my panic. Knowing wasn't enough. I still needed him to incriminate himself with this drug deal.

I raised my hands. 'OK, message received. Can we talk business now?'

Crichlow shrugged off Rags, put out a hand to me and pulled me to my feet. He didn't release his grip on my hand. 'Let's keep the chat to the business at hand. All right?'

I took that as code: Gates isn't to know about this. 'Yeah. Sure.'

'Rags says you've got a proposal. Let's hear it.'

'Car collectors around the world bring my grandfather their classic cars to restore. It's similar to the operation you have with Rags. Your customers send Steve their cars to work on. While they're in his workshop, I put the drugs in the tyres or wherever else I can. With all the cars coming in and out of Archway, no one will think twice.'

'What's in it for you?' Crichlow asked.

'What else? A steady income. The same reason you're in it – easy money.'

'The money is never easy,' Rags said. I felt the weight of personal experience behind his words.

'What are your terms?'

Terms? I didn't have a clue. How much did drug mules get? Was it a fixed fee or a percentage based on weight? I should have expected this question and been prepared to answer it.

'I'm not greedy. I'll take whatever you're paying Rags.'

Crichlow jerked a thumb at Rags. 'And him? What's in it for him?'

Rags seemed to shrink from us once Crichlow mentioned him. He folded his hands tight across his chest and kept his gaze on the floor.

'I realize I wouldn't have this opportunity without him, so I'll cut him in from whatever I get from you.'

'You've thought this all out, haven't you?'

'I've tried my best.' I got the feeling Crichlow didn't have a lot of faith in me. He only knew me from my dealings with Gates. He needed to see a different side of me. 'Look, the cops are on to this place when it comes to ferrying drugs around Europe. You can't continue, but you still need to move the coke. I can help you do it. And all I want is a nest egg to keep me out of the poorhouse. It's a win-win.'

'Do you know the risks you're taking?' Crichlow asked.

'I race cars. I take risks all the time.'

'This is different.'

'Yeah. It's safer. The cars will be freighted or hand-delivered by me. No one is going to suspect anything. It's no more dangerous than putting a letter in the post.'

'Who on your end will know about this?'

'No one.'

'Not your grandfather?'

'Like your boss, he wouldn't approve, and like your boss, he doesn't need to know. The fewer people who know, the less that can go wrong.' I'd had enough of the questions. It was time to force a decision. 'What do you think?'

Crichlow stepped back from Rags and me and paced a tight little circle. I could see him considering my offer, pulling at the fabric of it, looking for tears. I hoped the bait was tasty enough for him to go for it. If I got him on the hook, I was safe. Barrington might not like my off-the-books plan but he wouldn't care if I served up Crichlow's operation on a plate.

Crichlow stopped, jammed his hands in his trouser pockets and looked at us. 'I should confer with my people, but I don't feel I need to. Rags' operation has proved successful for us. I think your plan would prove just as successful. But you know what? I'm not interested.'

Relief swept across Rags' face. I felt panic spreading across mine. I was blowing it. I couldn't let Crichlow slip through my fingers.

'Hey, wait,' I said. 'You're missing out on a golden opportunity.'

'I don't think so. Hiding the dope in the wheels has been a great deception, but Customs is wise to it now. A variation on a theme won't cut it. I need something completely different.'

Barrington's instincts to cut his losses had been right. There was no way they were going to use Rags again to reopen their drug pipeline to Europe.

'Besides, there's a bigger reason why I'm walking away from your offer.'

'What's that?' I said.

'You know too damn much about my business.'

His hand flew from his pocket so fast that I didn't see the knife until it slashed across my stomach. The pain was so intense that it froze me in the moment. Thousands of severed nerve endings crackled with electricity and tried to jam my brain with the same message of pain at once. I clutched at the wound. Blood leaked between my fingers.

'No!' Rags yelled. He shoved me aside, sending me sprawling to the floor and lunged at Crichlow.

Crichlow sidestepped Rags' lunge. As Rags lumbered by, he swept the knife through the air again in an efficient arc. The blade caught Rags across the side of the neck. His legs went out from under him and he collapsed on to all fours. Blood poured from a deep and ugly wound. He clambered to his feet, but only half managed the feat before pitching forward on to his face.

I saw my fate if I didn't do something. I pushed myself upright, but I took too long. Crichlow charged at me. He caught me hard while my balance was off. I bounced off the side of my racecar, cracking my head on the door.

The moment I hit the floor, Crichlow jumped on top of me and pressed his knee into my stomach. It radiated pain, paralyzing the rest of me. Pouncing on my weakness, he grabbed the side of my head and smacked it on the concrete floor. The shockwave that went through my head stopped me from fighting back. The second blow put me in a stupor. The third left me clinging to consciousness.

Crichlow pushed himself off me and looked down at the mess he'd made of me. 'You know it had to end this way.'

I watched him walk over to one of the oil drums in the supply area. He broke the seal open and rolled the barrel over on to its side. A pool of amber spread slowly across the floor. He did the same to a second barrel before picking up a jerry can of petrol. I lost consciousness knowing what was going to happen next.

Lap Forty

The stench of smoke jerked me awake. In the short time I'd been out, the workshop had been turned into an inferno. Crichlow had doused everything that could burn in petrol and torched it. With all the chemicals and flammable materials, this fire would burn long and hot. The tyre rack burned black and ugly, spewing choking smoke. The office suite cracked and popped as something else succumbed to the fire. The oil barrels had been left to pump their contents over the floor. Black smoke billowed upward in a thick cloud off the oil pool and accumulated in the rafters. It swelled by the second and was now rolling back towards the floor. Where the oil burned slow and steady, the gasoline burned hot and fast. The rising temperature inside the workshop dried my face and I could feel it pricking my skin. Each breath hurt my lungs.

I was going to burn if the smoke didn't kill me first, but I refused to die in here. I wouldn't be another of Crichlow's victims.

I sat up and the knife that Crichlow had used to carve up Rags and me rolled from my hand. Clever. He wanted to leave a scenario for the world to believe.

My head ached. My brain seemed to be throbbing inside my skull. The edges of my vision stung as if someone had turned up the contrast. I had Crichlow's head-bashing to thank for that.

I pulled up my shirt and examined the gash. It was a foot long and bleeding, but it wasn't deep. Just surface damage, I told myself. As much as it seemed like a ridiculous thought, I'd survive.

I wasn't sure about Rags. A pool of blood two feet across circled his head. I scurried over to him and examined his neck. The cut was deep, but not accurate. Blood pulsed from the gash, but far too slowly for a major artery. I peeled off my shirt and pressed it to the wound. Again, I was trying to stop a man from bleeding to death. Rags stirred.

'You're OK,' I said. 'It's bad, but not that bad.'

Rags looked at the blaze and chuckled. 'You don't think this is bad? Look, we're not getting out of this. I need to tell you that Crichlow killed Jason. And now he's killed us.'

'Yeah, I know, but we're not dead yet.'

Crichlow was gone, but he'd been smart with his pyromania. We were pinned in the rear of the workshop away from the exits. If we wanted to get out, it meant going through a wall of fire. I looked up. The trapped smoke was swelling and dropping down to meet us. We had less than ten feet of clear headroom.

'The sprinklers?' Rags said.

The sprinkler system should have been dousing us, but nothing. Crichlow must have cut the water supply.

'Forget the sprinklers. Do you have your mobile?'

'Yeah. My pocket.' He tapped his right-trouser pocket.

I fished his phone out and punched in nine-nine-nine. I had to shout over the roar of the fire for the emergency-services operator to hear me. Her voice trembled when she told me the fire brigade would be there as soon as possible.

'I don't think they'll get here in time,' Rags said.

He was right. I ended the call by breaking into a cough. My throat was raw already.

'Keep the pressure on your wound. I'm getting us out of here,' I croaked.

The vapours inside a jerry can ignited and it flew across the workshop, smashing into a wall.

'I like your optimism,' Rags said.

'Shut up and don't move.'

I punched in Dylan's number. It rang until voicemail kicked in. I cursed and called Steve's number. He answered.

'Crichlow is the one who killed Jason. He's torched the workshop. Rags and I are trapped,' I said.

'Turn around! Turn around! Aidy's in trouble,' Steve yelled. 'How bad is it, son?'

I stared at the flames vaporising the paint off the walls. 'It's bad. Crichlow has dumped the oil barrels out and doused everything else in petrol.'

'Can you find a safe spot until we get there?' A tremor had entered Steve's voice. It hurt to hear it.

'No.'

'Stay low. Soak your clothes. We're coming. It's going to be OK. Say it.'

My head was aching. It felt as though the smoke was in my brain. 'It's going to be OK.' My words came out dry.

'Say it like you fucking mean it, goddamn you.'

I palmed away a tear. 'It's going to be OK.'

'That's my boy. Move this fucking car!' Steve said before hanging up.

I tossed the phone back to Rags and snatched a hose line from the hook on the wall. Even though Crichlow had cut off the mains, I was banking on there still being pressure in the lines.

'You won't put this out with that.' Rags laughed, but it immediately turned into a coughing fit.

'I'm just buying us some time. Prepare to get wet,' I said and doused him with water.

The moment I felt a change in pressure in the hose I turned it and doused myself.

The fire was spreading. The oil continued to expand across the floor. For every inch the pool grew, it set light to something else. Our safe haven wouldn't last. The speed at which the fire was consuming the workshop was staggering.

'We need more than this to stay alive,' Rags said.

We did and we had it. For all the combustible materials in the workshop, there were a few that weren't.

'Race suits? Do you have any?'

Rags' eyes lit up. 'In the bag over there.'

He pointed to a sports bag on top of a tool cabinet. I grabbed it and opened it up. It was Haulk's kit bag. It contained his suit, boots, gloves and helmet.

I stripped off my jeans and shoes and changed into Haulk's flame-retardant clothes. Since Haulk was taller and bigger than me, his clothes hung on me, but they didn't have to fit. They just had to protect me.

'Got another suit?'

'In my office.'

'Shit.'

'Do you think you can make it to the door?' Rags asked.

Racing suits are flame retardant, not fireproof. They are meant as a temporary barrier giving the driver a couple of minutes of protection at most. I could make it to one of the doors, but I'd never survive long enough to open it.

A thunderclap rocked the workshop. The fire had caught up with Haulk's car and the petrol tank had exploded, spraying burning petrol over a tool chest.

'How do you fancy driving out of here?' I said.

Haulk's car might be on fire, but the flames had yet to make it to mine. The only problem was that I had to cross through a lake of burning oil to get to it. I pointed at my car.

'Are you crazy?'

'Crazy is the only thing that's going to get us out of here.'

I pulled on Haulk's Nomex balaclava and his helmet, then snapped the visor down.

As Rags trickled out what water was left in the hose line, burning leaves dropped down and landed on his head and back. It was what was left of the many winners' wreaths hanging on the wall. He yelled out and I slapped them away with my gloved hands.

'You need to move fast.'

I stepped up to the roiling wall of fire. I had thirty feet of it to walk through. I tried not to think about how hot it was and walked into the flames.

The heat was immediate and intense. I felt it come at me from all angles, latch on to every inch of me and squeeze. It penetrated the suit immediately, hungry flames seeking a path through the fabric to get to my skin. It easily found the two weaknesses in my protection: where the legs of the suit slotted into the tops of my boots and where my balaclava was exposed under my chin. I felt my ankles and the underside of my jaw burn and the soles of my feet tingled as the burning oil ate my boots.

My view of the world vanished. The helmet's visor charred and turned opaque in seconds. I ignored the blindness and focused on where I'd seen my car before my vision disappeared.

I placed each foot as squarely on the ground as possible, but slipped on the burning oil. I pitched forward and landed on my hands and knees.

Panic knifed through me as quickly as the pain. I was on my hands and knees in a bed of flames. That one thought helped me scramble to my feet in a second.

I felt a new and more intense heat in my hands. I didn't understand it for a second, then I got it. The suede patches on my gloves were on fire. I fought the urge to yank them off and expose my naked hands to an oil fire.

'Keep going, Aidy!' Rags screamed.

That's it, I told myself, keep walking. You can do this. My mantra kept the panic in. I made it through the fire.

The second I was clear of the flames, I yanked the gloves free and tugged the helmet off. Every inch of the suit was scorched and blackened, including Haulk's helmet. The heat had destroyed the fancy design incorporating the Dutch flag. Nomex really was a lifesaver.

I ran up to my car. It was hot to the touch, so I used a burnt glove to open the door. I threw myself behind the wheel and slammed the door shut.

I felt safe inside the car, but it scared me to see what the oil- and water-temperature gauges were registering.

I put my finger on the starter. 'Please start.'

I pressed down. The engine turned over and over, but it wasn't catching. The fuel was probably evaporating in the engine.

Then the engine caught and fired. 'God bless Honda and their reliability.'

I put the car in gear and drove into the fire. The car pushed back the flames. I couldn't believe I'd just walked through this.

I punctured the flames and found Rags on his feet on the other side, holding his mobile in one hand and my shirt to his neck. I clambered from the car.

'It's your grandfather. He's outside. Jesus Christ, the tyres are on fire.'

He jammed the phone in my hands and aimed the hose at the tyres.

'Steve?' I said into the phone.

'We're outside. We've kicked in the door to the offices. Can you see us?'

I wiped my eyes. I'd been tearing up since I walked through the fire. I looked back. Between the smoke and the flames, I couldn't see them. I could barely make out the outline of the offices.

'No.'

'Fuck. We can't open the loading doors. They're locked from the inside.'

I coughed so hard I folded over. I felt the smoke in my lungs, choking me from inside. 'And I can't get to them.'

'We're going to get you out of there, son. Just keep believing that.'

He was clinging to that belief. I heard it in his voice. As long as he believed, I did too.

'We can plough through the doors,' I heard Dylan shout in the background.

'No, the inside of this place is a fireball,' I said. 'You'll burn up getting to us. I've got my car going. It's got extinguishers. I'll drive out from this side.'

'Are you going to smash through the door?' Steve asked.

Smash through it? I couldn't see it. It was lost in the smoke. In the gloom, I could miss the door and drive the car into a support pillar and that would be the end of the car and me. I went up to the prefab siding. It was corrugated metal. It was strong, but it wasn't reinforced like the rollup door.

'Steve, I'll never find the door in all this shit. This siding. How strong is it?'

'Not that strong.'

'I think I can rip through it. Come around to the other side.'

'Do it. We'll be waiting.'

I tossed the phone back to Rags. He dropped the hose to catch it.

I got back behind the wheel and strapped myself into the harness. I pulled hard on the straps. I needed to be in tight. Any slack and the impact would break my back.

I needed a long run up for this. I put the car in reverse and rolled it back into the smoke and the flames. Rags and the wall disappeared. Flames licked at the bodywork. Paint blistered. Smoke blackened the windows. I prayed the tyres wouldn't melt. I backed up until I bumped into the opposite wall.

'OK, here goes.'

I floored the accelerator, but the tyres slipped in the burning oil. The car barely accelerated while the tyres spun.

'Shit.'

I backed off and tried to feather the throttle, but the car still only reached fifteen miles an hour by the time it re-emerged from the smoke.

Rags lumbered over to me and opened the door. He looked awful. I couldn't tell if it was smoke inhalation or the blood loss.

'I can't get any traction on this sodding oil,' I said.

'Shit.' He thumped the roof of the Honda. 'He can't get any speed with all this fucking oil on the floor,' he yelled into the phone. A moment later, a grin broke out across his face. 'Your grandfather is a fucking genius. Get this thing on the rolling road.'

That would do it. The rolling road faced the prefab siding. If I built up enough speed on the rollers and jumped the car out, I'd have the force to tear a hole through this building without the run up.

Rags staggered over to the rolling road and pulled off the safety plates as I manoeuvred the car on to the rollers. Rags flashed me the thumbs-up and backed away.

I put the car in second and stepped on the accelerator. The car gathered speed fast on the near frictionless rollers. I watched the needle climb on the display. Thirty. Forty. Fifty. Sixty. Sixty miles an hour should do it. Now to jump it out of its rollers.

The car's weight kept sitting squarely in the rollers. To get it to fly out of them, I needed to give it a little help by rocking the car back and forth.

I stamped on the accelerator then jumped off the pedal, just for a moment. The car lurched forward on the rollers then rolled back. Before the car settled back entirely, I stamped on the power again then jerked my foot off.

Rags got in on the act. He dropped my shirt and threw his weight against the car to give it that little bump that could make all the difference. Blood poured from his uncovered wound.

'That's it!' Rags yelled. 'Faster now.'

The needle said I was doing seventy, but it wasn't coming out of the rollers. I took the car up to eighty. The tyres whined on the steel rollers.

I stamped down on the accelerator then jumped off. The car rocked back and forth in the rollers even more. As its momentum brought it forward, I stamped on the accelerator again. The car climbed high in the rollers before dropping back down. This was it. One more time. That was all it would take.

'You're almost there,' Rags said, before his words lost their strength. His eyes rolled back in his head and he collapsed, sliding from view. I couldn't stop now. Not when I was this close.

As the car bounced back down into the rollers and momentum

rocked it, it lurched forward again. I buried the accelerator into the floor. The car lurched up the rollers and over the top. The second the wheels touched the ground, the tyres screeched on the concrete floor and the Honda rocketed forward and slammed into the corrugated siding. The impact snapped my teeth together, but the car burst through the wall, tearing a sheet of the siding off as it went. There was a ledge on the other side and the car dropped three feet before coming to an abrupt stop in the bushes. The deceleration hit me across the chest like a four by two. I tried to breathe but my body had forgotten how. It took a moment for it to remember again. I released my harness, flung open the door and rolled out. Fire lit up the hole I'd punched through the side of the building.

Steve and Dylan raced towards me with Claudia and Barrington close behind.

'Get Rags. He's just inside.'

Claudia and Barrington broke off towards the hole.

Steve yanked me up into his arms. 'Are you OK?'

'I'm OK.' Those two words never sounded sweeter.

Last Lap

I was alone at home when DI Huston rang.

'How are you doing?'

'I'm fine.'

It had been four days since the fire at the Ragged workshop. The gash Crichlow had given me hadn't been serious. Soft tissue only, according to the doctor, but it was annoying. Every time I moved or stretched, the two edges of the wound seemed to shift. I was still coughing out the smoke from the fire and I'd picked up a couple of second-degree burns under my chin and around my ankles. I'd also come away with a mild case of whiplash when I crashed my car. These injuries would keep me out of racing for a couple of weeks. Not that I had any racing to go back to. Ragged Racing was no more.

'You up for a road trip?' Huston asked.

'Who's driving?'

'You. You'll have to meet me here.'

'Where are you?'

'At that factory you told me belonged to Andrew Gates.'

'I'm leaving now.'

I arrived at the factory to find Huston outside, leaning against her car. It had been a couple of days since I'd seen her. After the fire, Rags and I spent two days being questioned by HM Customs and the police from our hospital beds. Despite helping to identify a murderer and bringing down a drug-trafficking ring, no one seemed to be in a hurry to congratulate me. Oh, well. Huston opened my door and helped me out.

'I've got something to show you,' she said. 'This way.'

Crime-scene tape crisscrossed the entrance to the factory. I felt uneasy at the thought of what she'd show me. I prayed it wasn't a body. She snapped the tape and I followed her inside.

The area where Gates and Crichlow had interrogated me weeks earlier was staked out. A rust-coloured stain over four feet in diameter tainted the concrete floor.

'Is that blood?'

'Yes.'

I thought Rags had lost a lot of blood from his neck wound, but it paled in comparison to what had been lost here. I couldn't imagine anyone surviving that amount of blood loss.

'We've tested the blood. It's the same blood type as Dominic Crichlow's. It'll be a while before DNA testing proves whether it's his or not.'

No DNA testing was required. It was Crichlow's. Gates had caught up with his brother's killer and gotten his revenge. I winced at what Gates had done to spill so much blood.

'Have you found a body?' I asked.

'No.'

And I doubted that they would. With all the properties Gates owned, what was left of Crichlow was likely propping up a foundation somewhere.

'Have you spoken to Andrew Gates?' I asked.

'He's an absentee landlord now, so I doubt we'll get the chance.'

'He's gone?'

'He, his family and his mother left the country on different flights to different countries the day after the fire.'

'Where do you think they've gone?'

'I'm sure they're sunning themselves in a non-extradition country somewhere. We'll find out which one eventually. Not that we'll be looking too hard. It's only the guilty preying on themselves. The innocent have already been avenged. We have what we need. The only question I have is, did you tip him off about Crichlow?'

'No.'

'Someone told him. Now, I wouldn't blame you if you did after what Crichlow did to you.'

'I didn't.'

'Is that your official answer?'

'It's my only answer.'

She eyed me up, looking for a sign that would give me away. She wouldn't find one. There wasn't one to find.

'OK. I had to ask.' She had a file folder under her arm and held it out to me. 'I thought you'd like to take a look at these.'

The file contained eight-by-ten photos of Crichlow, Rags and a bunch of men I'd never seen before. Some of the shots showed them stripping the wheels off the Ragged cars. Others showed the tyres being pulled off the rims and packets of white powder being loaded into bags. Several of the pictures were taken at the accident-repair garage in Milton Keynes. The rest were taken at places I didn't recognize.

'After a ton of man-hours, our techs managed to get these off Jason's phone a few days ago. If you'd given me the phone when you'd found it, we could have prevented last night.'

It might have prevented the fire at Ragged, but it wouldn't have prevented any of the other collateral damage associated with the case.

'You might be interested to know that the crash centre you discovered belonged to Andrew Gates. I'm guessing we'll find out that all these buildings pictured belong to Gates and that Crichlow was using them as a front. I think these pictures are what Crichlow was after the night he killed Jason. He was scrabbling to cover his arse. It would explain why he ransacked Jason's flat and when you started getting close, he planted the razor on you.'

I'd guessed as much. Every time I updated Gates, I updated Crichlow. He knew my every step and so I made it easy for him to pull something to derail me.

'Have you shared this with Barrington?'

She nodded.

I handed the folder back. 'I'm sorry for all the trouble.'

'You should be.' A smile came with the put down. I saw the mother instead of the cop for once. 'Stick to the driving in the future.'

'I'll do my best, but no promises.'

I left Huston to her crime scene and drove to Archway. I found Steve and Dylan at work on Gates' cars. Now that Ragged Racing no longer existed, Dylan was back working for Steve. I broke the news that Gates had skipped the country while it was likely that Crichlow had skipped the planet.

'What are we going to do with all these cars?' Dylan asked.

'Gates paid us to restore them and that's what we'll do. We fix them up and return them,' Steve said.

'To who?' Dylan said. 'The man is gone and never coming back. I say we bloody keep them as compensation for all our trouble.'

'They don't belong to us,' Steve said. 'It'd be theft and I for one don't want to see any cops for a while.'

Both of them had more than a valid point. As much as I felt we were owed, Gates' cars weren't our property. 'How about this then? There's no one we can hand these cars over to, so I suggest we just hold on to them until Andrew asks for them back. Naturally, we would have to drive them to ensure they are in full operating condition.'

'Sounds more than fair,' Dylan said.

'I can't believe I'm agreeing to this crap, but OK,' Steve said. 'Pick a favourite. The rest I'll mothball until further notice.'

Dylan pounced on the red Triumph TR5, wrapping his arms around its flat bonnet. I sidled up to an original, canary yellow, 1970 TVR Tuscan with a V8 engine in it. It was a lot of engine for such a small car.

'OK,' Steve said. 'We'll dress up the other cars, but we'll give these two the full business.'

'Can I talk to you alone?' I said to Steve.

Steve looked to Dylan.

'You two talk. I'll get lunch. It's on me. Today is a good day.' Dylan grabbed his jacket and shot out the door.

'Please remind him he's only minding the car, not bloody keeping it,' Steve said.

'I'll try, but I'm not sure he's listening.'

'OK, what do you want to talk about?'

'The night of the fire. Someone tipped off Andrew Gates about Crichlow. I can only think of one person who'd do that.'

Steve opened the passenger door of the MGA he'd been working on and took a seat. He patted the driver's seat. I rounded the car and slipped behind the wheel. I remembered doing the exact same thing when I was so small my feet didn't reach the pedals and Steve telling me what I could expect when I grew big enough to drive the car. Those were great days that would always stick with me. I loved my grandfather so much.

'Crichlow was in the wind and with his connections he'd be out of the country,' Steve said. 'He'd left you to die and I couldn't let him get away with that. You're my family. My only family. So yes, I called Andrew and told him. Am I proud of it? No. Did I want justice at any cost? You bet your life.'

This wasn't what Steve had taught me. Doing right was his credo. Throwing Crichlow to someone like Gates was only justice if you wanted to delude yourself. Well, I wanted to be deluded.

'Thank you,' I said.

'You're welcome, son.'

Someone pulled back the workshop door and Claudia appeared in a blast of sunlight. 'Morning gentlemen. Time to crack the whip again, Aidy.'

Claudia had been dropping by daily to follow up on various points in the case. Barrington never showed his face. After pulling everyone off me and leaving me defenceless, he'd been smart to send Claudia.

'I won't be long,' I told Steve.

Claudia and I went around the corner to Alexandra Gardens. It was nice down there, especially by the river. It was quiet at this time of the day. Tourists were in short supply. She slipped her arm in mine as we walked.

She eyed the burn under my chin. 'It's 'ealing nicely. I don't think it will scar too badly.'

It was unlikely I'd ever have to shave there again.

'What's the latest on everything?' I asked. Where I'd been forthcoming with everything I knew, Barrington hadn't, but Claudia had been feeding me information as and when she could.

'About ten months ago, Rags asked Andrew Gates for a loan

after he lost a sponsor. Gates said no, but Crichlow offered 'im an alternative method for earning money. Things grew from there.'

'And Andrew Gates was never involved?'

'Not according to Rags. It was Crichlow's pet project. He carried the whole thing out under Gates' nose. Not 'ard, I suppose, considering the size of Gates' empire.'

'Crichlow was just a middleman,' I said. 'Who was the supplier and the distributor?'

'You know I can't tell you that. What are your plans now?'

'Face down at the moment. I think my days at the ESCC are done.'

With Ragged Racing in ashes, my drive had gone up in smoke with everyone else's job. Rumour was that Barry Nevin was going to start his own team, but it wasn't going to happen before the season's end. Naturally, Townsend Motorsport was in the frame to reclaim its factory-backed status. Despite this, it looked as if Russell Townsend wasn't going to honour our deal of taking me into his fold. The word was that Kurt Haulk would be Townsend's third team car. Mike Whelan was holding true to his word and scouting out some options for me.

'I sent out a statement to *Pit Lane* on the Tim Reid situation. They want to interview you about it.'

'They going to talk to Chloe too?'

Claudia smiled. 'Naturally. She's a victim too.'

I shook my head. Chloe Mercer would no doubt come out of this smelling like a rose. I took comfort in the fact that my title as *Pit Lane* magazine's Young Driver of the Year would remain intact and would stick in her throat.

'I wanted to let you know that my days with the ESCC are also over. I'm returning to France for reassignment.'

'Well, the ESCC will be worse off because of it.'

She smiled and curtsied for me. 'And so will 'er Majesty's Customs.'

'Barrington giving you the elbow?'

'I'm being sent on my way with a commendation.'

Barrington was taking all the praise for bringing down a major international drug-smuggling pipeline, although the success had nothing to do with him. It made sense that he was kicking her to touch. Her presence was potentially a major embarrassment for him.

'I hope your people appreciate your role in all this.'

'They do. That's why I'd like to make you an offer. I've been speaking to some of my connections in France. 'Ow would you like to compete in the Formula Renault Eurocup series? It would be with a good team.'

'How are their finances?'

Claudia laughed. 'Good. No loan sharks.'

Formula Renault meant I'd be back in single seaters, where I belonged. And France sounded good. It would put some distance between recent events and me.

'I like it, but I don't know any French.'

'I'd teach you.'

'I'm surprised you want to be in the same country as me after all the trouble I've caused you.'

'I'd like to get to know you better. So what do you say?'

After all my friends and I had gone through, it sounded better than good. 'I have a couple of conditions.'

'Name them?'

'Dylan comes with me. It's a package deal.'

'And what about Steve?'

'He's got Archway.'

'Not a problem. What else?'

'What's your real name?'

She kissed me on the cheek before whispering the answer in my ear. I liked it better than Claudia.

'Do we 'ave a deal?' she asked.

'I think we do.'